Praise for Lexxie Couper's *Savage Retribution*

"This is on rollercoaster ride of a story. The main characters are on the run throughout the story and the author has captured that feeling in telling their story. I definitely needed to catch my breath at the end...The combination of a very exciting plot, great characters, evil megalomaniac werewolves, and a sad back story make this a book that will be very difficult to put down."

~ *The Romance Studio*

"The pace of this story is rollercoaster fast with just about as many spins, twists, drops and turns in the plot. I thoroughly enjoyed Savage Retribution and I highly recommend it to all the wolf lovers among us."

~ *Just Erotic Romance Reviews*

"LexxieCouper's Savage Retribution is an action packed thrill ride. This story had me on the edge of my seat; start to finish. This story is so strong and well thought out, and the heat between Declan and Regan will have romance readers begging for more. I had a wonderful time reading this story. LexxieCouper can add another fan to her list."

~ *ParaNormalRomance.org*

Savage Retribution

Lexxie Couper

A Samhain Publishing, Ltd. publication.

Samhain Publishing, Ltd.
577 Mulberry Street, Suite 1520
Macon, GA 31201
www.samhainpublishing.com

Savage Retribution
Copyright © 2008 by Lexxie Couper
Print ISBN: 978-1-60504-019-6
Digital ISBN: 1-59998-506-3

Editing by Heidi Moore
Cover by Scott Carpenter

First Samhain Publishing, Ltd. electronic publication: February 2008
First Samhain Publishing, Ltd. print publication: December 2008

Dedication

For my husband, who knew I could do it and told me so every day. The keys to the Ferrari are getting closer, Sexy Man.

To Renee, Mariah, Daphne and Deviant Boy. Thank you. A million times over.

Prologue

Dublin—Four Months Ago

The stink of sex, sin and death seeped into Declan O'Connell's nostrils, overripe and acrid all at once. His lips curled into a silent snarl and he stepped deeper into the dank, dim building, the hair on his nape prickling.

This is not right.

The thought sent a ripple of tension through his already tight muscles. It *wasn't* right. The whole night hadn't been right; the anonymous tip about his sister's killer, the insistence he be here—at this place—at this time, the derelict, abandoned condition of the building. It didn't add up.

McCoy's not here, Dec. Shit, he's never been here. You can't even smell him on the air. Face it—this was a set up. And you've just walked right into it.

The snarl on his lips turned into a low growl and he felt the muscles in his body begin to coil tighter. Stretch. Grow.

Change.

Teeth grinding, Declan forced back the beast, denying it control of his body. He didn't know who had brought him here under false pretence—more than one person wanted him dead, and not all of them knew what he truly was. Better to walk out of the situation, not lope out on all fours.

A soft sound—barely louder than the snap of a dry blade of grass—shattered the silence of the derelict brothel and Declan froze.

He *wasn't* alone. Someone was—

The dark blur hit him from the left. Hard.

Something large and heavy crashed him to the ground. Teeth, long, sharp and slick with saliva, snapped at his face. He was barreled across the debris-strewn floor, chunks of concrete and shards of broken glass grinding into his knees and elbows, biting into his flesh even through the leather of his jacket. His favorite Levi's tore but he didn't give a rat's ass. Not with a fucking huge, black wolf trying to tear his throat out.

The animal lashed out, razor-sharp teeth missing his neck by a hair's width. Declan felt hot saliva splatter his cheek. He struggled on his back, pinned to the crap-covered floor by the wolf's writhing, savage weight. The stench of urine attacked his breath, invaded his senses with the mark of an animal Declan had tasted before.

His eyes snapped wide open, locked on the burning, iridescent gold stare of the wolf attacking him.

You!

The word formed in Declan's head. Cold. Furious.

Seconds before the beast in his own blood roared into existence and he changed. Human muscle into canine. Man into wolf.

He bucked the animal off him, snapping at its soft underbelly as it flipped and twisted to the side. Warm, coppery blood filled his mouth and throat. He leapt onto all fours, staring at the black *loup garou*, smelling apprehension and pain leech from it in thick, sickly waves.

Baring his teeth, he held its gold stare, his growl low.

You've fucked with the wrong wolf, asshole.

"Gotcha."

The voice—low, smug and female—sounded to Declan's left at the exact second something sharp, pointed and icy sank into his neck, right at the spot where vein became jugular. Intense cold, like the breath of Death itself, consumed him. His muscles contracted, his heart seemed to swell and, wracked in pain, he collapsed to the floor.

Incapable of movement.

Trapped. And utterly vulnerable.

Chapter One

Sydney, Australia.

Regan Thomas hated the dark. The dark kept secrets. Hideous secrets. Secrets of pain and torture and human brutality. The dark allowed man to commit all sorts of horrendous acts in the name of progress. In the name of science. The dark allowed rich men to get richer on the corpses of creatures unable to defend themselves.

Men like Nathan Epoc.

Turning the narrow beam of her flashlight on the solid, steel door before her, Regan felt her hackles rise. Of all the arrogant men of power in this country, Epoc was the worst. Every day his labs in Sydney discarded close to a hundred animal corpses—all maimed, sliced, injected and tortured to death.

A snarl curled Regan's lip. Science. To this day, she still could not decipher *what* Nathan Epoc produced in the name of science, apart from dead animals. Despite only arriving in the country two years ago, he was now one of the wealthiest men in Australia. No one, however, seemed to know what the hell he actually did. Mystery shrouded what went on behind the electrified fences and impenetrable walls of his windowless buildings, out here in the southern suburbs of Sydney.

Regan placed her black-gloved fingers on the door's security panel—flashlight beam a narrow point of illumination in the pitch black of the corridor—and keyed in a five-digit sequence. It had taken five tedious dinners with Epoc Industries' chief of security to procure the password: one night of bad food, bad personal hygiene and very bad wandering hands for each digit.

A chill of revulsion shot up Regan's spine at the memory but she shoved it aside. What was on the other side of the door was worth it. Seeing the animals running free from Epoc's building was worth it. Seeing the bastard's normally smug and composed face twisted with rage tomorrow night on the six o'clock news was worth it. Completely.

A soft click sounded and the door's locking mechanism deactivated, followed by a faint hiss of escaped, artificial air— rank with animal faeces and disinfectant.

Regan's lips spread into a grim smile. *Bingo.*

Muscles and nerves coiled, she gave the door a gentle and oh-so-minute push. So far, her "romance" of the security guard had landed her all the codes and schedules required to get to the main lab undetected, but she wasn't stupid. Being stupid led to being caught. Or shot.

She stood frozen, on the balls of her feet, ready to run. Or fight.

Nothing.

Except the low and mournful whimpers of animals locked in cages awaiting a slow and agonizing death.

"Not anymore."

Her voice was barely a breath. She pushed the door wider and stepped into the guts of Epoc Industries' Scientific Division, flashlight seeking those she had come to rescue.

The animals.

"Oh, shit."

A German Shepherd cowered in a cage before her, tail tucked between its bent hind legs. The sharp outlines of its ribs jutted out beside the hollow pit of its gut, the raw pink skin of its shaved neck and chest festered with weeping sores. It turned a sunken brown stare on her, its misery and pain clear in the liquid depths. Various tubes punctured its neck and chest, feeding something in and out of the emaciated dog.

"Epoc." Regan shook her head. "You bastard."

Stomach heavy, she took another step into the lab, moving her flashlight from one poor animal to another, throwing each into stark illumination as she did so. Here a bank of nine white cats, strapped into a device rendering them incapable of movement, eyelids wired open, a murky orange liquid dripping in slow, even drops onto the exposed eyeballs of each. Here a chimpanzee in a small cage, wires protruding from four stitched incisions on its spine, connecting the primate to what appeared to be a Geiger counter. Over there another bank of cats—these ones with their mouths braced shut around fat tubes filled with a black, viscous fluid.

Regan's stomach rolled and her grip on the flashlight grew hard. Fury surged through her. Fury and burning helplessness.

It didn't take a Zoology degree to see the animals in this lab would never run anywhere again.

Their eyes—their miserable, beseeching, dying eyes—held her. And asked for help.

Regan swallowed down the sudden lump in her throat and she thought of the small vial of Rimadyl in her backpack. It wasn't enough. Nothing would save these animals from their pain. Nothing. *Epoc. You inhuman bas—*

A low groan to her far right cut the dark thought short.

Fear and adrenaline scorching through her veins like electricity, Regan swung around. "Holy shit!"

The wolf was massive. Bigger than any Regan had ever seen. At least half the size of a buffalo, it stood on all fours in a heavily barred cage, bound by multiple leather straps completely restricting its movement. Two clear tubes jutted from a neat, little cut high on the base of its neck—one pumping in a thick, black liquid, the other empty, as if waiting for its use to commence.

Regan took a step forward, moving her flashlight over the wolf's muscled form.

It was sick. Possibly dying—the rapid, shallow breath, the dullness of its steel grey coat told her the animal was suffering. Big time. Yet even unwell, it still exuded primitive strength—a wild power almost frightening to behold. Regan's heart pounded in her chest and she slid the flashlight's beam to its head, careful to avoid shining the narrow but powerful light directly in the animal's eyes.

The wolf snarled silently, long teeth glistening, the twin silver discs of its eyes fixed on her.

Silver?

A slight frown pulled at Regan's eyebrows and her apprehension vanished immediately. A canine's eyes reflected green light in the dark, not silver, regardless of the genus. She shook her head, despair making her heart ache. "You poor thing," she whispered, throat tight. "What has Epoc done to you?"

The wolf's strange eyes stared at her. Seemed to delve into her soul. She pulled in a long, slow breath, unable to look away. *Wolf? Is it really a wolf?*

The wolf watched her from its cage, radiating power and rage.

And pain.

Regan blinked, shaking herself. What the hell was she doing standing around? God, did she want to get caught?

She placed the flashlight's barrel between her teeth before pulling her backpack from her shoulder. The heavy-duty bolt cutters tucked away inside would free the animals—she tossed a quick look at the still-staring wolf—*all* the animals of their metal-barred prisons.

Her hand brushed the hard plastic case of her anaesthetizing kit and she turned to the shepherd. At least the poor thing wouldn't die behind bars, even if its freedom only lasted a few moments.

On silent feet she crossed to the caged dog, holding her head down and to the side, right hand held out. She doubted the animal had the strength to bite but she wasn't taking any chances. Everything about her body language was by design: *I am not a threat to you.*

The dog's sad, brown eyes watched her approach, its tail giving a small, almost desperate wag as she drew closer and Regan's heart clenched again. She let her lips pull into a soft smile, careful not to show her teeth. "Yes, I know, boy," she murmured. "I'm going to take the pain away. I promise." Tail wagging weakly, the dog watched her.

As did the wolf.

Regan felt its silver gaze study her every move. It was unnerving somehow. Like the wolf judged her actions. She gave it a hurried look over her shoulder, butterflies flapping into frantic activity in her stomach. It looked like it could tear her apart with one simple snap of its jaws, sick or not. Lord, was she really going to set it free?

Of course you are. Would you really leave it behind? After seeing what Epoc is doing?

She turned back to the shepherd and quickened her pace. No. She wouldn't leave it behind, regardless of how it unnerved her. Reaching the dog, she placed her right hand through the bars of its cage, slowly raising it to the level of the dog's muzzle, allowing it to smell her scent. "It's okay, mate," she soothed. "I'm going to help." The dog's nose—drier than parchment— touched the small strip of exposed flesh between her glove and sleeve and its tail thumped weakly again.

Damn, I hate you, Nathan Epoc.

A soft snarl shattered the tense silence and Regan turned her head, the wolf catching her eye in the powerful glow of her flashlight. Its steady, silver stare bored into her before flicking to the left.

Her stomach twisted with unease. Pulling her bolt-cutters from her backpack, she severed the chain on the shepherd's cage, the noise like a gunshot in the silent lab. *Hurry, Woman. Hurry.* Pulling the chain free, she unlatched the lock and swung the door wide.

The dog stared at her, sunken eyes unblinking, tail wagging weakly.

Time pressing down on her, the weight of the wolf's gaze like a branding iron on her back, she withdrew her hypo kit from her backpack. "This won't hurt," she whispered, reaching into the cage. "I promise." The dog cowered, tail thumping in nervous swipes against the bars, its eyes fixed on her. With gentle fingers, she pinched a fold of skin on the back of its neck and injected the painkiller directly into its blood system. Tucking her torch under her armpit, she placed the hypodermic between her teeth and ran her hand down the dog's chest, feeling its wildly beating heart. "I'll do this as painlessly as I can," she said, her throat growing tighter at the animal's implicit faith. She moved her hands to one of the thick tubes inserted into dog's neck, readying to withdraw it.

A low grumble sounded behind her. Like a warning.

Muscles tense, Regan looked at the wolf again. *I'm coming. I can't rush this.*

The wolf studied her, before flicking its silver stare to the left again.

A chill shot up Regan's spine and the hair at the back of her neck stood on end. Fair dinkum, it was like the animal was trying to tell her something.

Yeah. To hurry up! Pull your finger out, Woman or you're going to get caught!

Gnawing on her bottom lip, she turned back to the shepherd. Hoping against hope the Rimadyl had started to take effect, she removed one tube. The dog whimpered but didn't flinch. "Good boy," she murmured, giving it a soft smile. Another tube followed. Another. Another. The dog gazed up at her, the thumps of its tail growing weaker. Regan's throat constricted. It wasn't going to last much longer.

"I need you to stay here for a moment, mate," she whispered, scratching it behind the ear. "Just until I see to the other animals. Then we're outta here, okay?"

Another tail wag, weaker this time. As if it knew what she wanted, the dog dropped into the down position and rested its muzzle on its extended front paws, liquid-brown eyes still locked on her. Trusting. Hopeful.

Tears burned at the back of Regan's eyes. She placed her palm on the shepherd's head...

And the wolf growled again.

"I'll be back," she said, knowing the high dose of painkiller would end the dog's misery before she returned. Blinking, refusing to let the tears fall, she moved silently. Across the lab.

To the wolf.

A flash of white in the dark told her its teeth were bared, but she continued forward. Pulling the bolt cutters from her backpack, she quickly severed a link in the chain wrapped around the cage's locked door.

A soft growl emanated from behind the bars and she looked up, her breath catching at the silver eyes staring at her. This close, the wolf's power was almost suffocating, as was its pain. "Not much longer," she muttered around the barrel of the flashlight. She slipped the bolt-cutter blades around one thick, shiny metal bar and—with considerable effort—managed to slice into the metal. Half an inch. She tried again. Maybe a bit more this time, but not much.

Regan scowled. This was going to take longer than she thought.

The wolf watched her, silent, before its hackles rose and it swung its head to the left. Seconds later, the chimp burst into screeching wails and a concealed door in the far left wall flung open.

Three armed security guards barged into the lab, guns and flashlights aimed at her. "Hands up, missy!"

Ah, shit!

"Hands up, *now!*"

Shit! Shit!

A whine filled the air, followed by the acrid stench of urine as the shepherd emptied its bladder.

"C'mon, girly," the largest of the three guards barked, something black and ominously shaped like a gun pointed straight at her chest. "Don't be stupid."

A wave of cold calm rolled through Regan. She gave the guards a slow smile, feeling the black paint smudged across her

17

face stretch and crack. "Someone should tell Nathan Epoc his security sucks." She pitched her flashlight at the largest guard's head.

Twenty-six years being the baby sister to one hulking, older brother stood Regan in good stead. When it came to defending herself, she was an expert.

The flashlight cut across the dark lab like a lethal pinwheel, narrow, white beam turning the room into a crazy lightshow. There was a loud clunk—metal on bone—as the flashlight struck the largest guard's forehead, followed by a bellowed, "*Mother fucker!*"

But Regan wasn't listening. She ran straight at the stunned and indignant man, flinging herself into a reverse spinning kick and smashing her booted heel against his thick jaw.

The guard went down. With a solid and somehow wet thud.

Blue eyes wild, Glock raised, the guard to Regan's left leapt at her. "Bitch!"

Without thought, she dropped into a crouch, taking out his legs with a tight, savage footsweep. She was up before he hit the floor, scooping up her torch and sprinting across the lab to the far door, the chimp's screeching wails like a Klaxon alarm in her head.

"Freeze, bitch!"

Shit, shit, shit!

The third guard—the rookie, if she remembered the schedule correctly—began running after her, stumbling over one of his fallen partners as he did so. *God help me if he remembers he has a—*

A shot fired, shattering the grim thought, and the rack of glass test tubes on the counter to Regan's immediate right.

SHIT!

"Shoot the fucking bitch!"

A metal chair flew through the air—*Christ! They're throwing furniture at me?*—before something large and heavy smashed into her, driving her to the floor.

Hot, wet breath snorted in her ear. "Gotcha, cunt." The largest guard—the one she'd hit with her flashlight—ground his flabby, sweaty bulk against her back, pinning her to the chilly, lab floor. "I'm gonna show you who sucks around here," he sneered. He dug his fingers into the soft underside of her wrists, ramming his hips against her ass. "You. On my hard cock."

"Shit!" A high-pitched shout cut across the guard's snarl. "She's let the dog out!"

Regan twisted her head, in time to see the shepherd, weak and trembling, launch itself from the cage, teeth bared, hackles up. *Oh, no!*

A gunshot split the air. Blood spurted from the dog's side, bright red and thick. Regan screamed, the anguished sound drowned out by loud, raucous laughter as the shepherd's lifeless body thudded to the floor.

"Got the fucker!" the tallest of the guards smirked, re-holstering his gun. Piercing blue eyes fell on Regan and his grin stretched wider. "Now, back to the fun."

Cold dread curdled in her throat. She bucked, trying to dislodge the guard pinning her to the floor. "Get off me, you fat fuck!"

He chuckled, dick grinding against her writhing butt. "Only when I'm done, cunt. Then my partners are gonna have their go." He pressed his open mouth to her ear and shoved his tongue into its shallow shell. "And you can scream all you want 'cause there ain't nobody here to hear you except these dumb-fuck animals." With a grunt, he flipped her onto her back and shoved his engorged dick hard against her crotch. "And they ain't gonna help you one little bit."

Regan stared up into his red, pudgy face, her dread turning to fear. *Oh please, no. Help me!*

"Hurry up, mate," the second guard said, stepping up beside his partner to leer down at her, depraved hunger burning in his blue eyes. "Shooting that mutt has made me hornier than—"

A low, savage growl cut him short.

"Aaah, Trev?" The rookie squeaked from across the lab, and even though Regan couldn't see him she heard something close to confused terror in his voice. "Trev, the wolf's gettin' bigger!"

The guard grinding his dick between Regan's thighs rolled his eyes. "It's in a fucking cage, Hicks. What's it gonna do? Join in?"

The wolf's growl filled the air—louder, longer. Two sets of flashlight beams fell on it immediately and, lying trapped under the grotesque and hideously aroused Trev, Regan watched the animal contort. Twist. Somehow grow bigger. The tubes poking from its neck quivered as, with an audible pop, they tore free, spurting black liquid all over the wolf's steel-grey fur. Regan's heart stopped. *Oh, my God...*

There was a low snarl, a sharp creak and the leather straps imprisoning it in the cage snapped. Just like that.

The rookie let out a yelp.

Trev stared at the snarling wolf, too stunned to get to his feet. "Jesus fuckin' Christ," he whispered. With a howl of brutal rage, the wolf burst through the bars of its cage. As if they were made of tin foil.

The rookie screamed. Blue Eyes stumbled backward. "Fucking hell!"

"Shoot it, shoot it!" squealed Trev, trying to scramble

upright and grab his gun at the same time.

He didn't make it.

The wolf smashed into him, driving him across the floor of the lab in a screaming blur of flailing arms and legs.

Regan scurried backward and stumbled to her feet, Trev's screams and the wolf's low, savage growls punching at her ears.

"Trev! Oh, fuck, Trev!" The rookie continued to wail, Glock completely forgotten.

"Shoot the wolf, you dumb fuck!" Blue Eyes shouted, throwing the rookie a murderous glare.

For a split second, Regan stood frozen, staring at the chaos around her. The smell of blood and piss stung her sinuses— *What in the name of God is going on?*—before primitive self-preservation kicked in and she turned and bolted for the exit door. Hot disgust rolled through her. She hadn't saved one single animal tonight. Not one.

Trev's screams, raw and wet and gurgling, rose above the rookie's wails and the chimp's screeching. Regan heard blood in the guard's throat and an image of the wolf's long teeth flashed through her head. Bloody hell, she'd caused this. Her feet faltered. She'd caused it all to—

A gun went off. Twice.

Trev howled. As did the wolf.

"*Get the fucking bitch!*" Blue Eyes screamed.

Regan didn't need any further prompting. Guilt bubbling like acid in her gut, she fled the room, the image of the dead German Shepherd haunting her. *I'm sorry, boy. I'm so sorry.*

Another scream pierced the terrible cacophony and the chimp screeched, manic and insane. A third gunshot rang out, a fourth, and the wolf howled again—long, loud and deadly—as Epoc Industries' high-tech security system finally activated, a

21

shrieking Klaxon squeal shattered the chaos.

Regan tore along the corridor, bleached in flooding white light. All around her, she heard the sound of metal cages rattling and shaking as the animals inside squealed and howled and tried to break free. She ran, their terrified calls drilling into her head, her heart. Another gunshot sounded behind her, a high-pitched scream rent the air, the wolf howled one more time...

And she burst from the building, wrapped immediately in the warm night air of an Australian summer.

Blinding spotlights swam across the surrounding walkways, slashing through the darkness like blades. Regan sprinted for the back entry gate, the same one she'd used to gain access to the secured grounds what felt like a lifetime ago. If someone had discovered it ajar, she was screwed. There was no way she could scale the twenty foot razor-wire fences enclosing Epoc's labs, no matter how loud the egging voice of her brother in her head. She looked over her shoulder, convinced she would see Trev, the rookie and Ol' Blue Eyes coming after her.

Nothing.

Except the stripping, swirling spotlights and the ear-piercing wail of the building's alarm, killing the peaceful stillness of pre-dawn.

Regan kept running. Until she cleared the perimeter, she was in danger. Even then, she couldn't relax. The black smudges on her face may have hid her true appearance in the lab, but it made her conspicuous as all hell out on the streets. An early morning jogger may wear all black—a *stupid* early morning jogger—but they wouldn't cover their faces in black shoe polish. If Epoc's men found her, they'd know who she was.

Run faster!

Her car was parked three blocks away, tank full, engine tuned to perfection. All she had to do to get away was get through the—

"Freeze, cunt!"

SHIT! Ol' Blue Eyes.

"Stop or I'll fuckin' shoot you down and fuck you as you die!"

Regan ran harder, the gate coming into sight. The *open* gate. *Yes!*

"I mean it, bitch!" Blue Eyes screeched. "The next thing you'll feel is my—"

He didn't finish. Regan prepared her body for the bullet but it never came. Throwing a look over her shoulder, she saw something that looked like a wolf but wasn't—something *huge*—thrash Blue Eyes's limp body about on the ground, its powerful jaws clamped around the security guard's blood-pissing throat.

Her blood ran cold. *Jesus! What is that?*

Feet stumbling, she fell to the ground, staring at the nightmarish sight as though hypnotized. *God. What IS that?*

"Over there!"

The furious shout snapped her out of her trance. Whipping her head around, she saw them. Five armed guards running towards her.

"Over there! Over there!"

She flung her stare back to the wolf, watched it raise its massive head from Blue Eyes's mutilated throat to regard her. Their eyes connected for a brief moment before it threw its head back and howled.

"There! There!" The approaching guards screamed. "Shit! Get it! Get it!"

They changed course, running at the wolf—the *beast*—

instead. Guns raised and aimed.

Blood flicking from its muzzle, the animal swung its silver stare to her once more before it ran away. Disappearing around the corner of the building, the yelling, bellowing guards close on its tail.

Regan stared at the motionless body of Ol' Blue Eyes—for exactly two seconds. Blood roaring in her ears, she scrambled to her feet and sprinted through the gate. Off Epoc Industries's grounds. Into the darkness of the street. Heading for her waiting car.

She was speeding through the quiet streets of North Sydney before her heartbeat returned to normal. "Holy shit!" Long dark fingers of pre-dawn shadows reached out for her car as she turned the wheel and sped down a narrow lane. "Holy shit!"

Had the wolf done what she thought? Had it saved her?

Regan shook her head and tried to force some calm into her screaming muscles. Wolves were smart, possibly the most intelligent of the canine genus, but *that* smart?

Was it really a wolf, though?

The question flitted through her stunned mind and her heart started thumping again.

She had no answer.

Not without seeing the animal again.

Turning the wheel once more, she pulled into her short driveway. Killing the engine, she stared out the windscreen at the closed door of her garage. Everything in her studies told her what she'd seen was lunacy. Wolves did not grow that big. They did not exhibit self-sacrificing behavior, *especially* not to protect a human. She made her living working with animals. She was Sydney's leading animal physiotherapist, damn it! She *knew* animals. And what she saw tonight *wasn't* normal.

But you did see it. The wolf did draw the guards' attention from you. It did save you. It did stop Trev.

A shiver raced up Regan's spine and her flesh broke out in goose bumps. Christ, what a fuckup. She pulled a deep breath and the cloying stench of Trev's sweat assaulted her senses. Urgh, she needed a shower.

She climbed from the car and began to cross the small patch of lawn she proudly called her front yard. She needed a shower and sleep. She needed normalcy again. In only a few hours she had an appointment with the director of Taronga Zoo. Following that a physio session with the Prime Minister's aging dachshund, after which came lunch with Rick at his...

A low and distant howl cut her thought dead.

A wolf's howl.

Regan spun around, expecting to see the steel-grey wolf behind her, its muzzle dripping with blood, its silver eyes burning into her soul.

Nothing.

As if there would be! Get a grip!

She stood still, ears straining to hear...

Nothing except the gentle roar of Bondi Beach half a mile away and the soft warbles of a nearby magpie out searching for breakfast.

Shaking her head, Regan climbed the steps of her porch and unlocked her front door. She entered her home, closed the door behind her and headed straight for the shower, stripping as she went. It was time for normal life to resume.

For her, at least.

The early-morning sun streamed into her bedroom through the open side window like a stroke of brilliant gold paint, casting everything in a warm hue and turning the dust motes on the air into dancing points of white-gold light.

Eyes still closed, Regan stretched, arms extending up and out, back bowing into a deep curve. Rick Deluca—a vet she'd known since her university days and had dated off and on for the past three months—had commented more than once how cat-like she looked when first waking. Regan took it as a compliment. She liked cats. They were creatures of grace and feline beauty. If she had to be compared to animal, a cat was fine and dandy with her.

A gust of warm wind blew through the window and the organza curtains billowed, brushing against her bare legs and tummy. Groaning low, Regan opened her eyes and stared at the ceiling. Why did her body ache like she'd been hit by a bus?

Her tired mind drew a complete blank.

For a disoriented second.

"Oh, bloody hell!" She smacked her palm to her forehead and dragged her hand down her face. "Epoc's lab."

Shit! What a complete cock up.

An image of a sad and dying German Shepherd filled her head and guilt flooded through her. She'd failed too many creatures this morning. The shepherd's brown eyes grew light, cooler, and suddenly it was the wolf's silver gaze staring at her. The wolf that saved her.

Saved her by ripping out the throat of a human.

A twinge of cold apprehension fluttered in her stomach and she swallowed. The guard, Blue Eyes, was never going to be a potential Nobel Peace Prize recipient, but no one deserved being mauled to death by a wolf, no matter how hideous they were.

Squinting against the bright morning sun, wishing like hell she could turn back time, Regan peered at her alarm clock.

Six twenty-seven.

She groaned again. "You've got to be kidding!" She'd only been asleep for two hours? What the hell woke her?

For a moment, Regan listened to the call of slumber beckoning her again: *Another thirty minutes, that's all. C'mon, y'know you want to.* She wiggled on the sheets, the cool cotton caressing her bare skin like soft kisses. Oh, how tempting...

Her stomach however, had other ideas. She had after all neglected it for the last twelve hours. Now it grumbled loud enough she expected the neighbors to run from their homes screaming "earthquake". With a very unladylike snort, she shook her head. There was no way she was going back to sleep now.

She climbed from her bed and padded barefoot across the polished floorboards of her bedroom, heading for the small but very cozy living room. Sydney wasn't the cheapest city in Australia to live. Finding an affordable place halfway decent had been almost as draining and traumatic as her regular lab raids. Her home, tucked high on the northern hill overlooking Bondi Beach, may be the size of a postage stamp, but it was hers, not the bank's and she loved it. Big enough for her king-size bed, third-hand sofa, old TV and a terrarium in the corner for Rex when he wanted to soak up some heat-lamp rays.

She studied the living room, wondering if the adult frill-neck lizard was waiting for his breakfast.

Nope.

A small grin pulled at her lips. He was probably sulking under the fridge. "Let me get my caffeine fix first, Rex!" she called to the absent lizard, shuffling toward the kitchen and its already percolating coffee machine. "Then I'll get dressed and tell you about the nightmare—"

A low whine stopped her dead.

With a frown creasing her brow, Regan turned.

And saw the wolf.

Chapter Two

Nathan Epoc stormed across the expansive floor of his opulent bedroom, his head aching with enraged agony.

Fucking do-gooder, animal-rights activists.

Activ*IST, Nathan. Activ*IST. *There was only one. A female. A single, unarmed female.*

Hot blood pulsed through his head like a molten trip-hammer and he scowled, running his palms over the smooth dome of his scalp. One little bitch. One little do-gooder, animal-rights activist bitch causing all this trouble. He glared out the glass wall of his bedroom.

Sydney Harbor sprawled before him, so blue it almost hurt to look at—a cerulean blanket bejeweled by the dazzling dawn sun and gleaming white boats. The bone-white arcs of the Sydney Opera House curved up and over the horizon to his right, a defining monument of architectural brilliance for a young country. Money could not buy the view afforded through every window of his home, only power. Absolute power. And he—Nathan Epoc—*had* absolute power. Had it. Wielded it. *Was* it.

He turned from the window, the sight of the arching Harbor Bridge in the distance catching his attention. The construction spanned the rippling channel dividing North Sydney from the commercial epicenter, another marvel of man's engineering genius.

Huh! If the world knew what *he* had achieved, these pitiful man-made constructions would be scorned for the triflings they were. If the world knew...

He ground his teeth. If the bitch who invaded his lab last night spoke of what she saw the world *would* know, well, begin to suspect, and that was not acceptable. He'd worked hard to present an immaculate, benevolent image to the people of this country and one little bitch could ruin it all.

A low growl rumbled in his chest and he felt his canines lengthen, digging into his lower lip. A ripple passed over his flesh. Fuck! Just thinking of the cunt and the trouble she could cause and he was close to shifting.

The drilling fire in his head flared and he growled again. Not at the pain, but at the thought of the female and the grief she could bring down on him. If she took photos while in the lab... If she had evidence...

He spun about, glaring out the window at the sublime day. "Fucking do-gooder bitch!"

He hadn't been this angry since Aine's death. Since the night the *Onchú* clan butchered her. The night his sweet lifemate was lost to him forever.

Bitter rage ripped through him, as fresh and biting as it had been over two hundred years ago. That night began a war unlike any the lycanthrope clans of the world had seen. A war led by him. His rivals had caught him off-guard once. They wouldn't do it again. He wouldn't let them. Any of them.

But now... Now this *human*...

He had to find her. Find her, find out what she knew and silence her.

And the second she was no longer a problem, find Declan

O'Connell again. He wasn't done with the Irish werewolf. The *conriocht.* Not this close to success. Not this close to punishment.

He crossed to his personal bureau and jabbed at a key recessed in the rose-cedar surface, impatience coursing through his veins.

"Yes, Mr. Epoc?" a husky voice sounded from the wall speaker above the bureau, both reverent and submissive—the way he expected all his staff and pack members to be.

"I want the bitch brought in," he said, canines growing longer, thicker with each word. "And I want her brought in now."

Regan's heart hammered.

The wolf lay on its side, taking up most of her old sofa, its eyes closed, its rib cage rising and falling with rapid, shallow breaths. Dry blood smattered the grey fur on its neck, cracked and thick like black mud. The cushions of her sofa bowed and compressed under the animal's massive bulk and, as she had in the lab, Regan wondered what species it was. None she was familiar with.

How can that be?

She frowned. She was at least passingly familiar with just about every species in existence—she had to be in her line of work. How could she not—

The wolf whined again, softer, weaker, and Regan's puzzlement vanished.

In a heartbeat she crossed the room and crouched by the wounded animal, skimming her hands over its body. A wave of

31

awe rolled through the cold worry knotted in her chest. It was unwell. Its limbs trembled and each breath seemed weaker than the last, yet its feral strength was undeniable. She'd thought it a creature of primitive power back in Epoc's lab but now, here in her room with its corded muscles under her examining fingers, its *mana* seemed almost tangible. "What genus are you, my friend?" she whispered, running her hands over steely quadriceps much bigger and longer than any wolf species she knew. Quadriceps turned to femur, femur to pelvic bone.

Regan frowned, confusion squirming in her gut. The animal's pelvis felt wrong, like some sick bastard with a Doctor Moreau complex had taken to it with a bone grinder in an attempt to reshape it into a human hipbone. "What *have* they been doing to you, mate?" she murmured, tracing the distorted bone. "My God, how can you even walk?"

She moved her hands up the wolf's spine, counting vertebrae, looking for wounds or injuries. Curiosity ate at her concern. Where had the creature come from? Wolves were not native to Australia and as far as she knew, the only ones in the country were those housed in zoos and animal enclosures. For this lone wolf to be in Epoc's lab...?

Imported illegally, perhaps?

But from where?

Her seeking fingers slid through a patch of wet fur low on the wolf's rib cage and Regan stilled her investigation. She parted the animal's dense coat, looking for... "There it is."

Fresh blood, bright red and warm on her fingers, seeped from a ragged hole puncturing the wolf's side. Regan prodded the surrounding flesh gently, worrying the bullet may be embedded in bone beneath. She'd have to get the animal to Rick. Whether the bullet was there or not, the wound needed to be—

The wolf whined. Low. Almost human.

"I'm sorry, mate," Regan soothed, removing her fingers from its rib cage. Chewing on her bottom lip, she smoothed her palms over its scapular and down first one foreleg and then the other. Both rippled with muscle and once again, uneasy wonderment wriggled in Regan's stomach. The humerus seemed too close to human in structure to be possible. She ran her hands over it and it seemed to shift. Grow longer. Straighter.

Regan scrubbed the back of her hand against her eyes. She must be sleep deprived. Bones didn't change structure. With a slight shake of her head, she went back to her examination. As soon as she was convinced the animal could be moved, she'd call Rick. He'd give his left nut to help her out, any excuse to try and impress her into his bed. But quite frankly, she had no hope of moving the animal herself, even if it would fit in her car.

Another whine whispered on the air, so soft Regan almost missed it. "Not much longer, my mysterious friend," she whispered, letting her hands settle on the wolf's rib cage again, careful to avoid its wound. Its coat felt like fine velvet under her palms and for a dreamlike moment, she felt like pressing her face to the animal's side. She leant forward, sliding her hands to its shoulder joint in search of wounds unseen and her bare nipples brushed against the wolf's chest, flesh to fur. Soft. Cool. So much more than she'd expected. So much more than any animal species she knew.

What type of wolf are you?

She returned her attention to the wolf's body. With the exception of the bullet wound, it seemed physically uninjured, but who knew *what* Epoc's scientists had been doing to it. She smoothed her hands over the silken fur, a distant more detached part of her mind admiring the wolf's superb biomechanical construct. It was a creature evolved for one purpose only—to kill—yet its beauty was undeniable. Strength, menace and deadly purpose all combined in the majestic somehow romantic form of—

The thigh muscle below her palm shifted, elongated, and Regan stumbled backward, landing flat on her bare butt with an ignominious thud. She stared at the massive, powerful and utterly lupine form. Watched it contort. Shudder.

The dense fur rippled, each strand seemingly alive with its own energy. The back legs grew long, straight. Thick, corded thigh muscles formed on bones no longer short and crooked. "What the..." Regan's stunned whisper barely left her lips.

Another shudder wracked the wolf's contorting form. Another. And another. Its fur grew thin, retracting into the flesh beneath, disappearing with each violent convulsion until its coat no longer existed and instead...

Regan's heart froze and she stared at the naked man laying full-length on her sofa.

The naked, trembling, gasping man laying full-length on her sofa.

Looking at her.

"What the *hell?*"

The man's eyes—the angry color of a stormy winter's sky— flicked over her face. Like oiled smoke, he was on his feet, hard, lean body coiling, pale flesh glistening with a faint sheen of sweat in the sun-filled room. Regan stared at him. Speechless. Unable to move.

Shaggy ink black hair fell across his forehead, brushed straight eyebrows of the same color, cheekbones high and angular. Smooth, curved pecs cut down to a hairless torso sculpted in muscle. Nothing detracted from the perfection of his body, not even the mean scar slashing his pale skin from navel to groin. Regan traced the ragged white line with her eye, her stomach clenching as it disappeared into a thick thatch of black pubic hair just above—

Oh, my God! He's huge!

A sharp intake of breath jerked her gaze back up to his face, in time to see nostrils flaring on a nose almost too long, almost too large. Those stormy eyes held hers. Kept her naked ass on the carpet. Frozen.

Compelling.

The word flittered through her head, disconnected and surreal and with it came a tight throb, low in the pit of her stomach. A clenching, warm beat between her thighs.

Shit, Woman! Have you lost your mind?

She sucked in her own swift breath, tasting his sweat on the air. "Who..." She began.

Those grey eyes flickered. Grew wild. Dangerous. "You're in a lotta trouble, love," he growled, a soft brogue lacing the foreboding words seconds before every muscle in his perfect body coiled and he leapt.

At her.

He slammed into her, flattening her to the floor. Back, shoulders, skull. Bright pain spiked through her head, cold and hot at the same time, and she cried out. Strong, long-fingered hands clamped around her wrists, pinning them to the floor beside her head with a grip so fierce her brother would have been jealous. Regan squealed, glaring up into grey, burning eyes. "Get off me, you bastard!" She bucked—all too aware of the muscled body pressed to hers. The *naked* body.

Fair Dinkum, Woman! Only seconds earlier he was a wolf! Wake up!

A hot breath feathered her face, ruffled her hair and she bucked again. This was no dream. *He* was no dream. "Get off me, you freak!"

Grey eyes flashed, all the more intense for the thick, black lashes framing them. "I'm no freak, lady."

The words flowed from well-defined lips, the soft Irish accent she'd heard earlier cut with anger. Long, corded legs battled hers, pinned them to the floor with a brutal strength. His knees shoved at hers, spreading her thighs wide until her lower body was completely trapped by his.

A rock-hard pressure nudged at the soft lips of her sex and Regan sucked in a sharp breath. Oh no, he was aroused!

Aren't you?

Hot, terrified shame tore through her. Yes. She was. "Get off me!" she screamed, thrashing underneath him in desperate fury. "Get off me! Get off me! Get off me!"

Declan stared down at the woman beneath him, fighting like hell to keep her in his hold. Christ, she was a wild cat. Even with her legs trapped under the considerable weight of his own, she'd almost thrown him off more than once. What the hell did she do for a living? Wrestle rhinos?

No, Dec. She takes on security guards.

"Get off me!" she screamed again, body like a live current of electricity. He pressed into her, trying to hold her still, trying *not* to think about the lithe muscles of her limbs and tummy, the sweat-slicked smoothness of her bare skin, the velvet heat between her thighs mashing against his ever-growing shaft with each whiplash buck she gave.

Should've thought about the fact you were both naked before *you jumped on her.*

"Listen, love," he growled, trying to shove the delicious

sensations stirring in his groin from his mind. "Just calm down and—"

Seismic rage erupted in her ice-green eyes. "*GET! OFF! ME!*"

Her body tensed with each bellowed word, thrusting her soft, damp heat harder against his now-throbbing cock.

Declan's head swam, the change still too fresh in his system, the primitive, elemental instincts of the werewolf still too powerful. The musky scent of her sweat and sex threaded into his every breath. Intoxicating. Potent. She was a fighter, a warrior... She'd risked her life to save those incapable of saving themselves. The wolf in his blood growled in ancient appreciation, in hunger...

Unable *not* to, he leant down to kiss her.

One second he stared down at her, struggling to hold her still, the next he captured her lips with his and tasted her with his tongue.

For a moment, she lay beneath him, her exquisitely bare body locked frozen with shock. And why not? A man she'd never met before was kissing her, a man who—only seconds earlier— had been a bloody, great big wolf stretched out on her sofa. He almost pulled away, rational thought smashing down on him. But then, a slight tremble rippled through her, her arms snaked up around his neck and she was kissing him back. Deeply.

Her tongue battled his, curled and delved and flicked. Her teeth nipped at his bottom lip and a jolt of liquid heat shot straight to his groin, bringing a low and utterly raw groan to his throat. He dragged his hands from her wrists, down the smooth columns of her arms, his thumbs brushing the heavy swell of her breasts pressed flat against his body. The contact, light and fleeting, sent another surge of wet heat into his balls and his already-hard cock pulsed with new, eager blood.

What are you doing?

He didn't know. The change had never left him so vulnerable to his werewolf's desires, so manipulated by those animalistic cravings before. All he knew, all he cared about at that very moment, was how wonderfully warm and sensual the woman beneath him felt. How completely she returned his kiss.

He plunged his tongue into her mouth again, shifting his weight to smooth a hand up the delicious curve of her breast. The soft feel of it under his palm, the puckered peak of her nipple under his fingertips made him groan again, made his breath catch in his tight throat. Praise Mary, she felt so damn wonder—

Something hard and small smacked into his temple.

Explosive, white-hot pain erupted in Declan's head. Eyes blurring, he rolled to the side. Christ, she'd hit him!

"Get off me!"

She lashed out, completely dislodging his weight before he recovered. She'd hit him! Christ, she'd almost knocked him out.

"Get the fuck off me!"

Another savage blow thumped against his head, this one narrowly missing his nose. He reeled back, pain and blood roaring in his ears. She'd hit him! While he was drowning in her taste and feel, she'd hit him!

Almost stumbling across the floor, Declan reached for his throbbing head, eyes still incapable of focusing. The blurred shape of the woman leapt to her feet, and he got the sense she was on the verge of kicking into him. A squirming wave of admiration rolled through him and his cock, still too full of hungry blood, twitched. "Shit, love, do you know how to throw a punch!"

The blurred shape loomed over him. "What the bloody hell *are* you and what have you done with my lizard?"

Declan blinked, both in confusion and in an attempt to clear his vision. "Your what?"

"Where the hell's my lizard?" Long, bare legs came into focus—briefly—drawing his attention up to their apex and a distant, devious part of Declan's mind—the part not in pain—noticed she not only knew how to punch, she also knew how to handle a razor.

Get your head out of the gutter. "Lady, I don't know anything about a—"

"Where's my lizard, you goddamn freak?"

Her roar split the room and sharp pain pounded through Declan's head. Hell, he liked it better when she thought he was a wolf. "I haven't seen your bloody lizard," he growled, staggering to his feet. He squinted at her, relief flooding through him when she appeared sharp. In focus. "Praise Mary, I thought you'd buggered up my sight for good!"

She stared at him, gloriously naked, her lithe, toned and very perfect body shaking with what he assumed was rage. Her hands were clenched into rock-hard fists beside her thighs, her legs spread, knees bent slightly. Her hair tumbled across her straight, tensed shoulders in a shaggy curtain of rich-chocolate waves, falling to her nipples, drawing his gaze to her heaving breasts. She looked ready to attack. To rip him limb from limb. Such a different creature to the one only moments earlier smoothing her soft, gentle hands over said limbs in an attempt to find any injuries. What a contradiction.

What a—

"*Where. Is. My. Lizard?*"

Hands raised, he took a step forward. "Listen, love. I don't know anything about a lizard, I haven't seen a lizard, I haven't even *smelt* a lizard." He stared at her, saw confusion shimmer in her ice-green eyes, saw her muscles tense with each word he said. He returned his eyes to her face, needing to keep his attention away from her body. It was too flawless. Too distracting. "Now, you need to listen to me because while you did a very brave and noble thing breaking into Epoc's lab, you also did a very stupid thing."

Her jaw clenched, and those striking eyes narrowed. "I'm beginning to realize that."

Declan didn't miss the caustic insinuation. He was a journalist, after all. Well, had been a journalist back in Dublin. Who knows what he'd call himself now? Lone wolf? He cringed at the cliché. And the black look of murder on the woman's face. "I'm going to say this as plainly as possible," he went on, risking another step closer, "and I don't want you to start screaming about your bloody lizard again. We have to get out of here. You have to come with me. Right now."

She straightened, and he swore he heard her spine snap straight. The fact she was stark naked seemed to have completely slipped her mind. She glared at him, bunched fists on hips too smooth and curved for Declan's peace of mind. "One kiss and you think I'm ready to elope?" She cocked a dark, arched eyebrow. "You had more chance when you were a wolf."

Declan raised one of his own eyebrows. "Yeah, I noticed."

Cool eyes bored into him. "What are you?"

"It's usual practice to ask '*who*' are you, the answer to which, is the man you just kissed."

The woman crossed her arms, stare flat and decidedly icy. "Put it down to temporary insanity. I'm not in the habit of kissing strange men."

Declan's lips twitched. "And yet..."

A dusky pink blush painted the woman's cheeks, a vision so innocent and beguiling a swelling wave of heat rolled through him and pooled low in his gut.

40

"I don't know who or *what* you are. But it's time for you to go."

The desire to step forward, curl his fingers around her arms and pull her to his body crashed over him. Christ, it had been so long since a female affected him like this. The search for Maggie's killer had consumed him. Nothing but finding his sister's murderer had existed—or mattered. Yet here he was, in—based on the accents he'd heard since being captured—Australia, the other side of the world, and he was horny.

And stupid. You think Epoc hasn't tracked you both down yet? Stop standing around thinking with your dick and start using your head. Her life depends on you now. Whether she likes it or not.

"You're right. It *is* time to go." He destroyed the distance between them, closed his hands around her arms and fixed her with a level stare. "Both of us."

Her reaction was swift and immediate. She kicked him.

The ball of her foot rammed straight into his shin. Bright pain shot up his leg, making his balls shrink. He bit back a shout, sinking his fingers harder into her biceps and glaring down at her. "Stop it. I'm not going to hurt you."

Green eyes flashed fury and—goddamn it—fear. "Let me go."

"I—"

She struck out before he finished, jerking her knee up fast and hard, and it was only the grace of God—and his preternatural reflexes—that saved his balls being mashed up into the base of his spine. He twisted his body, right thigh taking the blow, the awkward action making the bullet wound in his side erupt with fresh, blistering pain. *Jesus Christ!*

Declan's patience snapped. In one fluid move he spun about, flung the woman onto the cushions of the sofa he'd been

41

lying on only minutes earlier and followed the path of her body with his own, pinning her to the piece of furniture with his hands, hips and legs. A growl burst from his throat and, temper boiling, he bared his teeth. "Listen to me, love. We don't have time for this. Nathan Epoc's mongrels will be here any second and if they find us, they'll kill you." He tightened his grip on her wrists, staring hard at her. "After they rape you. As men and then as wolves."

The blood drained from the woman's face and she froze, body stiller than a statue. "Wolves..." The word fell from her lips in a stunned breath. "My God, what the hell is going on?"

Declan clenched his jaw. "Unfortunately, more than you ever wanted to know." He relaxed his hold on her wrists. A little. "Now you have exactly sixty seconds to pull on some clothes and get ready to leave. After that we're out of here, dressed or not."

The woman tensed and he saw rage ignite in her eyes again. "I'm not going anywhere with you. My lizard... The cops..."

Declan shook his head. "Epoc owns the cops. Perhaps you didn't hear me earlier when I said rape and murder. I wasn't kidding. They will do things to you no human mind could imagine. Unless you come with me." He shifted his weight, tight impatience eating at him. "Trust me, I'll explain everything I can later, but we have to go. Now."

He rose to his feet, hoping to God he'd made his point. His heart hammered and his blood roared. He tried to tell himself it was adrenaline making his body behave so, but he knew otherwise. Lust scorched through his veins—and at that very moment, lust was almost more dangerous than Epoc.

The woman stared up at him, naked body vulnerable, sharp eyes defiant. A second passed before, with fluid grace, she leapt to her feet, sprinting across the room to disappear through a far door, the flexing muscles of her toned ass playing merry hell with his senses. He studied the door she'd passed through, listening to what was happening in the room. The sound of drawers opening and clothes rustling satisfied him and, dragging his hands through his hair, he turned and surveyed the room around him. She didn't trust him, yet—and really, was there any wonder? But maybe if he found this missing lizard of hers...

A very faint click sounded in his ear and he flicked his head slightly to the left, tuning into the noises emanating from her room. His eyes narrowed. Damn it, she'd picked up a phone.

He crossed the room to her bedroom in two leaps, the urge to transform like a weight on his chest. Flinging open the door, he stepped in, fists balled, nostrils flaring. "Not sure we have time for a phone call, love."

She spun about, staring at him with wide eyes, looking for all the world like a small animal frozen in the lights of a speeding truck. A small animal holding the handset of a cordless phone, that was. "How did you—?"

He ignored her question. She'd figure the answer out in due course. If she was what he thought she was—an animal expert of some kind—it wouldn't take long for the penny to drop. No matter what form he was in, his hearing was phenomenal. It came with the whole werewolf package. He stormed across the room, taking in the short running shorts and black tank top she now wore with a surreal mix of disappointment and relief. "I'm full of surprises."

The woman's muscles flexed and her grip on the handset tightened. "So am I."

Declan gave her a bleak scowl. The low, almost inaudible beep beep of a dial tone spilled from the phone in her hand and his scowl turned to a frustrated snarl. Shit. She'd called someone. "As much as I'm enjoying this whole tête-à-tête," he said, reaching for the handset, "there are more important things we have to be doing. Like..."

He didn't finish. The low sound of an engine thrummed into his head, vibrated through his body into his gut. He sucked in a swift breath and the scent of wolf assaulted his sinuses. Bad wolf. He spun about, staring through the door across the woman's living room, watching as a large, black van slowed to a complete stop by the curb out the front of her house. *Fuck.* Spinning back to the woman, he shook his head. "Time's up."

"Time's up?" Her forehead creased. "What does that mean?"

Declan gave her a level look. "It means this. Sorry." And he smashed his fist against her jaw.

Stunned rage filled her eyes—a heartbeat before her body went limp and she slumped forward. The phone fell from her hand, hitting the floor with a soft thud.

He grabbed her and threw her over his shoulder, her unconscious frame like pliable rubber. "This is *not* how I wanted to do this," he growled, hitching her weight closer to his head and anchoring his arm snugly around her waist. He shot a look over his shoulder, blood hot with the need to transform. He stared at the van on the street through the gauzy length of curtain hanging over the living room window. Watched its doors swing open. Watched a hulking shape he knew all too well climb out of the passenger side seat. Watched the man with flaming red hair and muscles on muscles bend his short, wide neck to the side in an action designed to intimidate. *McCoy.*

He bared his teeth and turned back to the woman's bedroom. In time to see a greenish-grey lizard roughly the size of a small dog, go skittering across the floor and disappear under the far wardrobe. A short, sharp snort escaped Declan.

"You're on your own, lizard."

And without further adieu, he crossed the room, kicked out the flyscreen of the main window, leapt through it and took off across the woman's small backyard. The sound of the van door slamming shut behind him thumped at his senses as he cleared the dividing fence in a single bound, sprinting across the neighbor's lawn. Just a naked Irishman with a bleeding side, running through the early-morning streets with an unconscious, animal liberationist slung over his shoulder. Nothing unusual about that.

Nothing unusual at all.

Chapter Three

Peter frowned at the phone in his hand. What the bloody hell was going on? "Hello?"

Nothing.

His frown pulled deeper. The caller ID display told him it was his baby sister on the other end, but since when did Reggie think it was funny to call and not say anything?

She wouldn't.

Unease twisted in Peter's gut—cold and tight. She'd pulled a lab raid last night. She hadn't told him which lab she was hitting in their last conversation but he knew when she was going in and when she'd planned to be out. He made it his business to know when she went on one of her freedom missions. No one else in the family knew what she got up to in the wee hours of the morning. Dad would kill her, even if he did agree with her motives, and Mum would chain her to the sofa, but someone had to be there for her if she was ever—God forbid—arrested, or worse yet, shot. She didn't like it, but too bloody bad. It's what big brothers did; they pissed off their little sisters, even if it was for their own good.

Peter placed the phone back to his ear. "Reggie? Can you hear me?"

Still nothing. Well, nothing except the irritating scratch and hum of the connection. His gut twisted again. Damn it. What if

46

she was in trouble?

In trouble? Reggie's always in trouble.

Peter shook his head. She'd been after someone big last night. He'd seen it in her eyes. Someone she considered the enemy. Perhaps she'd finally been caught. Goddamn it, what if she was—

"You're on your own, lizard."

The muffled words, almost inaudible, fell from the phone. Male? Irish? Peter snapped straight in his chair. *Lizard?* Shit. Rex. "Hey?" His sharp shout lifted the heads of quite a few people surrounding him but he ignored their curious stares. They were in a cop shop, for Christ sake. Someone shouted down a phone just about every other minute. "Hey? Regan?"

Nothing.

Cold worry gnawed at him, joining the tension squirming in his gut. Fuck.

For a terrible moment, he didn't know what to do. His gut, as churned as it was, told him to get over to Regan's house now, but to do so meant hanging up the phone in his hand and what if his little sister *was* in her home, *was* on the other end trying to talk to him, *needing* his help?

"Thomas?"

Peter stared at the far window, the blue, cloudless sky outside seeming to mock him. Goddamn it, what the hell should he do? Was Reggie—

"Thomas!"

A gruff and very belligerent voice barking his name yanked Peter's attention away from the window and the ominous thought of his sister's silent phone. He stared up into his boss's bloodshot eyes, unable to miss the sour expression on his round, unshaven face. "Yeah, Inspector?"

"Your wife's been tryin' to call you for the last ten minutes." Tony Muriciano glared at him, leathery skin yellow and dry from far too many cigarettes.

"*Ex*-wife, Inspector," Peter corrected, his grip on his phone curling tight.

Fat, nicotine-stained fingers jerked on the waistline of wrinkled chinos and Muriciano's ample gut wobbled under his white shirt. "Whatever. Tell her next time she's tryin' to get hold of you to call the switch. I'm too busy to deal with her shit."

Peter looked up at his boss, suppressing a snarl of frustration. Reggie. What was going on with Reggie?

Muriciano managed to look annoyed. "How the fuck she get my number anyhow?"

Maybe it was when you hit on her last Christmas party, you fat fuck. "I don't know, Inspector."

Muriciano's lips pulled away from yellow teeth in a snide smile. "Of course." His red-rimmed eyes glinted. "So, was that your sister's name I heard you shoutin' out a second ago? She okay?" He swiped a hand over his pate, licking his lips. "You can give her my number anytime. I'd hate for such a pretty young thing to be in trouble." He snorted, mouth stretching into a wide leer. "Unless it's trouble with me."

Peter's fist clenched and he shoved aside the urge to pull his own gun from its holster and shoot his captain in the head. "She's fine, Inspector." He held up the phone still clenched in his grip. "Just a lousy connection."

Muriciano gave his head a nod. "Hmmm. Well, if she needs a hand..." He chuckled, the sound both low and crude, and Peter had to sink his nails into his palm to keep his hand from wrapping around his Glock.

The Inspector turned and began weaving his way back to his office on the other side of the room, barking orders and insults at various detectives and uniformed officers as he went. "Your wife's on line ten, Thomas," he shot back over his shoulder. "She sounds pissed."

"*Ex*-wife," Peter growled, returning the phone in his hand to his ear. How the hell the man ever made detective, let alone Insp—

"Fuck! She's not here!"

The harsh shout spat from the handset and Peter jumped.

"The bitch isn't here! They're not here! Where the fuck is O'Connell?"

"McCoy, look! Near the bed. On the floor. Why's that red light blinking on the phone?"

There was a scuffle, the distinctive sound of cotton sheets being disturbed followed by a guttural male voice with a broad Scottish accent saying, "Hello?"

The phone creaked as Peter's grip curled harder. "Who's this? Where's my sister?"

"Now? Or after I fuck her?"

Peter's blood ran cold. "You touch my sister and you're—"

A sharp clunk stabbed at Peter's ear, followed by the drilling beep of a disconnect tone. *Shit!* He leapt to his feet, chair tumbling over. *Shit!*

It would take approximately forty-five minutes to get to Reggie's house, thirty with the blue and reds on. Too long. He'd have to call in a Bondi unit.

Snatching up his wallet and badge, he grabbed his jacket from under his chair and took off across the room. Blood roared in his ears. Christ, what had Reggie got herself into now?

"Thomas! What the fuck you think you're doin'?"

Muriciano's bellow bounced around the room, and more cops lifted their heads from their paperwork.

Hot impatience tore through Peter and he slowed down, scowling at his boss. "Gotta go, Inspector."

"Detective Thomas!"

Grinding his teeth, Peter stopped, turning to watch Muriciano lumber toward him. "Sorry, Inspector. I've got to—"

"Just received a call from HQ, Thomas." Muriciano gave him a smug grin and for a second Peter saw utter belligerence flare in the man's eyes. "Williams broke his shoulder. Ya getting a new partner. They'll be here within the hour. Unless someone's dying, you're not going anywhere." The grin stretched wider and Muriciano chuckled, flabby gut wobbling like jello. "Understand?"

Jaw clenched, Peter nodded. "Understand, Inspector." And, before rational thought took over, he punched his superior in the nose and sent the fat fuck to the floor. "But as I said before, I've got to go."

Regan's house was a shambles. More than a shambles. When Peter crossed the threshold, he felt as though he'd stepped into a scene from a cliché-ridden movie—one of those where a house is ransacked by a crazed criminal looking for something highly important and highly illegal. A crazed criminal who smelt like a filthy animal. Jesus! What was that *stench*?

A chill ran up his spine and, nose creasing at the pungent smell, his hand moved toward his gun.

"There was no one here when we arrived, Detective. Just the mess and the smell."

Peter turned to the uniformed cop stepping up beside him, not missing the trepidation in the young man's face. "What's causing the stench? Do you know?"

The cop's face scrunched in distaste. "From what I can tell, someone's pissed all over the furniture. Especially the bed. But I can't be sure."

Cold worry thumped through Peter's chest. "Piss?" He took a step deeper into his sister's house. "Nothing's been touched?"

The cop shook his head. "No."

Peter surveyed the mess around him. Whoever had done this, had done so out of anger. There were no signs of struggle. Overturned furniture littered the room, the cushions were shredded, the curtains ripped from the windows but nothing in the chaos told him Reggie had been involved in its making. Someone angry had done this. Peter hoped to Christ they were angry because his sister had not been here. The piss could be a disgusting, infantile response to their failure, although to Peter's farm-boy nose it smelt more animalistic than human.

You're on your own, lizard. The words floated through his head and he gripped his gun harder.

"Detective Thomas?"

Peter started, swinging his attention back to the cop waiting beside him. "Sorry, Officer...?"

"Paterson. Detective, shall I call in a CSU?"

Peter looked around the mayhem of his sister's normally tidy home. He highly doubted the crime scene guys would find anything but, after punching Muriciano in the face, he'd better stick to protocol.

Yeah, not a wise move back at Command. You ready to be suspended?

A dry snort burst from Peter's nose. Muriciano wouldn't suspend him. He'd bluster and rant and rave and pour a ton of public humiliation down on Peter, but he wouldn't suspend him. Peter knew where Muriciano had buried the bodies—figuratively speaking. His superior wouldn't risk the skeletons tumbling from the closet, no matter how shattered his nose and pride.

"Detective? The CSU?"

Peter nodded, re-holstering his gun. "Do that, Officer Paterson. The Bondi crew can handle it. I'm outta my jurisdiction here."

He scanned the overturned room, trying like hell to ignore the sparks of cold fear in his chest. Jesus, what a mess. *I'm coming, Reggie. Just be safe until I get there.*

But where was she?

Peter's fists clenched. He didn't know. But he'd find out.

"Can I ask whose house this is, Detective?"

The young cop hovered beside him and Peter gave him a quick look. "Yes you can." He crossed the room, stepping over upended side tables, shattered lamps, gutted cushions and their exposed innards on his way to the sofa. Something had caught his eye. Something...

He stopped at the overturned piece of furniture, the overpowering stench of urine almost making him gag. Which was saying something, considering he'd grown up crutching sheep. Crouching down, he ran a slow inspection over the abused sofa, feeling his chest grow tight. Reggie loved the sofa. It had been their great-grandparents' and their father told—to their mother's absolute dismay—quite a bawdy tale of Reggie's conception involving the old, paisley-covered cushions and too many bottles of champagne. She'd be heartbroken to see it in such a degraded state.

Yeah, but what caught your eyes? What made you come over here?

A frown pulled at Peter's forehead and he reached out, removing something small and soft from the armrest of the sofa. *This* is what caught his eye. Still crouching, he studied the tuft of grey fur, rubbing the soft, almost silken strands between thumb and forefinger. An animal had been laying on the sofa recently. He brought the tuft closer, eyes narrowing at the still slightly tacky, faint crimson stain coloring a few of the soft strands. A bleeding animal. He flicked his gaze to the sofa, knowing what he hoped to find wouldn't be there.

Shit.

Either the Irishman he'd heard talking to Rex had taken the cushions or whoever destroyed Regan's house had. Peter's gut twisted. Something told him it was the latter. It seemed they didn't want the cops finding the injured animal's blood.

And yet they piss everywhere?

Peter's frown deepened. Something very odd was going on here. And Reggie was right in the middle of—

A gunshot shattered the air.

Peter sprang to his feet, spinning toward the direction of the report, Glock drawn.

"What the fuck was that?" The young cop screeched, aiming his weapon—waveringly, Peter was disgusted to see—at the kitchen entryway.

Gun raised, breath even, Peter crossed the room, staring hard at the opening before him.

"There it is again!" Paterson's gun swung wide, aimed straight at Peter's feet.

Peter dropped his gaze to see what Paterson was about to shoot and the breath gushed out of him in a raw laugh. Lips twitching, he dropped into another crouch, scooping up the long, grey-green, scaly creature casually walking toward him.

"G'day, Rex," he said, lifting the lizard up to his face to give it a slight smile. "You wouldn't be able to tell me what happened to that sister of mine, would you?"

Rex looked back at him, flat tongue flicking out in nervous, little jabs at the air.

Peter's smile disappeared. "No. I didn't think so."

Shit.

Regan opened her eyes. Slowly. She peered around the dark room, squinting at the thin shards of bright light pushing through a narrow crack in the curtains on the far wall. Where was she?

She pressed her palms to the spongy mattress beneath her and struggled into a sitting position, taking in the kitsch, framed prints on the wall and the sunken bed beside her. A hotel room? Was she in a hotel room? The sound of traffic hummed beyond the walls; cars, trucks, motorcycles, and behind those typical urban noises the distant cries and squawks of seagulls. God, she could be anywhere.

Swinging her legs around, she placed her bare feet on the floor and pushed herself upright. Black swirling stars filled her head immediately and she flopped back down to the bed, a dull throb pounding up her jaw into her temple. She lifted her hand, running her fingers along the aching beat.

Damn it! He'd hit her! He'd actually hit her.

"I'm sorry about that."

The softly spoken words with their even softer accent caressed her ears and she spun around, staring through a fresh wave of black stars at the man sitting in the armchair behind her.

At some stage he'd found himself some clothes. A pair of very faded blue jeans hugged his long, lean legs, emphasizing the corded strength of his thighs and impressive bulge between them, and a black Ramones t-shirt covered a torso Regan remembered being hard and smooth and wonderful to touch. A squeezing sensation rolled through her belly into the warm centre between her legs. Regan scowled. Goddamn it! The man had kidnapped her and here she was feeling horny? She steadied herself on the bed, giving her abductor a mean glare. "Yeah, well sorry doesn't cut it, mate. If you wanted me to leave that badly you could've asked."

To her surprise, the man laughed, the sound rich and relaxed. "I *did* ask. You decided to make a phone call, remember?"

Regan closed her eyes. Shit. Peter would be going out of his mind. Probably had the entire Sydney City Police Force out looking for her.

And with good reason?

She flicked a shuttered gaze to the man watching her. She didn't know. Yet.

"I truly am sorry about the jaw." The Irish lilt played over her senses like a feather and she suppressed a shiver. She really needed to get her act together. Who knew what he had in store for her? "But we had to go. I couldn't wait." Grey storm-cloud eyes grew intense. "*We* couldn't wait."

Regan edged into a more comfortable, but easy-to-spring-from position on the bed, checking out how close and easy to reach the phone was in case she needed to swing it. "What are you?"

The blunt question didn't seem to offend him. In fact, those defined lips curled into a small smile. "Apart from a freak, you mean?"

Regan didn't bat an eyelid. "Yes. Apart from that."

"A werewolf."

It was Regan's turn to laugh. "Oh, right. A werewolf. Of course. Why didn't *I* think of that?"

The man's smile stretched wider. "I thought it was pretty obvious myself, love. Considering one minute you were stroking my fur and running your fingers up and down my *four* legs— which I enjoyed immensely, I might add—and the next I was standing before you on *two*. Furless."

A very large, hard lump suddenly stuck in Regan's throat and her head swam again. The memory of the wolf's unusual humerus and pelvic bone crashed over her, as did her surreal response to the animal's inherent power. Her skin prickled into clammy gooseflesh. She stared at the man still watching her from his chair, her pulse a rapid hammer pounding in her neck. "Holy shit."

The man's smile turned dry. "There's nothing holy about werewolves, love."

Frazzled anger shot through Regan and she gave her abductor a glare. "Stop calling me love."

Even blacker eyebrows shot up, a light she could only describe as mischievous glinting in his grey eyes. His smile grew wider. *Wolfish.* "And what would you be having me call you, then?"

"My name's Regan."

With a speed she'd seen from him before, both as man and wolf, he was on his feet, across the short distance between them and beside the bed. He extended his right hand, the mischievous light in his eyes now devilish. "Declan O'Connell. Your kidnapper for the day."

Regan ignored his hand, even as a tight, wet heat unfurled in the pit of her stomach at his proximity. His clean but musky scent threaded through her breath and she pressed her thighs closer together, trying her best to ignore the constricting pressure between them. "For the day?" she repeated, looking at him squarely in the face. "So this is just a twenty-four hour thing? Like a twenty-four hour flu?" She paused. "Only more annoying?"

The man—Declan—chuckled, but Regan didn't miss the dark tension in his gaze. "Perhaps 'for the day' was a poor choice of words."

Regan clenched her fists and jaw. "*Perhaps* you should tell me what the hell is going on. Because at this point in time, I'm very close to picking up the phone and braining you with it. Hard." She narrowed her eyes. "I'm still not convinced this isn't all just a bad dream left over from my run-in with Epoc's security guards."

Strong fingers pinched her shoulder before she could move. "Feel that?"

Damn, he's fast. The thought sent a chill straight up her spine. How the hell was she to get away when he moved like a...

Like an animal?

Stomach fluttering, Regan looked up into the smoldering grey eyes. Damn it, she was in trouble. A heavy lump formed in her throat again and she swallowed. "What's going on? No bullshit, no Irish charm, okay?"

Declan's face turned serious and he perched on the edge of the bed, studying her with a look so intent the muscles in the pit of her stomach twisted. "Nathan Epoc is a lycanthrope. A werewolf. The Alpha male of the *Eudeyrn* clan, an ancient and sadistic pack. He's been experimenting on our species for centuries, trying to perfect a way to extract our *croí*, our life essence." His expression turned deadly and for a brief moment his grey eyes shimmered with a rancorous silver glow. "The process drains the victim of their life-force, sucking their spirit from their body in an agonizing and protracted process until they're an empty, inert shell. Not dead, but not living either." His eyes slid to her. "The dog you tried to save in Epoc's lab was in the early stages of the extraction."

Stomach churning, Regan stared at Declan. Disbelief and horror coursed through her veins. She shook her head. "But that dog was a German Shepherd, not a wolf. You said..."

"I said 'trying to perfect'." He swallowed, Adam's apple rising and falling with the harsh action. "Every living thing has a life essence, Regan. Epoc has killed more than one animal, more than one *person*, to reach the stage he's at now. The dog was in the latter stages of the procedure, the last animal tested, before the bastard moved onto his real subject."

Regan's mouth felt coated in dust. "Which was...?"

A bleak, frightening smile pulled at Declan's lips. "Not which, Regan. Who. Nathan Epoc and I have a very long history. None of it amicable."

She looked at him for a long moment, heart trying to beat its way from her chest. "Why?"

"Why do we have a history?"

"Why the tests? Why the..." She stopped, unable to continue.

Declan's jaw bunched. "For the creation of an elixir. The drinker—Epoc—will not only gain the victim's strength but their *croí* as well, making them virtually immortal. Invulnerable." His grey eyes flashed with cold rage. "Unstoppable."

No! It couldn't be true. Could it? She shook her head, scrambling off the bed. "No. I don't believe it." She backed across the room, hugging herself. "I can't believe it."

Declan rose to his feet, watching her from the other side of the bed. "Why not, Regan? You saw with your own eyes what I am. You felt with your own hands..."

"Okay, I've seen *you* change, so maybe it's true—or maybe you just hypnotized me—but c'mon! You want me to believe Australia is riddled with werewolves plotting to take over the world?" Her skin prickled with what felt like a million biting ants. She'd fallen into a cheesy, fifties horror movie and she wanted out. "I've seen Nathan Epoc. He's no wolf. Blood-sucking, demon-spawn from Hell, maybe—but *werewolf?*" She shook her head. "Not possible. I can't believe it."

Declan didn't move, but his eyes seemed to reach for her. Hold her frozen. "Yes, you can, Regan. You have to. Because Epoc won't only be after me now."

It was too much. Regan turned and, heart hammering, sprinted for the door.

Declan smashed into her before her fingers closed around the door knob, his incredibly hard body crushing her against the solid wooden door with such force her teeth clicked shut. Strong fingers curled around her wrists and rammed them beside her head, thighs she already knew impossible to escape pinned hers still. "I can't let you go, Regan. Not now."

"Why not?" she snapped. Declan's heat melted into her, made her breath short. She glared at him—but her pussy was throbbing a traitorous beat. "You think Nathan Epoc's really going to come after me? An insignificant human?"

His eyes were grey, turbulent pools. "I know he will. You've seen too much. You know too much. He will send the meanest mongrels of his pack to hunt you down and make the last few moments of your life the worst you've ever imagined. I can protect you. *Only* I can protect you. Keep you safe."

Regan tilted her chin. "Safe? That's why you can't let me

go?"

Declan's nostrils flared. "No, Regan." He pressed closer into her. "*This* is." And his mouth claimed hers.

A jolt of exquisite tension stabbed into the pit of Regan's stomach. Her pussy fluttered an erratic pulse equal to the frantic beat of her heart. A growl rumbled deep in Declan's chest and he plunged his tongue further into her mouth, demanding she return the kiss. His body pressed her to the door, thighs to thighs, hips to hips. The contact felt like a branding iron. Left her dizzy and wet with want. The thick, solid length of desire between his thighs ground against her belly, as undeniable as his hold was inescapable. Regan whimpered, the sensations roaring through her both intoxicating and petrifying. What the hell was going on? She was in a hotel room who knows where, she'd been abducted by a man she'd first met as a wolf and she was more wet with lust than she'd ever been in her entire life. Nothing made sense.

Does it matter?

Regan's heart froze. Yes. It did. It had too.

She shoved against his weight, dismay and delight ripping through her when he didn't budge. His mouth continued its assault, his heat continued to seep into her body. His teeth nipped at her bottom lip and she whimpered again, eyes fluttering closed, tongue mating with his.

God, Woman. What are you doing?

Drowning? Or dreaming?

Declan's hands left her wrists and scorched a path down her arms. For one brief moment the thought of escape shot through Regan's head—all she'd need do was slam her palms against his ears and shatter his eardrums. But then his large, strong hands closed over her breasts and the thought, like reality, vanished.

He squeezed. Hard. Shots of pleasure stabbed into Regan's stomach, igniting squirming spasms of tension in her pussy. She moaned, arching into his grip, her breasts growing heavy with a desire she knew was wrong but couldn't deny. His fingers found her nipples and pinched them through her shirt, the soft friction from the material adding to the blistering rapture of the savage caress. *Hell, Woman. You've lost your mind.*

Who cared when it feels like this?

She arched again, wrapping her right leg around his left. Holding him as surely as he held her. Wanting to feel the molten shaft of steel pressed to her belly pressed instead to something far wetter and more intimate.

A very low *gnarr* rumbled up Declan's chest and he tore his mouth from hers, staring down into her face, chest heaving. "Christ, Regan." His eyes burned. "Who are you? What have you done to me?"

Regan rolled her hips, grinding her mons to the thick shaft between his thighs contained only by snug, stolen denim. "I'm asking you the same question."

He dragged in a ragged breath. "The answers need greater consideration, then." Without breaking eye contact, he raked his hands down her rib cage, under her tank and took complete possession of her breasts. Skin to skin, flesh to fevered flesh. "Starting here."

"Hell, yes." The words burst from Regan's lips. She threw back her head, the hotel door behind her resounding with a dull thud as her skull smacked against it but she didn't care. Nothing existed except Declan's hands cupping her breasts, fondling them with languid attention. "Oh, yes."

His mouth found her neck, scorched a line up to her ear. He sucked and bit at her lobe, sending a tiny shard of painful bliss into her constricting sex. She writhed beneath him, shoving her pussy to his cock with greater force. Declan squeezed her breasts again, knuckles pinching her nipples with almost brutal force until she whimpered with impatient pleasure. Every muscle in her body quivered, thrummed with raw, base energy. She stared sightlessly at the ceiling, feeling like she was about to explode.

How can that be? All he's doing is squeezing your—

With savage speed, Declan ripped her tank top open and captured her right nipple with his mouth.

Regan sank her nails into his bunched shoulders. *Oh, God. Yes.*

Sharp teeth closed down on the puckered peak, flooding her pussy with cream. He drew her breast deeper into his mouth, suckled on its distended tip. His tongue laved her sensitive flesh with rapid strokes, flicked and circled her aching nipple. She tossed her head from side to side, eyes closed, lips parted, her throbbing cunt greedily closing down on a phantom cock she wished was there.

Declan's lips scorched a line from her right breast to her left, replacing his mouth on the heavy, abandoned swell of flesh with his masterful hand. He pulled at her nipples, with teeth and fingers, and Regan's pussy gushed with eager moisture.

She shoved her hips harder into his rigid cock. "Please..." The single word fell from her lips, barely more than a breath.

Declan's mouth continued to feast on her breast. He tortured her nipple with his teeth, sucked it so hard she saw stars. She gasped and drove her nails into his shoulders. A distant part of her mind screamed at her to stop him, get away from him, get away now. A louder, more primitive part however, squealed in ecstasy at each drawing pressure on her nipple and demanded she rip the shirt from his torso, granting her access to skin she knew to be smooth and perfect under her palms. Granting her access to the small circles of his nipples, tracing them with first her fingertips and then her tongue.

The thought sent a sizzling stab of liquid heat into her core and she moaned, both in frustration and rapture. She'd never wanted someone like this. It was wild. Animalistic. Consuming and overwhelming. She wanted him. Every mysterious, reality-bending inch of him.

As if Declan heard her craving, he slid his palms down her torso. Long-fingered hands wavered at the elasticized waistband of her running shorts for a frozen second before, with an abrupt move, he jerked her harder to his cock, plunged his hands into her shorts and grabbed the cheeks of her ass.

Regan's heart skipped a beat and she sucked in a swift breath. "Holy fuck!"

Declan lifted his head from her breast with an audible pop. "I keep telling you, Regan, there's nothing holy about me."

His eyes seemed to glow silver. They bored into her like a drill, making her cunt constrict and her head giddy. Trapped her as surely as his hands and body did. *Nothing holy…*

She stared back at him. Felt the branding heat of his hands on her ass sink into her core. Felt the thick, turgid length of his impressive cock press to her mons, just as branding, just as commanding. The crisp cotton of her shorts served as no barrier, no protection. A shiver rippled up her spine and a soft moan sounded in her throat.

The sound shattered the heavy silence and in a heartbeat, Declan's eyes—those untamed, thunderous eyes—dilated. Became an animal's eyes. A *wolf's* eyes. An utterly inhuman growl filled the air.

Regan's throat squeezed tight. *Oh, no.*

The wolf's eyes stared at her from Declan's face. His fingers sank into her ass and, as he pulled her sex closer to his, she felt his short blunt nails grow harder, longer.

Her heart stopped. Her pussy constricted. And, before her wanton body could take charge of her actions, she swung her arms into two sharp arcs and whacked them against Declan's head, smacking her flattened palms to his ears.

He threw back his head and howled, staggering backward, clawed hands pressed to each side of his head, eyes squeezed shut, agony etching his face.

Regan watched him. For a split second. Heart pounding, throat tight, she grabbed the doorknob and flung the door open. Running out into the sun-filled car park of the motel and sprinting down the footpath.

Away from Declan O'Connell. Away from the creature he was becoming.

Chapter Four

She bolted. Faster than she'd ever run before. A lifetime spent chasing wandering cows on her family's farm and irritated animals at Sydney's zoos and animal parks meant she knew how to run fast. Right at that very moment Regan figured she was close to breaking not only her own personal best, but the current world sprint record. With a frown, she pushed more speed from her legs. The Lord help her if she needed to run a marathon at this pace. She was fit, but not *that* fit.

A noise behind sent her already frantic pulse into acceleration. Damn it. Was he on her tail already? She risked a quick look over her shoulder.

No. Just what appeared to be a kindergarten class out on a field trip with their teacher, the frazzled-looking woman trying to keep twenty-odd riotous kids under control, on the footpath and off the road.

"Miss Bristow." A squeaky voice called out. "I saw that lady's boobies."

Boobies.

The word punched Regan in the stomach and she stumbled, hitting the concrete with both hands and knees. *Boobies?* Damn it. She'd been so intent on getting away she'd forgot Declan had torn her top.

How the hell could you forget that? His mouth on your nipples felt like—

She leapt to her feet, the giggles of the children behind her and the treacherous thought in her head making her face burn. Fair Dinkum, she'd let him touch her, kiss her. They'd be on the floor of the motel right now, fucking each other senseless if it hadn't been for his eyes changing. An excited chill shot up her spine, despite the scorching sun beating down on her. Her pussy pulsed and she scowled. She had to get away. She couldn't outrun the perfidious ache in her sex, but she could outrun the man she'd left in the motel. For a while, at least. Taking off again, sweat trickling down her forehead and spine, she crossed the road, hugging her tattered top to her body as she dodged more than one speeding car. She needed a phone.

The screech of cicadas filled the morning air like a dentist's drill, following her every step. She wished they'd shut up. Their noise made it impossible to hear if anyone came up behind her.

Do you think you'd hear him?

Stomach churning, she cast a look over her shoulder. Just an old lady walking a Bichon Frise and a teenage boy resplendent in full Goth attire muttering to himself. No stalking wolf. No hint where she was. She had no idea where Declan had taken her, but she guessed they were still in Sydney. The baking heat, screeching insects and yellow haze told her as much. As did the maniacal way the cars whizzed by, like their drivers were determined to break the land-speed record on their way to wherever they were going.

Or maybe they're trying to escape a drop-dead gorgeous, Irish werewolf too?

Her feet stumbled again but she caught herself before she fell. Damn it. She had to get her act together. Vaulting a low, brick fence she cut across a corner, and headed down another street, following the main road. She'd come across a gas station soon. It was Sydney Law of Probability Number Two: Every main road had at least five gas stations in a ten-mile stretch.

"Nice arse, honey!"

The shouted words bounced off her as a lowered hatchback filled to the brim with pimple-faced youths shot by, as did their following whistles and lewd suggestions. Something far more important had caught her eye—the green, red and white Caltex star, towering over all. A faint whiff of gasoline tickled her nose and she smiled, pushing out a new burst of speed.

The gas station was deserted when she reached it. The only sign of life a pair of very grubby jeans and worn-down boots sticking out from under a Ford coupe jacked up in the adjoining mechanic's workshop. She scanned the signage around her, searching for any clue to what suburb she was in. Nothing.

Tossing a quick look behind her, expecting to see Declan or, worse still, an unnaturally large, grey wolf, she crossed the oil-stained concrete, stopping at the Ford's tailgate. "Excuse me? May I use your phone, please?"

"Pay phone's near the john, honey," a muffled voice answered from under the car.

"I don't have any money." Regan fought the urge to fidget. Time was pressing down on her like a wrecking ball. "I'm sorry, but it's an emergency."

An impatient snort of disgust came from beneath the car, followed by a muttered, "It always is." The filthy jeans shifted and out shot a man even more filthy, the wheels of his trolley squealing louder than the surrounding cicadas. Sullen eyes glared up at her, contempt etching his grease-smudged face...until he took in her torn shirt and red, sweaty face. "Crikey, lady!" He scrambled to his feet. "Are you awright?"

"Please." Regan gave him a harried smile. "I need to use the phone." Apprehension was beginning to get the better of her. She *felt* Declan's warm breath on the back of her neck, *felt* the wolf's whiskers feather her sweaty skin.

"Sure, sure." The man barreled past her, shoving open the connecting door to the store with such force Regan expected the glass to shatter. It didn't, and she followed him in, the icy bite of its air-conditioner making her fevered flesh ripple into goose bumps.

The man charged around the counter, worried gaze continually flicking to her. "Here." He held out a cordless phone smudged with greasy fingerprints, and Regan almost smiled in sympathy at the nervous energy radiating off him. "Are you sure you're okay? Is the bastard who did this to you close by? Do you want me to go get 'im? I've got a tire-arm in the garage. Are you callin' the cops? You should call the cops."

Regan removed the phone from his trembling grip with her free hand, keeping the other tightly clamped on her torn top. "Thanks. I'm okay."

"You're callin' the cops, right?"

A tight, dull beat began to thud in her throat and she nodded. "I am."

Peter would not believe what she was going to tell him, but she had to ring someone, and after Declan busted her on the phone in her bedroom, her brother was probably on the verge of a mental breakdown. Pressing her arm against her chest, she punched in Peter's cell number, gnawing on her lip as she waited for him to answer. Perhaps Declan—if Declan really was his name—had drugged her? Perhaps he'd seen her running from Epoc's lab last night and followed her, breaking into her home and injecting her with something as she slept. Perhaps—

Don't be stupid, Woman. After growing up with Peter and his regular "snake-in-the-bed" attacks, do you really think anyone could do anything to you while you slept? Get real.

Real? What was real anymore?

Declan O'Connell?

Vivid, wild memories whirled through her head. The wolf's unusual bone structure, the feel of its coat under her palms, the way its powerful body shuddered as it changed to a man, the feel of said man's tongue on her flesh, his teeth biting on her nipple...

"Lady? Are you awright?"

The mechanic's alarmed voice made Regan jump and she gave him a startled look.

Worried blue eyes stared at her. "You were moanin' a little. Are you in pain?"

Regan's face erupted in hot shame. Moaning? Where the hell was her brain? In her pants? In Declan's? She gave the hovering man what she hoped was a reassuring smile, wishing her pussy would stop clenching with eager want. "I'm okay."

Turning her attention back to the handset, she scowled. Peter wasn't answering. She'd have to ring his command.

Still chewing on her bottom lip, she looked out through the grimy front window of the store. No grey wolf. No black-haired, silver-eyed Irishman.

Maybe it's all in your head?

"Detective Thomas's desk."

The smooth, female voice with a faint German accent on the other end of the line made Regan blink. An uneasy shiver shot up her spine. "May I speak to Peter Thomas please?"

There was a short pause. "I am sorry, Detective Thomas is not available at the moment."

Regan bit back a curse. "This is his sister. Do you know when he'll be back?"

"I am sorry, no." The woman paused again, and inexplicably, an image of a tall, voluptuous blonde filled Regan's head. "This is Peter's partner. Can I help with something?"

Regan frowned. Partner? Peter's partner was a gruff man called Michael Williams, Doughnut to just about everyone. The woman on the other end did not sound like Doughnut at all. Unless Doughnut had been taking voice-acting lessons, that was. Or had undergone a sex change.

"Miss?" The female voice floated down the phone line. Low. Calm. Confident. "Regan?"

Regan gripped the phone harder. Something felt wrong here. Surely Peter would have told her he was getting a new partner? Yet how else would the woman on the other end know her name? Another icy chill shot up her back.

"Regan?" The woman repeated, and this time Regan detected an edge in her otherwise poised voice. "Are you alone? Tell me where you are and I will come get you."

"Lady?"

Rough fingers touched Regan's shoulder and she jumped, almost dropping the phone.

The mechanic stood beside her, looking more anxious than ever. "You don't look well. Your face's gone all white. Are you sure you're okay?"

"She's fine," a deep, rumbling and oh-so-familiar voice answered, the exact second a long arm reached forward and took the phone from Regan's hand.

She turned, heart thumping, pussy fluttering and stared up into stormy, grey eyes.

Declan shook his head slightly, very deliberately hitting the disconnect button on the hand piece. "Just a little stubborn, is all."

"Who the fuck're you?" The mechanic blustered, wide-eyed stare darting between Regan and Declan. "Is this the guy who did this to you?"

Declan turned his head, giving the man a level stare. "Go away."

The mechanic's mouth fell open. "Listen, mate, I don't know who you think you are, but—"

He didn't get any further. The low, animalistic, savage growl sounding in Declan's throat stopped him dead and he took a stumbling step backward.

"I'm the man keeping this woman alive," Declan said. He turned back to Regan, eyes a smoldering, angry silver. "No matter how hard she's making it."

Rex's tail was scratchy. Peter swiped at it and the lizard sank its needle-like claws into his shoulder in retaliation, climbing closer to his neck.

The low hum of the rising elevator did little to soothe Peter's agitated nerves and the almost undetectable pull of gravity only made his already churning gut feel worse. Jesus, what the fuck was going on?

The Bondi CS crew had been thorough, and while it was too early for a complete report, Peter knew by the grim expressions on their faces as they'd moved about Regan's house they'd find nothing. The only hope for a lead from what was undeniably a crime scene was the piss sprayed all about the house. But something in Peter's gut told him even that bizarre piece of evidence would reveal sweet, fuck all. The tire tracks out in front of her house obviously belonged to a van but, despite what movies and TV shows told the viewing world, tire tracks rarely lead the cops to a suspect. All he had to go on were the two names and the two male voices he'd heard on the end of the phone call what felt like a lifetime ago. One Irish, one Scottish. O'Connell and McCoy. How many O'Connells and McCoys were there in Australia?

Too many to do a door knock, that's for sure.

The elevator jolted to a halt and Rex's claws punctured Peter's shoulder again. Wincing, he reached up and gave the skittish lizard a soft scratch under its frilled neck. "Steady, mate. It's okay."

The jarring clunk of the opening doors earned him a fresh set of holes in his flesh and he grimaced. *Nothing but a prelude to the pain Muriciano's going to bring down on you, Thomas.*

With Rex digging deeper into his flesh, he crossed the room, paying little attention to the curious and almost sheepish looks from his colleagues. Only one thing occupied his mind and it had nothing to do with his boss. He had to find Reggie.

Rex wormed higher up his shoulder and Peter gave the lizard another, albeit distracted, scratch. *A male with an Irish accent, someone called O'Connell, a male with a Scottish accent, someone called McCoy, a house covered in urine, a tuft of what looks like grey dog hair and two missing sofa cushions...Where the fuck do I start?*

"Muriciano told me you were an odd one."

A low and supremely confident female voice jerked Peter out of his dark thoughts. He started, snapping his attention to the svelte blonde wrapped in snug, black linen perched on the edge of his desk.

Finely arched, blonde eyebrows rose above a direct ocean-blue gaze. Blood-red lips curled into a mocking smile. "Do you always wear a lizard on your shoulder or is this a one time thing?"

Peter gave the woman a level look. "I'm hoping to start a new trend." He stepped over her long, stretched-out legs, unable to miss their incredible shape under the snug black fabric. Dropping his wallet onto his desk, he shot a quick glance at the ID card clipped to her hip pocket. "Any reason you're sitting on my desk, Detective Vischka?" He turned and stared straight into her striking eyes. His gut however, told him the answer before the blonde said a word.

"I am your new partner, Detective Thomas." The husky words rolled with a very faint German accent. "The one Muriciano told you was coming over two hours ago. You can call me Yolanda."

Peter flicked his gaze over her relaxed frame and an unexpected tightness stirred in his loins. Long, long legs, a flat stomach, finely muscled arms and breasts more than capable of filling his hands to capacity. In other words, a distraction.

He didn't need a distraction. He needed to find his sister.

The blonde straightened, her razor-blunt hair cascading over her shoulders to brush the heavy swell of her breasts hidden by her pristine, black shirt. "I have been waiting for you." She brushed the caressing strands of hair back over her shoulder. Her tight nipples pressed at the material of her shirt like neon targets and Peter felt his body tense in primal interest. "I spoke to your sister, in fact."

His throat slammed shut, his new partner's nipples forgotten immediately. "Where is she?"

Yolanda's full lips curled into a slow smile. "I will tell you on one condition."

Anger shot through Peter and, before he could stop himself, he grabbed her smoothly curved biceps and glared into her face. Rex hissed at the abrupt move and sank his claws in deeper,

73

but Peter ignored him. "What did she say?"

For a split second, Peter thought the muscles under his palms shifted, even though she remained utterly motionless. Her deep blue eyes never wavered from his and her lips stretched wider. "Touchy, are we?"

Peter clenched his jaw. "I don't have time for games, Detective. What did my sister say?"

Yolanda studied him, the heady yet somehow delicate scent of her perfume invading his breath. With slow deliberation, she closed the miniscule distance between them, the tips of her breasts brushing his chest in a soft nudge. "She said 'come save me'. Seconds before an Irishman hung up the phone."

Peter's pulse hammered.

Yolanda raised her eyebrows. "Well? Are you going to get rid of the crawling handbag, or is it coming along?"

Gripping her seatbelt in a death-grip, Regan stared in caustic horror at the man currently driving like a madman through the congested streets leading out of Sydney's CBD. "So, we're adding Grand Theft Auto to your list of criminal offences, are we?"

Declan flashed her a quick grin, grey eyes glinting with something close to mischief. "Hey, I'm not stealing. I'm borrowing."

"I think the mechanic back at the gas station would beg to differ. Especially after the whole lengthening canines and growling like a savage beast thing you did when he said you couldn't take his car. I think you scared the poor bloke witless. Do you always turn on the 'animal' to get what you want?"

The corner of Declan's mouth curled into a disturbing grin. "Not until you came along, love."

Regan glared at him, pressing her butt harder into the passenger seat of the mechanic's old but finely tuned pick-up, trying to keep stable as Declan flung the car through the maze of lanes leading to Sydney Harbor Bridge. Menace radiated from him in waves, sending a chill up her spine and making her nipples pinch into hard, little points under her tattered shirt. "You know, there are posted speed limits," she said, closing her fingers tighter around her seat belt.

Declan's thigh flexed as he pushed his foot harder to the accelerator. "There's also a sadistic bastard on our tail, something you seem to keep forgetting."

Regan suppressed her own growl. Declan's insistence Nathan Epoc was a mad-scientist werewolf was beginning to get tired. She cast him a sideward glance, taking in his brooding profile, his strong nose, high, chiseled cheekbones. Her pussy gave a tiny flutter of appreciation and she groaned silently. *Damnit, I've fallen in lust with a nut-job.* "Okay, hero," she said, trying to ignore the traitorous tension in her sex. "What's your plan? Are we going to aimlessly drive around Sydney all day or are you actually headed somewhere?" She raised another eyebrow at him. "Do you even *know* where you're going?"

"I'm getting you as far away from Epoc and his mongrel pack as I can."

"Oh, good. And here I was thinking you were going to do something stupid, like leave Sydney."

Declan's jaw bunched. "You still don't believe me, do you?" He slipped the mechanic's pickup into a break in traffic the size of a kid's tricycle. "You think either I'm delusional or you're still asleep." He flicked an enigmatic look her way. "Even after what happened back in the hotel room."

A blush hotter than the sun flooded Regan's face and she turned away from him, watching instead the rapidly approaching pylons of the Harbor Bridge. She let out a soft sigh and dragged a trembling hand through her hair. "I don't know what to think," she answered truthfully, gripping her seatbelt tight. "I wake this morning to find a wolf who's really a man on my sofa. He tells me I'm in danger, knocks me unconscious and takes me to some hotel who knows where, giving me a cockamamie story about a werewolf-slash-scientist with a demented Dracula complex, and even though I should be petrified or madder than hell, every time I look at him all I can think about is sex." Her face flushed again at the unexpected admission but she continued, even with the heat on her cheeks. "Every time he touches me I almost orgasm, despite the utterly surreal fact he has a tendency to grow long teeth and claws and growl like a wild beast if he doesn't get his way."

She turned back to Declan, noting with a small sense of dry satisfaction his white-knuckled grip on the steering wheel. "Can you see my predicament?"

He didn't answer. Not until the Sydney Harbor Bridge and the expanse of water it spanned was long behind them, the pick-up heading through the opulent northern suburbs at kamikaze speeds. "I don't know what to do or say to convince you you're in danger, Regan," he said, voice low, accent thicker than ever. "Save drive to Epoc himself and there's not a chance in hell I'm doing that." His gaze flicked to her and Regan sucked in a swift breath at the turbulent desire she saw in his eyes' stormy depths. "As for making you come...I've wanted to do that from the second I saw you in Epoc's lab. Covered head to toe in black, risking your life to save a—"

An explosive crunch cut his words dead. As did the lurching jolt of the pick-up.

Regan grabbed the dash, heart thumping up into her

throat, seatbelt biting into her neck. "What the hell?" The car jolted again and this time, she saw why.

A black van charged along the road beside them, crumpled nose almost level with theirs. Almost. It swerved, a violent and deliberate arc. There was a deafening bang, the sickening squeal of metal on metal filled the cab, and the mechanic's pick-up shuddered.

"Fuck," Declan growled.

Regan's heart hammered, hot rage roaring through her veins. "They're trying to run us off the road!"

The van crashed into them again and Declan let out a sharp snarl. Sweat popping out on his forehead, he spun the wheel to the right. "The fucker found us quicker than I thought."

Another crunching collision jarred them, hard enough to make Regan's skull smack the side window. Her teeth snapped shut on her bottom lip and the coppery ting of blood slicked her tongue. Head throbbing, she watched Declan fling the pick-up up a narrow side street. She held on for dear life as the now badly beaten automobile tilted so far to the left, its right tires lost contact with the road and the world abruptly skewed on its axis. "Who's found us?" she demanded. "Who's in that van?"

Tires screeching, the van followed. Gaining.

Declan's jaw clenched and his knuckles grew whiter. "McCoy."

Regan blinked. "Who the fuck is McCoy?"

Declan didn't answer. Slamming his foot to the accelerator, he pushed the pick-up harder, its finely worked engine roaring to new life just as McCoy's van rammed straight into the back of it.

The pick-up lurched forward violently, careening into a RV

parked at the curb. More metal screamed, the hood concertinaed, the windshield shattered into a thousand pieces and, before Regan could scream, the pick-up spun into a sickeningly fast one-eighty, slammed into another parked car and jolted to a shuddering halt.

"Get out!"

Declan was growling at her before her head stopped spinning.

"Get out! Get out now!"

He turned in his seat, raised his knees up to his chest and struck out at Regan's door with his heels. It flung open, the sharp ting of salt air biting immediately at her sinuses as summer flooded into the cab.

"Get out, Regan," He ordered, ripping her seatbelt off and shoving her from the car. "We've got to run."

Regan stumbled across the footpath, swiping at the small trickle of blood running down her temple. "Jesus. What..." Her head felt like it was about to erupt. "What..."

A demoniac, bestial growl assaulted her ears and her stomach dropped. *Oh, no.*

"Regan!" Declan grabbed her arm. Stared hard into her eyes. "Run!"

He shoved her away and spun about.

Just as a man, roughly the size of a gorilla threw himself against his body.

The pair rolled across the ground, crashed against the mechanic's crumpled pick-up. A howl filled the air. Loud and piercing. Followed by a growl equally as loud.

People—curious about the noise and carnage—began to appear on the surrounding footpaths, more than one gasping and calling for someone to call the cops, but Regan couldn't move, unable to drag her stare from the sight before her.

The brutish man forced Declan to the ground, driving punch after punch into his chest, face and ribs. "Thought you'd get away from us, you dumb-fuck, Irish shit."

Declan struck back. "You been rolling in your own filth again, McCoy?"

McCoy bared vicious canines, a chilling snarl cutting the air. He grabbed at Declan's throat, his long, thick fingers sinking into the corded column.

Regan's blood turned to ice. "Declan!"

McCoy's head shot up, burning red-gold eyes fixing on her. "She's a sexy piece of ass, O'Connell. I'm going to enjoy fucking her."

A growl ripped from Declan's throat. He whipped his knees up to his chest and rammed his feet into McCoy's gut, launching him into the air.

The snarling man flew high. And transformed—mid-arc—into a huge, charcoal-grey wolf.

The street erupted. Squeals and cries of shock rent the air, followed by the sound of feet pounding the pavement as the terrified onlookers fled.

Regan staggered backward, heart pounding beneath her breast, eyes fixed on the slathering wolf staring at her.

"Regan!" Declan roared. "Run!"

She shot him a frantic look. In time to see his body shimmer as he transformed into the massive wolf she'd first seen caged in Epoc's lab.

Regan. Run.

The words sounded in her head—but whether in her voice or Declan's she couldn't tell. It didn't matter. The snarl bursting from McCoy's muzzle set her feet in motion. She turned and sprinted away from the two wolves. But not before seeing the frightening grey wolf—Declan—leap at the even bigger wolf preparing to pounce on her.

She tore down the deserted street, the sound of fighting wolves almost drowning out the screech of the ubiquitous cicadas and the squeal of an approaching siren. Her feet stumbled at the ominous wail and a picture of Declan shot dead by cops filled her head. *Bloody Hell. Declan. What am I doing?*

Run!

The bellow filled her head. Desperate. Furious.

Heart pounding, mouth dry, she took off again, vaulting a low corner fence, heading deeper into suburbia. Lush, opulent, ridiculously expensive suburbia.

With the growls, snarls and howls of Declan and McCoy in her ears.

The low branches of an ancient Morton Bay fig hid her. She stood, palms pressed to her bent knees, sucking in breath after breath in an attempt to ease her frantic pulse. Peering through the foliage-dense branches brushing her cheeks and shoulders, Regan watched the path.

She heard nothing but the screech of cicadas.

What if Declan was dead? What would she do?

A sharp shard of ice stabbed at her thumping heart at the thought and she shook her head. No. He couldn't be. Not after all this. Not after dragging her into this craziness. He wouldn't dare.

She swallowed the lump in her throat, staring down the path she'd sprinted up not fifteen minutes ago, willing him to be there. Wolf or man, she didn't care, as long as he was there.

A hot, summer gust brought with it a distant siren, the wail a long way off but still making Regan's chest clench. *C'mon, Declan. C'mon. Don't leave me like this...*

The fervent order made Regan blink and she snorted with wry amusement. Only a short while ago she was trying to get away from him. Now...

A faint rustle down the street made her tense and she shrank closer to the fig's colossal trunk, making herself as invisible as possible. A woman jogged by, decked out in designer sportswear with thin, white cords dangling from her ears to the slim MP3 player on her arm. Regan let out a silent sigh, slumping against the rough trunk pressing her ass. What should she do? Go looking for him? Keep running? Call Peter?

Peter. Damnit, he'd be tearing the city apart by now.

And she'd missed lunch with Rick. Who knew what *he'd* be—

A prickling sensation rippled up her spine and she *felt* eyes on her. Stiffening, Regan straightened from the trunk and saw the wolf. Staring at her through the concealing branches of the fig tree.

Mottled shadows played over the animal's coat. Made it impossible to know just which wolf had found her. Throat tight, mouth dry, Regan studied it. She couldn't run. Not if it was Declan coming to her. *But what if it's McCoy?* Her pulse leapt into erratic life and she squeezed her fists tight. Ready to fight. Hoping she didn't need to. "Declan?"

Wicked, blood-smeared teeth flashed at her, and a soft growl rumbled low in the animal's chest.

"Declan?"

The wolf's haunches bunched, its muzzle creased. Regan

sucked in a short breath, lifting her fists. Adrenaline surged through her. And then she gasped in relief as a slight tremble shook the animal's body and Declan stood before her. Naked once more, covered in cuts and bruises, the wound on his side weeping fresh blood again.

Silver eyes shimmered to grey and his lips curled into a dark grin. "I'm going to need to find some new clothes."

Chapter Five

The heavy oak doors swung open, revealing an entry foyer more magnificent and lavish than any Regan had seen. Declan's grey eyes flashed silver, an unreadable expression flicking across his face before he waved his arm wide. "Your castle awaits, my fair abductee."

Regan took a step in to the foyer, the gleaming white marble floor stretching before her, the cool, dim silence beyond beckoning. She hesitated, ready for the Klaxon squeal of a security system.

"I've disengaged it."

She gave Declan a quick look, doing her best to keep her eyes on his. It was difficult, knowing, as she did, how completely naked he was. "How do you know how to break into a house?"

He raised a straight, black eyebrow. "I'm not always a wolf, Regan. My 'day' job required I knew how to get in—and out—of locked premises."

"What is your day job, exactly?"

"Journalist."

"And journalists break into mansions often, do they?"

He gave her one of those wolfish grins she was already getting to know well. "I'm from Ireland, love. Remember? I didn't write articles on what to wear to Bondi Beach."

A frown pulled at Regan's forehead. "*Didn't?* What do you mean, 'didn't'?"

Declan ignored the question. "I've hidden our tracks. McCoy won't be able to find us here." He moved past her, striding deeper into the silent mansion.

A shiver raced up Regan's spine and she closed her eyes. Immediately an image of Declan's tight, naked ass filled her head and her stomach fluttered, a delicious, little dance worming its way down to the damp junction of her thighs. "I'm losing my mind," she mumbled.

Declan chuckled. "No you're not."

She opened her eyes, ready to give him a piece of her mind.

But the foyer stood empty before her.

Pulling in a slow, steadying breath, Regan moved into the house. *So, abduction, car theft and now breaking and entering. Not the day you had planned, is it?*

She looked around herself. She should find a phone. Let Peter know she was okay.

Are you okay? Are *you?*

A tremble began in her stomach, a soft, rapid spasm like a million butterflies beating their wings in blind panic. God. She'd just witnessed two—damn it—two *werewolves* fighting. How did one's brain deal with that? Especially when she now stood in someone else's home with one of them. She frowned, rubbing her palms up and down her suddenly cold arms. And why wasn't she trying to get away?

Well?

She didn't have an answer, only the weird trembling sensation in her gut well on its way to consuming her whole body. Hugging herself, she walked across the expansive foyer, looking for somewhere to sit. Her legs felt wobbly. Twin, marble columns caught her eye and, shaking, she walked toward them, staring in stunned amazement at what lay beyond them, a room so large it could only be described as an exorbitant ballroom.

"Bit over the top, isn't it?"

She jumped, spinning about to glare at Declan who, at some stage, had silently joined her between the columns. "Don't *do* that."

He dropped her a wink, walking backward into the extravagant room, bare feet silent on the white marble floor. "Care to dance?"

Regan's heart leapt up into her throat and she swallowed. It seemed he'd found himself something to wear.

Black, silk boxers hung low on his hips, leaving his lean but finely muscled, upper body bare, drawing her eyes to its untamed perfection. She pulled in a steadying breath, the tremble in her stomach gaining in strength. Unable not to, she gazed at him, at his smooth, defined shoulders, chiseled chest, sculpted stomach..."Shit, Declan. Your wound." She ran to him, heart leaping into her throat. She touched the flesh around the bleeding gash in his side, feeling sick. The skin was ragged, torn open again by his battle with McCoy, an angry laceration burning with obvious infection. Fine, grey hairs matted in blood circled the wound, as if the injury had trapped the animal part of Declan, preventing his complete transformation. "I need to clean this, sterilize it before it—"

His hands closed around hers, soft yet commanding. "It's fine."

She looked up at him. Stared into his eyes. Her heart clenched. So did her pussy. "What if the owners come home?"

"They won't."

"How do you know?"

"I can smell it." A small smile tugged at the corners of his mouth. "Plus I checked their answering machine. They're in New York. Not expected back for another week."

A frown dipped Regan's eyebrows. "How can you joke?"

The smile on his lips vanished and he gazed down at her, face an unreadable mask of intensity. "I'm alive, Regan. *You're* alive. Is there any better reason to laugh at danger?"

Her chest tightened. "Let me help you," she murmured.

He didn't reply. Just stared back at her, devouring her face with his eyes as though her very countenance was his only nourishment.

Her breath quickened and she dropped her head, turning her attention back to his side. The trembling in her stomach, her limbs, was now a shudder, a bone-rattling shake threatening to rob her of her strength. Sightlessly, she stared at the bloody gash on Declan's side, trembling fingers wavering above its raw surface. Oh, God. What was happening to her? A violent sob burst from her, and she fell to her knees, pressing her feverish forehead to Declan's strong, hard thigh. "Wh-what's wrong w-wi-with me? I can't st-stop sh-sh-shaking." The words were almost inaudible, a stuttered, choked breath. "I'm c-cold."

Warm hands ran down her arms, under her knees and back, and suddenly she was lifted from the floor, held firmly against Declan's chest. He gazed into her face, his heat folding around her like a velvet blanket. "It's shock, love. That's all." He gave her a gentle smile. "You've had a wild day. You're allowed to be a little shaken."

They didn't move for a long moment; Regan's body shaking, Declan's as still and solid as a statue. Until, heart pounding, Regan leant forward and placed her trembling, parted lips on his mouth.

Their tongues met. Slowly at first, each tasting the other

with tender flicks and stabs. Regan traced the soft line of Declan's bottom lip, drawing it into her mouth. He moaned his appreciation, crushing her closer to his chest. She placed her palm to his jaw, loving its angular strength, its stubbled texture on her skin.

A slight tremble shook her body and Declan pulled her tighter to his, as though willing to absorb the shock coursing through her. His tongue mated with hers, seeking, growing fierce with each penetrating caress. Demanding hers to be the same.

A wild beat erupted in her sex and she whimpered, tangling her fingers in his hair, tugging on the silken strands until his head lifted. "Your side," she murmured, gazing into his smoldering eyes.

"My side is already healing," he murmured back, brushing her lips with a feather-light kiss. "You are what counts now."

"Warm me, Declan," she whispered. "Make me burn."

Desire flared in his eyes. He crushed her mouth with his, dragged his lips along her jaw line, up to her ear. "And burn..." In three strides he crossed the room, lowering her onto a golden, velvet chaise covered in over-sized, plush cushions. For a moment he did nothing but stare at her, smooth, broad chest rising and falling in ragged rhythm, muscles coiled, nostrils flaring. She couldn't take it. She lifted her hand—a wordless plea. He took it, placed the soft flesh of her palm to his mouth, touching the tip of his tongue to the faint crease of her lifeline.

Her eyelids wanted to flutter closed but she kept them open. How could she close them? What would she do if, on closing them, she woke to discover it *was* all a dream?

She watched his mouth worship her palm, her fingers. Watched him linger over the sensitive, almost ticklish underside of each knuckle, her pussy clenching with each nip and nibble.

A hitching moan caught in her throat. Lord, just her hand...just her hand and she was liquid heat!

Blunt, even teeth worked a delicious path to the tip of her middle finger and, eyes still holding hers, he drew the long digit into his warm, wet mouth and sucked on its length in gentle pulses of pressure. Sending shards of electricity into her sex. She gasped, eyelids fluttering at the sublime pleasure engulfing her.

Lips circling that one finger, he curled his tongue around its base, flicking at the slight hollow between it and her index finger. Again, scorching jolts shot into Regan's pussy. Again, she gasped. "Declan..." His name fell from her dry, parted lips in a hoarse breath. "Please..."

The word ignited silver fire in his grey eyes. He withdrew her finger from his mouth, the tiny nip he gave its tip filling her cunt with sodden rapture. With slow and ever-so-steady intent, he lowered her hand to his chest. The hard pebble of his nipple rubbed against her palm and the overwhelming desire to trace its puckered form crashed over Regan. Yet before she spread her fingers to capture it, he slid her hand lower, down the flat curves of his stomach, along the jagged ridge of his scar, to the waistband of his boxers.

Regan's heart froze.

The jutting head of his turgid shaft tenting the stolen boxers nudged her wrist. The contact sent her pulse flying. Declan sucked in a sharp breath, the connection obviously affecting him equally. The reaction shifted his body slightly, but it was enough. The bulbous dome of his cock head pressed to her wrist again and she sucked in her own swift breath.

It was too much. Such a simple caress, but it was too much.

The burning intensity of Declan's stare stole her breath. As did the scalding bead of pre-come wetting her flesh, even through the silken boxers. Unable to take it any more, Regan let her eyes close and succumbed to the sensations consuming her.

The second Regan's long lashes brushed her cheekbones, Declan moved.

Cock an aching, straining rod of steel, he leant forward and pressed his mouth to the smooth column of her neck, letting the kiss push her backward until he lay on top of her. Her firm, toned thighs hugged his hips, held him to her in an embrace he never wanted to break. Elbows resting on either side of her torso, he moved his hands to the torn edges of her tank top. With a reverence he couldn't fathom, he pulled the material aside, his mouth drying at what he revealed.

Her breasts were perfect. Smooth, round and swollen with a desire he knew surged through her. He touched the tips of his fingers to each pinched nipple, a small smile playing with his lips at Regan's hissed intake of breath. She moved under him, arching her body into his, pushing her hot sex closer to his throbbing cock.

Christ Mary, he wanted her. Wanted to bury his aching shaft into her creamy folds. But he forced himself to be slow. The poison of McCoy's bites and scratches still laced his blood, made his control of the beast tenuous. He'd never had a problem containing his werewolf side—not in all the decades of his existence. But then, he hadn't known Regan Thomas. The mystical power she wove over his body was far greater than the ancient power of his species. He wanted to bring her to climax after climax after screaming climax, but as a man. If he rushed now, he didn't think he could keep control over what he was. And, even though it made his heart ache, he knew he still scared her.

So instead, he feathered his fingertips over her nipples, gently, reverently, worshipping their tight dusky-pink tips. Her breast grew rounder under his touch and Regan lifted her arms, placed her hands on his and pressed them harder to her flesh. Made him squeeze the swollen curves with his fingers.

Hot, hungry blood surged into his cock. His balls felt ready to rupture.

"Please, Declan…"

That soft plea. And his name.

Declan's head swam with roaring desire.

"Please…"

Incapable of denying her—and himself—he lowered his mouth to one straining peak and drew it past his lips, past his teeth.

Regan arched beneath him, shoved her dampening pussy harder to his cock. "Yes. Oh, Goddamn it, yes."

He suckled, the feel of her nipple on his tongue, against his teeth unlike any experience he'd had. The swell of her breast pushed gently on his cheeks, chin and nose and he dragged in a long breath, luxuriating in the musky, slightly saliferous scent of her flesh. She'd done little but run since he'd come into her life and the perspiration of that physical exertion still slicked her skin, making the velvet surface sweet and salty at once. The contradiction drove him wild. He closed his hand harder on her breasts, sucking greedily at one peak as his fingers pulled and pinched and twisted the other.

Regan writhed, her nails sinking into his hands for a painful second before she moved them to his shoulders. "Jesus Christ, that's good."

Frenzied lust almost overwhelmed him. He ravaged her

nipple, gnawed it between his teeth. Pulled the distended nub of flesh deeper into his mouth and suckled on its glorious form. She moaned and thrashed beneath him, scoring savage lines up into his hair with her nails, forcing his head harder to her breast.

The wordless demand sent fresh blood pumping into his shaft and he bucked against the spread junction of her thighs, hungering for greater contact.

"Christ, oh, Christ..." The exclamation dissolved into hitching, breathless moans. "Fuck. It feels so good."

The cry was like liquid fire on Declan's control. He shoved his hips forward, needing to feel the heat of her sex on his cock like never before. Dragging his mouth from her breast, he bowed his back, her nails scoring lines over his flesh as he thrust at her pussy with an urgency he couldn't ignore or deny. "Christ, Regan. What have you done to me?"

She didn't answer. Instead, she cupped her breasts in her hands, kneading them in unison with the frantic pounding of his heart.

The sight tore a growl from Declan's chest. He leapt to his feet, grabbed the waistline of her shorts and ripped them from her hips.

Her feet fell back to the floor before her shorts did, her thighs spreading to reveal the glistening cleft of her cunt. Dropping to his knees, Declan curled his fingers around her hips, yanked her down the chaise and plunged his tongue into her sex.

"Fuck. Oh, fuck. Yes."

He heard Regan pound her fist into the cushions, felt her body quiver as he drove his tongue first past the sodden folds of her cunt and then over the hidden button of her clit. She bucked against his mouth, thighs spreading further open, cries punching the air. He captured the nub with his teeth, suckled its tiny form. She rammed her sex harder to his mouth, fingers knotting in his hair.

Raking his nails over her hips, he squeezed her ass, kneading the toned muscles of each cheek until his fingers worked their way to the tight hole of her rectum. He circled it with the pad of his right finger, his already engorged cock growing stiffer at the keening moan slipping from Regan's throat. A wave of lust crashed over him. She would let him sink his finger into that puckered hole, but he wouldn't. Not yet.

With a control he didn't believe he had, he slid his hands from her ass and found her drenched pussy instead. He tongued her clit faster, shifting his head slightly and sinking his middle finger into her cunt.

The constriction of her creamy, slick muscles closing around his flesh almost made his cock spurt there and then.

"Oh, my *God!*"

Regan's raw cry filled the room. Declan lapped at the juices oozing from her sex, drowning in the taste of her desire. His cock, so flooded with blood its skin felt ready to tear, pushed the cool material of his borrowed boxer shorts. Blindly he reached for it. Pushing his free hand past the boxer's elasticized waistline, he wrapped his fingers around the venous, aching length of his shaft. Pre-come leaked from the head, slicked his stretched skin. He pumped his tight fist once, twice, knowing he was dangerously close to the precipice of a climax more forceful than he'd ever experienced before. Christ, was he close. The urge to straighten and ram his cock deep into Regan's sodden sex, bury himself to the balls in her tight sheath almost drove him insane. The wolf inside roared for it. Demanded it. But Regan's cunt tasted too good, her cries and moans of ecstasy too intoxicating to bear even the briefest loss of contact. He wanted to fill her with utter pleasure. Wanted to burn away all her fears. Wanted to consume her in the way she—in such a short span of time—had consumed him. Totally. Utterly.

As if feeling his powerful need transmitted through his mouth, Regan lifted her legs and planted her feet on his shoulders, her cunt spreading wider still. She didn't say a word, just arched her body in such a severe bow her clit ground against his tongue and her perineum nudged the base knuckle of his middle finger.

The temptation was too great.

Withdrawing his hand and mouth from her cunt, he smeared the slick, pungent juices of her desire from her nether lips to the clenched hole of her rectum, coating the tight opening with a viscous film of her own lubrication. Twisting his wrist, he plunged his thumb into her cunt and placed the pad of his middle finger to her ass, caressing it once.

For a split second, Regan's body stilled. He lifted his head, wanting to see her face. Her head was thrown back, her lips parted in a silent gasp, her eyes closed. He pressed his finger gently against her hole. Once.

Regan sucked in a sharp breath and her hips rose, her cunt taking his thumb deeper.

He pressed again, harder this time, the puckered opening yielding slightly.

A moan followed. Low. Raw. A moan and then: "Yes. Yes."

Scalding, hungry heat surged into his swollen sac and cock. With infinite care and devouring urgency, he pushed into her anus. Gripping her with thumb and middle finger. He pressed the two together, the thin wall between cervix and rectum like velvet fog under his flesh. Regan cried out, grabbing at the cushions around her. "God damn it, Declan. Don't stop. Don't stop."

He wriggled both fingers and Regan bucked again, thrashing against his hand. "Fuck. Fuck, yes."

"Tell me how much you like that, Regan," Declan murmured, his cock an inferno of burning hunger between his thighs. He rubbed his thumb and fingers against each other through the membrane of her sex and her cunt convulsed, fresh liquid seeping from her cleft. The distinct scent of sexual bliss filled the room and Declan's blood turned even hotter, his every fiber imbued with the powerful musk of Regan's pleasure.

Her breath burst from her in ragged, shallow pants. "It's good. It's *so* good."

He dipped his head a little and blew a fine stream of air onto her sodden, pulsating sex. "Shall I stop?"

For an answer, she bucked her hips harder into his hand and thrashed her head from side to side.

Her absolute surrender to the pleasure in her body detonated a carnal lust deep in Declan's being. He sucked in another musk-heavy breath and, heart pounding, balls throbbing, lowered his mouth to her cunt once again. Needing to taste her pleasure as well as feel it drench his hand.

Her muscles constricted. Sucked at his fingers as surely as he sucked at her clit. His balls rose up and he squeezed his cock painfully, struggling for control. The scent of her sex, the clamping of her pussy and rectum, the sounds of her rapturous desire were pushing him so close to the edge he felt his scrotum swell.

Regan's hands fisted in his hair. "I'm going to come, Declan. Oh, my God, I'm going to come."

Declan's cock throbbed eagerly at the panted exclamation. He drove his thumb harder into her cunt, his finger deeper into her ass, wriggling and twisting them, seeking the sweetest of spots that would release the building, mounting pressure of her orgasm and flood her pussy with creamy juice. His tongue flicked and rolled and tortured her clit. He didn't want her to come. He wanted her to *erupt.*

Her hands jerked on his hair, her toes curled into his shoulders. He sucked her clit, wiggled his fingers, stroked the inner wall of heaven.

Regan snapped into a sharp arc and her fists yanked convulsively on his hair. *"Oh, my fucking God!"*

Cream gushed from her. Warm ambrosia. Declan lapped at her gushing climax, his balls two scorching worlds of exquisite agony. He dragged his thumb up the throbbing length of his cock, over the bulbous bulge of its head, readying to slam it into Regan's sopping cunt.

He lifted his head, saw her face contorted in release. And felt his wolf's blood thicken...

Mary, Mother of God. No!

The change shuddered through him. His canines lengthened. His flesh rippled. The wolf inside roared—demanding release, existence, fulfillment.

No! No! No!

Staring hard at Regan, at her thrashing head and squeezed-shut eyes, he sank his teeth into his bottom lip and his nails into his engorged, distended cock. Blood flooded his tongue. Pain exploded through him. Before, body screaming with denial, desire and fury, he collapsed to the floor. The sound of Regan's explosive climax ringing in his ears.

Epoc watched the Manly ferry cross Sydney Harbor under the mid-morning sun, carrying—no doubt—the maximum limit of passengers, ninety percent of which would be tourists. Tourists heading to the zoo to gawk in brainless amusement at the animals imprisoned there. What would they do if they saw the *real* animals of the world? Those not trapped in just one form?

Turning his gaze from the over-burdened vessel, Epoc flicked a glance at the man standing beside him, noticed with a certain sense of satisfaction the wildly pounding pulse in his thick neck. Good. He was scared. As he should be. "I don't care how many people saw you change, McCoy," he said, returning his gaze to the busy harbor below. "People are stupid. Almost as stupid as you, it seems, if you let O'Connell best you in human form."

Off to the left sat Kirrabilli House, the Prime Minister's private harbor-side residence. The PM was coming for dinner tonight—an intimate little occasion during which Epoc planned to suggest that Australia needed a biological warfare assault division. Controlled by Epoc, of course. The PM would go for it. When the suggestion came from Epoc, he always did.

Casting McCoy a barely concealed look of contempt, he threaded his fingers behind his back, power making his cock thick and heavy. "Find the Irish son of a bitch and the cunt with him or it'll be you I strap into the shackles and drain, do you understand?"

McCoy's red-gold eyes widened but he straightened, his mammoth frame towering over Epoc's even as sour capitulation threaded through his scent. "I understand, sir."

Epoc stared out the window, agitation flaying at his calm. The first successful extraction was but an inserted plastic tube away. The lab but awaited the subject. If it weren't for Regan Thomas, Declan O'Connell's life-force—that powerful, existential elixir of spirit and being—would already be a part of his own, leaving the bastard's blood dry, worthless corpuscles in withered, useless veins. The last of the *Onchú* clan destroyed. Aine's brutal death avenged.

But plans had gone awry. Very awry.

He pulled in a silent breath, tasting McCoy's submission and fear on the particles in the air. Declan O'Connell would suffer for the annoyance, as would the human bitch. He would see to it. It wasn't *just* werewolves he could perform the extraction on. It would not garner him anything of use, but to a human, the procedure would be like having every fiber of their body shredded.

"I want them both," he growled, letting McCoy hear his consuming rage. "Before sunset. Or everyone the cunt knows and loves will suffer. Starting with her brother."

Chapter Six

Pulling the front door of his apartment closed behind him, Peter strode along the hallway to the elevator. Distantly, he hoped Rex would be okay. Reggie would have his nuts if something happened to that damn lizard of hers. He didn't have a terrarium so the best he could come up with on short notice was turning every reading lamp he owned on, trying to emulate its baking heat. If Rex wanted to warm his cold-blooded body while "visiting" Peter's home, he'd have to stretch out on a copy of the February edition of *Playboy*. Or the January edition, if he wasn't into redheads.

He shoved his keys into his hip pocket, the unnerving sense of unease he'd first experienced at seeing Yolanda Vischka still gnawing at him. She'd waited for him while he dropped Rex off, preferring to sit in his car. "I have a phone call to make," she'd said, the husky tones of her voice playing with his senses in ways he couldn't fathom. Jesus, the way he reacted to her anyone would think he was a horny sixteen-year-old, not a thirty-nine-year-old, seasoned divorcé.

He walked quickly along the hallway to the elevator, playing over everything that had happened so far, doing his best to do so as a cop, not a worried-sick brother: Reggie's disappearance, the unknown men on the end of her phone line, her trashed home, Detective Vischka...

An image of the blonde filled his mind and Peter's feet stumbled.

Scowling, he jabbed at the elevator's down button. The drive to deposit Rex at his apartment had been disturbing. The woman sitting beside him oozed with sensuality and mystery even as she questioned him about Reggie's disappearance. She kept creeping into his head, taking up space and time that he should have been dedicating on his sister.

Christ, he didn't need this now.

But you have it now. What are you going to do about it?

The ding of the elevator's door opening saved him from the answer. He stepped into the small cubicle, punched the "door closed" button and forced his attention back to his sister. Forensics would have the results of the urine samples taken from Reggie's house in the next hour or so. He would head over to the labs and see if the results gave him any clue where to head next. If they didn't...

Don't think about that. Not yet.

He stormed from the elevator, scrubbing at his face as he headed toward his parked car. Jesus, what would he do if he couldn't find her? What would he tell their parents?

"The walking handbag is going to be fine, yes?"

He dropped his hands from his face, his throat growing tight and dry at what he saw. Perched on his car's hood, her long legs crossed at slim ankles, her arms folded under breasts high and full and heavy, was Yolanda.

She's sin and heaven all bundled into one enticing, distracting package, you know that, don't you?

"Rex will be okay," he replied, keeping his voice calm and detached. "Did you make your call?"

The skin around Yolanda's eyes seemed to tighten. "Yes."

Peter studied her. He'd known her for less than an hour but already she was worming her way under his skin. Not just the way she looked, but the way she acted, like a fragile creature pretending to be a vixen. Or a vixen masquerading as a lost soul. He couldn't figure out which. But she was getting to him in a way a woman hadn't for years when he needed to concentrate the most. Damn it, he never had this problem with Doughnut.

Frowning, he walked past her, too aware of her perfume for peace of mind. Shooting her a quick look, he yanked open his door. "I need to see the guys at Forensics. Do you want me to drop you off somewhere?"

Eyes suddenly sharp, she straightened from the hood. "I will come with you."

He shook his head. "That's not necessary. I'm sure you have quite a bit to do. Getting settled into a new city and—"

His cell phone cut him short.

Snatching it from his jacket pocket, he whipped it to his ear. Damn it, let this be Reggie..."Thomas."

"Detective Thomas?" the gruff voice sounded on the other end of the connection. Cold disappointment flooded through Peter. "This is Senior Sergeant Garrett, Bondi Local Area Command. Damn, it's taken me a while to track you down. Do you know how many Detective Thomases there are in Sydney?"

Peter frowned, impatience making him edgy. "What can I do for you, Sergeant?"

"I have a gas station mechanic from North Bondi who tells me your sister's been abducted by an Irishman. Do you know what he's going on about?"

The pulse in Peter's neck leapt into furious life. "I do," he said, his grip on the cell phone increasing. He flicked another look at Yolanda, unable to suppress his grin. "Tell me where he is."

Peter followed his new partner into the gas station, agitation setting his teeth on edge. She'd peppered him with questions the whole way here: *Where would your sister go? Does she know any Irishmen? Have any secrets?* He was certain the questions were meant to help, but for some reason they seemed dogged, overly insistent.

His eyes—almost of their own accord—dropped for a fleeting second to Yolanda's butt as she took a step up into the gas station's store and, noticing its seam-free firmness, he suppressed a moan. Damn it, he was going to kick Doughnut's flabby ass when he returned from medical leave. If it were Doughnut walking in front of him, his mind would be firmly focused on the job at hand, not whether his partner was wearing a thong or no underwear at all.

"I tell ya, the bastard growled at me. Like an animal."

The shouted words snatched Peter's attention from his partner's ass to the short, wiry and very greasy man in even greasier coveralls, yelling from behind the counter at a silent uniformed cop.

Yolanda stepped forward, placing glossy, blood-red tipped fingers on the cop's shoulder and a completely unexpected, irrational twinge of jealousy stirred in Peter's gut. "We will take over, Officer." She turned to the agitated man coated in grease. "What type of animal, sir?"

The mechanic's eyes grew wider. Wilder. "A great big fuckin' dog."

Yolanda's shoulders tensed. "Hmmm. And you gave him

your car because...?"

"Because he growled at me like a great big fuckin' *dog*. Aren't you listenin' to me? Struth! You broads with badges. The bloke's eyes turned silver, for Chrissake. Silver!"

A heavy lump filled Peter's throat. "Tell me about the woman with him."

Wild eyes swung to him. "She looked shit scared. Especially after gettin' off the phone from the cops. An' her shirt was all torn, like someone had tried to rape her."

Molten rage threatened to consume Peter. *Rape*. The word curdled in his mouth like sour milk. He gave the man a level look, forcing calm through his veins and muscles. "Did she go with him willingly?"

The mechanic looked at Yolanda. "She didn't put up a fight, but she didn't look happy about it either."

Peter's fist bunched. Not putting up a fight was *not* Reggie's style. Unless this Irish son-of-a-bitch had something over her, she'd fight tooth and nail to escape him. Something was wrong about this whole situation. It just didn't feel right.

He flicked his own quick glance at Yolanda, not missing the intense way she was staring at him. She started, as if caught doing something wrong and, face poised and composed, turned her attention back to the mechanic, quick smart.

The knot in Peter's gut—the one twisting there from the second he'd received Reggie's aborted phone call too long ago—tightened. Not right. Something was just not right...

"I am assuming you have given the arriving officer your registration details, yes?" Yolanda's smooth, deep voice played over his nerves and he scowled. He was too aware of her sensuality. He needed to focus. Jesus. His sister had been abducted.

Disgust rolled through him and he stepped up to the counter, staring hard at the mechanic. "I want to know every detail about this growling Irishman. I want to know everything he said. To you and to her. Word for word, inflection to Irish-Goddamn-inflection."

"Are you her brother? The cop I spoke to earlier said he was tryin' to find her brother."

Peter clenched his fists. "Yeah, I'm her brother. Now what did the Irishman say?"

"He didn't look like he was gonna hurt her, but he was a scary bastard."

Peter ground his teeth. "What. Did. He. Say?"

The mechanic turned his stare from Peter to Yolanda and back to Peter again. "He said he was keepin' her alive. Safe from—"

"Detective..." Yolanda's hand brushed Peter's arm, her intoxicating warmth invading his body as she stepped closer to him. He flicked her a look and his gut twisted. Direct blue eyes held his. Kept him frozen. "I think you are a touch too close to this situation, yes? Leave the questioning with me." Heavily mascaraed lashes fluttered before her mesmerizing gaze returned to Peter. "Getting what I want is my specialty."

Peter scowled again and he narrowed his eyes. *Is she working you? Does she know what she's doing to you or is it all an act?*

He didn't know. Things just didn't feel right. *According to the brother in you? Or the cop?*

"It's fine, Yolanda. I can handle this."

"I know you can," she said, understanding sympathy softening the sensual haughtiness of her face. "But let me be your partner."

He stared at her, his pulse hammering. The brother in him was worried sick, but she was right, he was too close to the situation at the moment to think rationally. He took a step back, letting her take charge of the questioning.

He needed to clear his head. Of his fear for Reggie's safety, of his anger at her abductor and his increasing attraction to his new partner. God only knew how though. All three emotions were growing in strength with each passing second, and it made his already churning gut churn more. With desire *and* disgust.

"I have all the details the mechanic could recall of the man last seen with your sister plus a *very* detailed description of the stolen pick-up." Yolanda's sensual heat reached out for Peter all the way from the passenger seat of his car. "He sounds quite menacing. Tall, dark hair, eyes that may or may not be grey. Irish accent. Lean but muscular. The mechanic described him as..." she referred to a small notebook in her hand, "'fucking two roos short of the paddock and nastier than a cut snake'. I am assuming he means the suspect is not friendly, yes? The uniform has posted an APB on both the Irishman and the pickup." She turned her inescapable gaze on him and his skin prickled, making him want to squirm in his own seat. Instead, he gripped the wheel harder, turning into the quiet street she had directed him to. Long, slender fingers feathered over his thigh, high, so close to the bulge of his groin he almost swerved off the road. "She will be fine, Peter. I promise."

He ground his teeth, trying to focus on her words but distracted beyond belief. There was that touch again. That sensual brush. Making his body respond on an utterly physical, utterly *male* level. Was it innocent? Or calculated? He didn't like being played, and something about his new partner told him she was doing just that. But why? He studied her from the corner of his eye. "Who is the bastard supposedly saving her from?"

Yolanda gave him a blank expression. A *practiced* blank expression. "I don't understand."

Peter accelerated through an amber light, his pulse quick, his knuckles white. "The mechanic said the Irishman claimed to be keeping my sister safe from someone. Who is it?"

A long pause followed, before Yolanda shifted in her seat, fidgeting with the notebook. "The bad guys."

Taken aback, Peter raised his eyebrows. "The *bad* guys?"

Another shift in her seat, a dismissive curl of her lips. "The bad guys."

Peter suppressed a growl of disgust. Damn it. Why didn't he believe her? "What did Reggie say?"

The hand on his thigh stilled. "Reggie?"

"My sister. What did the mechanic remember her saying?"

"Not much. He said she tried to call you but before she spoke to anyone at the station the Irishman arrived. That is it."

Peter bit back a curse. Everything felt wrong, but be damned if he knew why.

Yolanda's hand pressed firmer against his leg, the warmth of its contact making his skin tingle. "We will find her, Peter. We will find her and the Irishman will get what he deserves. I promise."

Eyes narrowing, he turned a corner. "Tell me why you transferred to Sydney City, Vischka?"

The hand on his thigh stilled. "Why?"

"Because unless you're after something, I'm buggered if I can figure out why you're all over me like a rash."

An unreadable expression flittered across her face, somehow lost and vulnerable, before, with a sharp sniff, she lifted her chin and turned away, looking out the window. "Maybe my transfer had something to do with the fact I told my captain to fuck off when he suggested a 'quickie' in the evidence room." She fell silent, watching the houses pass.

Ah, fuck. Way to go, dickhead.

"This is it," she suddenly said, voice distant, as she pointed to a small semi-detached house on the high side of the street.

Peter pulled to the curb, self-contempt bubbling through him like boiling acid. Damn it. What was going on here? He killed the ignition, staring blankly at Yolanda's house. Maybe he'd misread her? Maybe she was one of those touchy-feely people? Maybe she was more sensitive than she let on? A fragile female hiding in the vixen, after all?

His ex-wife had spent the last four years of their marriage complaining he was a cold fish. Perhaps she was right all along? He suppressed a wry sigh. Fuck. Years of being a cop and he couldn't tell if a woman was coming on to him or just being friendly. He shook his head. "Sorry, Yolanda. That wasn't called for. I didn't mean to imply…" He petered off, unsure what to say. He didn't mean to imply she was a slut?

For a moment his partner didn't respond, her attention fixed on something outside the car, before she shrugged and turned back to him, expression ambiguous. "Do I intimidate you, Detective? Or intrigue you?"

Peter clenched his jaw, the question throwing him completely.

A slow grin curled one side of glossy red lips, any hint of vulnerability disappearing. "Because I am hoping the answer is intrigue." Confident sexuality oozed from her once more. "I will not be long," she stated, blue eyes direct. "I need to change my clothes. Grease is not easy to remove from linen and that gas station was literally painted in it." The fingers returned to his thigh. Higher this time. Almost brushing the swell of his crotch through the material of his trousers. "Do not wait in the car. Not in this heat."

Peter narrowed his eyes on the immaculate presentation of Yolanda's small house, fully aware the sweat trickling down his back was caused, not by the summer day, but by her words.

You're not going in there are you?

Another brush of his thigh, this time high enough to tickle the swell of his balls. If he didn't know better, he'd think it was all an accident. But he did know better. Didn't he?

He climbed from the car, the mid-morning heat hitting him like a wave, wringing new sweat from his skin. He followed her up the path to the front door, impatience eating at him, edgy anticipation feeding it. What he anticipated he didn't know, but it itched at the back of his mind, in the pit of his gut. His gaze dropped to Yolanda's butt and he suppressed a groan. *Bloody hell. Concentrate.*

Her living room was a study in minimalism. Black angular sofa, black leather sling chair, a low, glass coffee table and two matching lamp tables on which sat short, fat polished steel lights. A small plasma screen hung on the wall above a glass shelf displaying a single *objet d'art*—a sculpture of the ancient Roman babes Remus and Romulus suckling on a wild wolf's teats. Minimalism at its extreme.

Peter took it all in, unease licking at his gut again. Cozy.

Yolanda stepped past him, trailing warm fingers over his shoulder, setting his skin afire. "Come in." She cast him a lidded look through the razor-sharp bangs falling over her eyes. "I won't bite." Those glossy blood-red lips curled when Peter didn't move. "Not unless you want me to, that is."

Maggie looked at him with those large, liquid-chocolate eyes. Puppy-dog eyes, he'd called them, a term Maggie both loathed and loved since she was young enough to understand the pun behind the expression. Except tonight, those puppy-dog eyes were shining with tears. And agony.

"I'm sorry, Dec." Pain made the words almost indecipherable. Pain and the bloody knifepoint pressed to her throat.

The ground underneath Declan's paws vibrated with her terror and his body responded. There would be more blood spilt tonight. Just not Maggie's.

He took a step forward.

"Enough, O'Connell." McCoy's hand—the one not holding the knife—curled harder over Maggie's left breast. Maggie whimpered, a single tear marking her cheek as she cringed against the cruel assault.

Declan bared his teeth, his growl low. Deadly.

"Revenge is but a sweet thing, isn't it?" Epoc stepped from the looming darkness surrounding them, his smooth pate gleaming in the silver moonlight. Even in human form, he stank of deranged insanity. Eyes glowing with an unnatural power, he stared at Declan, making Declan's hackles rise. "How does it feel, knowing your sweet sister is the property of my clan, O'Connell? That I can taste her whenever I want. That I can do whatever I want to her and there's nothing you can do about it?"

White rage tore through Declan but he remained motionless. The knife at Maggie's throat punctured the skin directly above her jugular. All it would take was one quick slash and she would be dead. He couldn't risk it.

"Dec..." Maggie's cry was cut short. McCoy yanked her back against his body, wicked-sharp canines flashing as he laughed a silent laugh.

Epoc's own laugh wasn't so silent. He stared at Declan, dominance oozing from him in waves. "So sweet. So innocent. To think, she actually believed McCoy loved her. To forsake her own clan to be with the werewolf of her dreams..." He laughed again. "She came willingly, do you know that, O'Connell? She followed McCoy like a love-sick puppy." The laugh turned to a snort. "Not sure she loves him now, though. Not after everything he's done to her. Everything he's let be done to her."

"They shouldn't have expelled you," Epoc continued, eyeing Declan closely. "It left her lost, looking for an emotional connection. Someone to love after her brother was removed."

"Help..." The raw sob burst from Maggie's lips. McCoy's fingers sank deeper into her breast, his face as expressionless as a mask.

Fury overwhelmed Declan, made his muscles coil. The screaming desire to tear the Scottish mongrel's throat out consumed him. In one snap of his muzzle, the bastard would be nothing but a twitching corpse on the ground.

But for the knife...

"She puts up a fight, Onchú," Epoc continued, glowing golden eyes flaring brighter. "Every night she fights. What my pack does to her. What I do to her...in my lab. Such ferocious spirit. If it weren't for the blood in her veins, I'd consider letting her live. But of course, I can't do that. She is, after all, a filthy Onchú bitch. She doesn't deserve to live." Epoc's teeth glinted as he gave a wide, reassuring smile. "But don't worry. I'll let you watch McCoy fuck her before I gouge out your eyes. Then it'll only be her screams you have to listen to as I drain her very

essence from her worthless body."

It was too much. Declan couldn't bear it anymore.

*Blood scalding with indescribable rage, he leapt, teeth bared. And landed on...*soft cushions.

Declan snapped awake, chest heaving, heart hammering, images of Maggie crashing through his pounding head—a tsunami of torturous memories. He stared at the sparkling chandelier hanging above him, totally disorientated. Where the fuck was he? *When* the fuck was he?

He struggled up to his elbows, the blood in his veins feeling like boiling acid. Fuck. His body was on fire, the wound in his side an inferno of agony. Gingerly, he moved his hand to the rupture, its poisonous heat baking his fingertips. He traced the fused knot of angry flesh, wincing at the hot pain stabbing into his gut with the delicate contact. The epidermal layer was healing, but the flesh and sinews and muscles beneath... Damn it, he was in trouble.

Slumping back to the cushions, black pain folding over him in a greedy wave, he rolled his head to the side, trying to remember where he was through the dark fog reaching out for him.

Luxury. An expansive room. White marble and gold...

A woman walked into the room, pulling his blurring vision. A woman with long, firmly toned legs, and long, thick brown hair the color of burnished chestnuts. A woman with a torn tank top knotted between high, full breasts, a flat stomach and a phone in her hand.

A woman he should know...

Regan.

Arresting light-green eyes fell on him and she froze. "Declan?"

Worry etching her beautiful face, she dropped the phone and ran toward him. He tried to smile, to tell her everything was fine, *not* to worry, he was fine, but before his lips parted dark, hideous fingers of pain curled around his being and pulled him under. Into the fog. The dark. Into the hideous memories of Maggie and Epoc and McCoy. Into Hell.

The caller ID came up "private." Whoever had called him had done so from an unlisted number. Peter frowned at his cell's screen. No message, no voice. Just a connection cut before a word was exchanged.

Something to do with Reggie?

Perhaps. Could also be his ex-wife. He still hadn't returned her earlier call, a fact she would be psychotic about by now.

No. It was Reggie. Peter's gut clenched and he stared harder at the silent cell phone in his hand.

"Who was that?"

Yolanda's voice—like smoke and honey—jerked Peter's head up and he shoved his cell into his jacket pocket.

She stood in the doorway of her bedroom, the black linen she'd worn previously replaced by a snug white t-shirt and faded denim jeans. Jeans, he couldn't help but notice, still unzipped. He saw a flash of a tattoo low on her belly, just below her navel—a full moon? Silvery clouds?—before lifting his gaze to her face. "No one," he answered. "Wrong number."

A knowing smile curled her lips and she leisurely zipped up her fly. "Really?"

He scowled. "Yes. Really. You doubting me?"

One finely arched, blonde eyebrow rose. "No. But you are

playing things very close to your chest which makes it hard to help you find your sister." She tilted her head to the side, her hair cascading over her shoulder in a shimmering curtain, her blue eyes direct. "You do not trust me yet, yes?"

Peter crossed his arms, studying her. Did he trust her? Trust was not easy to earn. Just because she was a cop, his new partner, didn't mean he automatically trusted her. And her appointment coming on the day Reggie disappeared? It raised too many questions in his head for him to be comfortable, let alone the elemental way she made his body act. "No," he answered. "I don't."

"Is there anything I can do to change that?"

"Stop trying to distract me."

The eyebrow cocked again. "Distract you?" Her glossy red lips twitched. "Is that what I am trying to do?"

"Aren't you? Every time I get my head focused on Reggie, you touch me, or look at me..."

"And I am not supposed to look at you, yes?"

Peter stared at her, confusion eating at him. He should be out looking for his sister, not having a conversation with a woman who made his baser male responses come to life. He shook his head. Maybe he was reading her all wrong? Maybe Yolanda was just a woman extremely confident with her sexuality? Maybe he was more fucked up than his ex-wife accused him of being? Or more sex-deprived than he realized? An angry thump sounded in his temple and he swallowed down a sudden bad taste in his mouth. "I need to get over to Forensics. The results have come in for the urine swabs conducted on Regan's furniture."

An ambiguous light flashed in Yolanda's eyes. Eager but reluctant at once. "I will come with you."

"No."

An irritated frown pulled at Yolanda's eyebrows and for a moment Peter thought he heard a low growl rumble somewhere in the room. "I am your partner, Detective, whether you like it or not. Stop treating me like an annoyance."

You are an annoyance, Yolanda, he almost snapped. *I don't trust you, I don't know you but you make my body react in ways it never has. And that makes me all the more suspicious of you.*

She crossed the room, placing her hand on his arm, gazing into his eyes as her fingertips brushed his biceps through his jacket. "I believe partners should have no secrets. Secrets are not conducive to trust. I want to help you find your sister, Peter. Let me."

He closed his hand around her wrist, feeling her palm on his arm like a brand, even through his clothes. "Is this the way you break in all your new partners, Vischka?"

Her eyes stayed locked on his. "No."

"Why am I different, then?"

She studied him, and for a still moment, he saw a hint of vulnerability shimmer in her eyes again. *She's been hurt. And she's trying to hide it.*

But by whom? And why?

He brushed a strand of her hair from her forehead, the slight contact of fingertips and skin sending a ripple up his spine. *Tell me your secrets, Yolanda.* Self-contempt gnawed at him and he dropped his hand, glaring at her. "What aren't you telling me, Detective?"

Her face grew still, and the vulnerability in her face grew haunting. Stronger. Before, with a curl of her lips, her haughty expression returned and she scored a line up his torso with her nail. "I like to be in control."

The smoldering sensuality in her words, the mass of

contradictions she presented...everything about her, about the moment, made his pulse quicken and his mouth dry. "So do I."

But you're not now! You're thinking with your dick when you should be thinking of Reggie.

He jerked away from Yolanda, so on fire he could barely draw breath. "What are you doing to me, Vischka?"

Another one of those ambiguous flashes gleamed in her eyes and she pulled a soft breath. "I do not know."

He turned and stormed across the room, needing to distance himself from her. If he didn't..."It's time to go," he threw over his shoulder, confusion, irritation and—damn it, lust—boiling in his gut. "I've wasted too much time already."

Yolanda studied him. "Go where? Did your wrong number tell you that?"

He ground his teeth and flung open the door. It hadn't. But he needed to move. Out of Yolanda's home. Away from the confusing temptation she presented.

Chapter Seven

Regan watched Declan's eyes open, the shining silver wolf pupils locking on her immediately. He blinked—an almost imperceptible action—and the dark, turbulent grey of his human eyes gazed up at her.

"You're still here."

The soft surprise in his voice made Regan smile. "Where else would I be?"

A wry grin stretched Declan's lips. "Oh, I don't know." He repositioned himself so his feet were planted on the floor and his elbows rested on his knees. "Mars, maybe."

"As far away from you, you mean?"

His grin grew wider and he dropped his head a little. The slight tilt and twist in his torso told Regan he was inspecting the wound in his side, a wound she had watched, in stunned amazement, re-knit and heal completely while he was unconscious—an agonizing twenty minutes and fifty-four seconds. "It's gone," she said from her crouching position before him, the joints of her knees aching like mad. She hadn't moved since he'd gained a fleeting consciousness, some twelve minutes ago, the name *Maggie* a hoarse cry bursting from his lips, his eyes the wolf's eyes—wild, savage and haunted.

Declan lifted his head. "Took a bit longer than normal, this time."

Regan frowned. "This time?"

He snorted. "The life of a werewolf isn't all getting massages from beautiful naked women on their sofas, love."

His answer made her cheeks fill with heat. Fair Dinkum, that innocent moment felt like a lifetime ago. Everything in her world was different now. Thanks to the man before her. A man who had taken her to sexual bliss and back. A man more strange and mysterious than she'd ever met. "Who's Maggie?"

Her own question took Regan by surprise, as did the tight knot of jealousy in her stomach as the name passed her lips. Declan's eyes widened and every muscle in his body tensed. "Why?"

"You called out her name. While you were unconscious. A few times, actually. Along with 'get your fucking hands off her, you bastard'."

For a long moment it didn't seem as though he was going to answer. Just like he'd avoided answering her repeated question of how he escaped McCoy as they broke into their current "hideout". It seemed secrets and her abductor were close mates, and her chest grew heavy at the thought. But then he pulled in a long breath and let out an even longer sigh, something very much like anguish etching deep lines alongside his nose and mouth. "Maggie was my baby sister. Three years younger than me and the most innocent pup in our clan. She fell hard for a beta wolf in a rival clan and, before I could stop her, she left ours. The laws of our kind are very simple—you forsake one clan for another, you may never return. Loyalty is not just a creation of poets and artists for canines and, despite the genetic differences, werewolves still are a member of the *canis* genus. Just a more...advanced one."

Regan frowned again, the dull ache in her knees forgotten. "Why did you want to stop her?"

The haunted light she'd seen in his eyes before flared once again and a tense stillness seem to invade his muscles. "McCoy was the wolf she fell for. McCoy is Epoc's main beta."

Regan's mouth went dry and her heart gave a hard thump. She didn't need to ask why he'd wanted his sister not to go, not after coming face to face with the Scottish werewolf herself. "Why couldn't you stop her?"

Long silence followed her whispered question. And then, in a voice devoid of emotion: "I was identified as a threat to our Alpha before I reached maturity. Despite the arguments of the rest of the clan, I was expelled. Our Alpha was growing long in the tooth and he knew his dominance would not last much longer. An immature male Alpha may not challenge a clan's leader. The penalty is death for those that do so, but an Alpha may initiate a physical *reprimand* if they see fit. Our Alpha created an excuse to engage me in a confrontation he and I both knew I would win. My *impertinence* was punished and my expulsion ordered. Once I was no longer a member of the *Onchú* clan I was powerless to prevent Maggie from doing anything. And powerless to protect her." A very menacing, very low growl rumbled in his chest and he stared over her shoulder, eyes more haunted than ever. "There is nothing romantic about being a 'lone wolf', Regan, no matter what Hollywood tells you."

Regan swallowed. She knew what Declan was inferring. The *Canidae* family of carnivorous mammals were pack animals, social order and connection meant everything to them. How it differed for *were*wolves, she had no idea, but the look of loss and torment on Declan's face told her it wasn't by much. And why would it be? Even humans craved family and a sense of social belonging. For a creature both canine *and* homo sapien, it must be an instinctual, emotional need deeper than anything she hoped to understand. She thought of Peter, and how broken she would be if denied contact with him. Snakes in the bed aside, he was a brilliant brother. Caring, thoughtful and protective. How would she cope if she knew he was in danger?

Probably the same way he's coping now.

A chill rippled up her spine at the thought. She knew her brother well. God help anyone who got in his road trying to save her.

"When did you last see Maggie?" she asked softly.

Declan scrubbed his palms up and down his face, as if trying to erase the pain deeply etched there. "Two years ago. The night of her murder. I've been hunting her killer since."

Bile coated Regan's throat. "McCoy?"

Fierce rage turned Declan's face to granite. "By Epoc's direct order."

Regan stared at him, fear and sorrow and anger twisting her heart. "Why? Why did they kill her?"

"Epoc hates the *Onchú* clan. He has spent centuries destroying almost every *Onchú* on the planet." He gave her a black smile, eyes chips of grey ice. "I'm the last."

"I don't get it. If Epoc's a werewolf too, why does he hate...?"

"Centuries ago his lifemate was butchered in their bed by my clan, decades before Maggie and I were born." Another look passed across his unforgiving features—Contempt. "The *Onchú* are not the most noble clan in the world, but the *Eudeyrn* are the cruelest. The *Onchú* and the *Eudeyrn* have been warring clans since time began but it all came to a head that terrible night. They attacked Epoc's home while he was out on a hunt. Their target was Epoc himself. He'd hit my clan in an unprovoked attack a month earlier, killing the youngest male pups as they played in our territory, literally tearing them limb from limb. The then Alpha of my clan wanted Epoc's blood. And his head. He ordered an assault on Epoc's home. Unfortunately, Aine was killed defending her own pups. Epoc swore revenge. And he's spent the last two centuries extracting it."

The chilling pun was not lost on Regan. She'd seen Epoc's lab. Knew of the experiments he performed within. She pulled in a steadying breath, her body so tense she felt ready to snap. She saw Declan didn't want to say anymore, everything about him screamed the subject was over but she *needed* to know one more thing. She was inescapably caught up in it now. "So, the history between you and Epoc you spoke of earlier..."

His lips twisted into a bitter grin. "Our clans, Maggie and my bloodline. I am the direct, male descendant of the werewolf that killed Aine. The werewolf that killed Epoc's lifemate."

He watched her eyes. Waiting for her reaction. Her judgment. Fire burned through him, the wound in his side— now totally healed on the surface—a cancerous poison sending out wave after burning wave of pain. But he kept it from Regan. She didn't need to know. What she'd just heard was enough for one day. Shit, for a human ignorant of his world and his kind until but a few hours ago, it was enough for one *lifetime*. Telling her his wound was not healing as it should would only make her worry.

Clear green eyes gazed at him, their color like *bhoireann* spring moss. Every emotion Regan felt shone in their mesmerizing depths—sorrow, concern, anger, fear.

His throat grew tight. Fear. But of what? Epoc? McCoy?

Him?

He wanted to reach for her. Wanted to fold his arms around her slim, warm body and hold her close, his face pressed to her hair, their hearts beating as one. Instead he stayed still, elbows on his knees, side an inferno of red pain. Watching her eyes.

He didn't know what his future held. But he knew—for the next few days at least, until he'd dealt with Epoc and his mongrel, McCoy—he could never leave her. *She* was now his world as much as Maggie had been. He'd burn in Hell before he let anything happen to her.

Didn't you say that about Maggie, Dec?

Yeah. Yeah, he had.

"My father was a farmer," Regan said suddenly, holding his gaze with her own. The statement was unexpected and Declan blinked. A soft smile flittered over Regan's lips at his reaction but she continued, never changing her position. "His father before that, and his father's father. Our land was in our blood. When the drought of 'eighty-three hit we lost the majority of our stock and crops. Do you know what it's like to watch animals starve to death? To go out every morning with a .44, knowing you will be putting a bullet between the eyes of at least five dying animals?"

She dragged in a slow breath, a frown pulling at her eyebrows. "The bank foreclosed on Dad's bridging loan and we were forced off our farm. Forced out by city money. Dad went to work in the local abattoir, slaughtering sheep and cattle almost starved, to feed the country's population—the majority of which complained because the cost of milk had gone up, meat was becoming too expensive and farmers were just winging for a government hand-out. He came home every night stinking of blood and offal. Emotionally he died the day we had to leave the farm, but the abattoir killed his spirit. The only thing that pulled us through it all—living in Dad's old work truck, surviving on stale bread and food-coupons—was our love for each other."

She sighed, raking her hands through her hair before

continuing, each word she spoke making Declan's gut wrench. "Mum did everything she could to make the nightmare an adventure, but I'll never forget those months. They were the worst of my life. And the best. It showed me who I was, who my family was, and I was proud of those revelations. But I couldn't have walked away the person I am now if it wasn't for my brother—Peter. He was my rock. *Is* my rock."

She stopped, the calmly delivered account both horrific and moving for the simplicity of her words. Declan stared at her. He'd wondered when he first met her what type of person risked their life for animals incapable of defending themselves and now he knew.

"Regan..."

She shook her head, leaning forward to place the ends of her fingers on his lips. "What I'm saying, Declan, is this. I know how strong the love of family is. I know what heartache is." Her eyes held his for a long moment. Declan's breath caught in his throat and his heart pounded in his chest, an increasing rhythm so strong he felt his body quake under its beat.

"I know," she said. Before leaning closer still and replacing her fingers on his lips with hers.

The kiss was gentle. Almost hesitant. He felt the apprehension still holding her, but he felt something else. Something more powerful. A longing to be released of the memory. A desire to create a new one. A smoldering passion surging through her blood. As it did his.

He opened his mouth, the touch of her tongue against his teeth like a surge of raw energy, charging his body with concentrated need. He buried his hands in the tumble of her hair, pulled their bodies together. She fit so well between his legs, her hips pressed to his inner thighs, her soft mound brushing his stiffening shaft. He took her tongue deeper into his mouth, reveling in the way she tasted, the way she felt.

Her hands smoothed up his back, her palms like mist on his fevered flesh. She traced his spine down, fluttered her fingertips along the waistband of his borrowed boxers. Hot blood flooded his groin at the contact, his cock growing full and heavy. Its stiff length nudged the warm junction of her thighs and a deep moan sounded in her throat.

Nails scoring a wickedly delicious path back up to his shoulders, as if to hold him a prisoner in her embrace, she broke the kiss, green eyes heady as she looked into his. "You scare the shit out of me, Declan O'Connell."

"You scare the shit out of me, Regan Thomas."

Regan chuckled, dragging her hands from his shoulders, under his armpits to flatten her palms on his chest. She captured his nipples, rolling them gently between her fingers as she pushed her sex closer to his. "Well, at least we're even then."

He shook his head slightly. "Oh, no, Regan. There's nothing remotely 'even' about this relationship. When it comes to the balance of power, you have me firmly in the palm of your hand."

One of Regan's eyebrows arched and her lips—those extremely kissable lips—twitched. Eyes holding his, she shifted slightly, sliding one hand down his torso, past the elastic band of his boxers to enclose his rigid cock in a snug grip. "This hand?"

He sucked in a sharp breath. "That would be the one."

"Hmmmm." Her thumb rolled over the head of his cock and he pulled in another breath, heartbeat tripling. "Best not be letting my power go to waste then."

She pushed him backward, her other hand smoothing over his stomach as he stretched out on the chaise. With almost tender fingers, she traced the line of his scar, the hideous mark left by Epoc almost two years ago. He closed his eyes, her touch like a feather on the violent path. It soothed him. Dulled the angry burn of his side. When her lips brushed the white, jagged line of scar tissue, when she touched it with the tip of her tongue, his breath caught in his throat and his hands fisted the cushions.

So much of his life was about pain, and here was a creature wanting to take it away. The pain, the heartache. With a kiss...

Her tongue traced the scar. From its knotted starting point in the dip of his navel, to where its ragged path disappeared behind the thick thatch of his pubic hair. And still she didn't stop. Her lips continued their journey, nibbling a steady trail over the black curls, the hand gripping his cock slowly pumping up and down as her tongue flicked at its wide, swollen base before moving on to his balls. She licked one then the other, drawing his right nut into the wet, warm well of her mouth.

A rolling tsunami of searing heat spread through his body, stealing his breath and making his heart pound. "Jesus, Mary!"

Regan's tongue curled and flicked and licked at his balls. Her fingers stroked his cock, the organ so hard he felt its veins coursing with eager blood. Damn, it felt good. So good he thought sure he was going to come. Or transform.

Control it, Dec. If you change now...

The beast roared. Denied. Hungry for the pleasure Regan would bring.

He dug his nails into the softness of the cushions, wishing—wanting—them to be the softness of Regan's breasts or thighs or butt, but knowing if he so much as touched her he would come. Fuck, he was going insane. Driving mad with desire, lust and agony. His side burned like fire, his blood sang like demons. His cock felt like a pillar of steel...

...and then Regan's lips closed over its tip and it felt nothing like steel. It felt like existence. Scorching, consuming existence surrounded by Heaven. Hot, wet, sucking Heaven.

She slid her tongue up and down the underside, teased the web of skin below its head, circled the distended edge, all the while massaging and fondling his balls with a hand both gentle and aggressive. Every inch of his body quivered, every fiber of his being—both the man and the wolf—trembled, like the note held by a maestro, played by her amazing tongue and hands. He arched his back, drove his shoulders harder into the chaise and his shaft harder into her taking mouth. Praise Mary, he couldn't hold on much longer.

The hands on his balls skimmed down to his ass cheeks, squeezing each as her mouth plundered his cock. He bucked, feeling an exquisite tingle begin in the soles of his feet, the base of his spine...

Hold it, Dec. Hold it.

"Fuck, Regan," he ground out, gripping at the cushions, knowing he punctured the fabric with claws, not human fingernails. Knowing, but incapable of retracting them. "I'm going to come if you don't stop."

The suction on his cock lessened, the hands on his ass stilled. Before, as though weighing up his raw statement and deciding her course of action, she plunged her mouth savagely down his shaft. So deep her lips pressed against his balls and he felt his cock-head press the back of her throat. "Jesus."

Blistering pleasure ripped through him. He threw back his head and howled, the sound purely wolf, purely wild. Crushing heat possessed his sac, smashed up into his cock, making his body buck in violent spasms. He thrashed his head from side to side, fighting to stay a man, fighting to stay alive. Fighting to stay on his back when what he wanted to do more than anything was leap to his feet, throw Regan to the floor and fuck her until they both were drained beyond movement, his cock locked in her tight cunt, his scent forever on her flesh. Marking her his forever. "Yes, Regan. Yes. Yes. Yes."

His cock was a rod of burning steel. His body a building crescendo of rapturous tension. "Fuck," he cried out, claws shredding the cushions as her teeth sank into his shaft. "Holy fucking Christ."

The hands on his ass moved back to his balls, squeezed them. A steady finger pressed his perineum in perfect rhythm with the ruptures of heat consuming him and he snapped into an arc, explosion after explosion of pleasure detonating in his balls. Cohesive thought deserted him. The wolf and the man blurred. He had no idea *which* he was.

And then Regan's mouth slid from his cock.

He flung open his eyes. Stared at her as she suddenly rose to her feet, stepped out of her shorts and—green stare holding him frozen—impaled herself on his throbbing length. *"Jesus Christ."*

Her slick folds engulfed him, an exquisite sheath of tight, wet muscles. Fluid filled his balls, pleasure pulsated through his being. Christ, how could she be doing this to him? How could he *not* being coming now? Unbelievable bliss pressed against his prostate, his cock, his scrotum. He gazed into her face, sweat stinging his eyes. "Jesus." His voice was choked. Hoarse.

Her lids fluttered closed, a soft moan fell from her lips. She rocked against him in gentle rhythm, taking him deeper into her pussy with each slight move, grinding her clit against his pelvic bone. Her hands stole to her breasts, cupping them, mauling them.

Another wave of throbbing heat crashed through Declan at

the sight. Another and another. Pre-cum spurt from his cock, sucked away by Regan's pussy. He felt it. Felt it leave his slit. Fuck. He felt *every*thing. He felt the tension in her thighs as she undulated over him. Felt her clit swell full. Hard. The wolf howled again—but in his mind or from his throat, Declan didn't know. Or care.

He reared up, dragging his hands up her back as his mouth claimed one perfect, puckered nipple.

"Oh." Regan's gasp lit a fire in his already burning blood. As did the feel of the rock-hard tip of flesh between his lips. He rolled it between his teeth, suckled it deeper into his mouth. She hissed, arching into him, her hands burying in his hair as she ground her clit against the root of his thrusting cock. "Oh, yes."

He pulled back, sucking on her nipple as he did so, taking her down with him. Her pussy rode up his cock and for a moment he felt sure he would slip from her creamy channel, but Regan shoved her hips backward and he filled her again, her ass cheeks slapping against his balls in frenzied strikes both exquisitely painful and blissful at once.

"Fuck, that feels so good," Regan moaned, arching her back, dragging one hand from his hair to score five lines of heat down his torso. She flattened her palm on his wounded side, the heat of his hidden injury a glacier compared to the heat of her hand. He felt like she was branding him—with her hand and her cunt. "Bite it," she growled, shoving her breast harder to his suckling mouth. "Bite it now."

He did as she commanded, her cunt clamping on his pulsating shaft each time he closed his teeth down on her nipple.

"Oh, fuck. Yes," she called, riding his cock in unison.

He flicked at her nipple with his tongue, wild pleasure

tearing through him when she closed her fingers around his nipple and pinched. Delicious pain shot through his chest, straight down to his balls. Heat detonated in his sac, an eruption of pure sensations making his head swim and his cock swell harder. He thrust up into her, taking total and complete possession of her pussy.

His cock throbbed and ached with an inexplicable response. It grew longer, stiffer with each punching thrust into the sweetness of her sex. With each groan and whimper and cry falling from her parted lips.

As if sex was just a thing of his imagination until he'd filled her.

Sucking and gnawing and flicking on her nipple, he grabbed her ass. He was about to explode. There was nothing for it. Every time the velvet-wet walls of Regan's cunt slid up and down his cock, he felt the tension build. Felt his essence flood to his balls, ready to burst forth in a forceful gush so powerful he feared he would pass out.

He dragged his mouth from her breast, replacing it with his hand and pushing her straighter. "Jesus, Regan," he ground out on a ragged breath. "I can't hold on much longer."

Eyes smoldering, breath shallow, Regan gazed down at him. "I'm so close..."

"I've been *so* close from the moment your tongue touched my flesh," he growled, muscles quivering as another molten wave of tension surged through him. He thrust into her, ramming his cock deeper and deeper, explosion after explosion of agonizing bliss detonating through him.

She moaned, eyes closing, hands sliding to his stomach, up to his chest. She pressed her palms flat over his nipples, shifted her hips slightly, drew up and down his rigid shaft in deepening penetrations.

He couldn't take anymore. He sank his nails into her hips, his side screaming in agony as his whole being screamed in rapture. "I can't—"

"Now," she cried out. "Oh, yes. Now."

A slight shudder wracked her body. Her cunt closed around him—squeeze, squeeze, squeeze—and, as a raw, keening noise tore from her lips, he finally came, powerful eruptions of come that left him gasping and holding on to her, never wanting it to end, never wanting to let her go.

Never.

Declan's heart beat gently against her cheek, a steady, slow rhythm that had returned almost immediately after their twin climaxes. Eyes closed, Regan lay beside him, their legs entwined, her head resting on his chest. The fact his body seemed to recover so quickly from not only the terrible wound in his side, but the most mind-blowing sex she'd imagined, niggled at her. It was easy to forget what he was, until an animalistic growl rumbled in his throat, or a wild howl filled the air, or claws not nails pressed to her skin. And then it crashed over her again—a frightening surreal realization she was falling for a man not *really* a man but a creature she'd always believed fictitious.

She pulled in a silent breath, wishing her *own* heart would ease its rapid beat as quickly as Declan's had. But then, she was just a normal human, wasn't she? It would take quite some time for her body to recover from what they'd shared, no matter how fit she was. Sliding her palm over his stomach, she traced the twisted line of scar tissue along its path. He truly was a mystery. Yes, he'd shared so much with her. Yes, her heart wept whenever she let her mind turn to the horrific tale of his sister. Yes, she knew he was from Dublin, was once a reporter. But how could a simple human such as herself ever truly understand a being such as he? Even with all her animal training?

She trailed her nails up to his chest, drawing distracted circles on the hard planes.

"Hmmmm, that's nice." Declan's murmur tickled the top of her head and he smoothed his own palm up and down her back, following the curve of her hip until his hand rested on the dip of waist. "Have I told you you have the most amazing hands I know?"

The proclamation made Regan's lips curl into a soft smile. "No."

He chuckled, low and sleepy. *Well, you do.*

Regan opened her eyes, staring sightlessly at the enormous oil painting of a reclining nude on the far wall. Her heartbeat quickened. Again. It had happened again. Declan's words—or his thoughts—sounding directly in her mind, just as they had on the street when McCoy attacked them. On the street it had been a screamed order to flee, now it was a languid declaration of admiration, but still...

He's in your head. In your head as well as your heart.

Declan stirred underneath her, muscles lax and fluid. "Did you say something?" he asked, rapidly descending sleep slurring his words.

Regan shook her head against his chest. "No." She forced her muscles to mirror his. "Sleep. You need it."

A drowsy, almost inaudible "yes, ma'am" followed and soon, within one beat of his heart, Declan's body relaxed.

She lay there for a while, listening to his heart, his ever-so-soft snoring. Conflict and confusion churned through her stomach and up into her chest, not quite chilling the warmth of their love making but making her skin prickle all the same. With infinite care, she disengaged herself from his embrace and placed the hand once cupping her waist on to his flat stomach. A snorting intake of breath made her freeze, but all he did was wriggle deeper into the cushions of the chaise and throw his other arm up over his head, the perfect picture of complete slumber.

She stood beside him for a while, watching him sleep. He was gorgeous. Not metro-sexual gorgeous, not Hollywood gorgeous. Just gorgeous. Edgy, rugged and brooding. Her pussy constricted with desire and the urge to drop to her knees and press her body to his again was so powerful she almost did. Her heart clenched, wanting it as much as her sex did. Maybe more.

Shaking her head, she turned and padded across the ballroom floor on silent, bare feet. She needed to think. She needed to clear her head of Declan's voice, of the memory of his taste, his touch. Falling in lust with a werewolf was one thing, falling in love with them was a...

She froze, barely a step into the foyer. *In love?*

Her heart leapt up into her throat and she swallowed it down in a painful gulp. Fuck. How could she be falling in love with Declan when what he was still scared the crap out of her?

Her pussy fluttered. Her palms grew sweaty, her skin clammy.

Running up the massive central staircase, she headed in the direction she hoped would be a bathroom, pulse hammering in her temples and throat. She needed a clear head, a composed state of mind. She needed a shower. A cold one. A very cold one.

And afterward, she needed to see a psychiatrist.

Falling in love with an Irish werewolf? She'd definitely lost the plot.

Declan listened to her go. The faint vibrations of her feet on the staircase pounded through the wooden floorboards up into the chaise, like a nail driving into his being. He didn't move. The pain in his side engulfed him, made him grit his teeth and curse Epoc a million times over, but he lay still, eyes closed, breath even, throwing in the odd soft snore here and there.

He could guess what was going on in Regan's head. And he knew she needed a moment alone.

A sigh welled up in his chest and he released it slowly. Christ, what would she do when he told her his next move?

Kill him?

He suppressed the dry snort before it left his nose. No, she wouldn't kill him, but she wasn't going to be happy either. In fact, she'd probably put up a fight, a pretty good fight, knowing her. He couldn't imagine her letting him lock her up, no matter how persuasive he was. Still...

The faint sound of running water trickled into his consciousness and a small smile pulled at Declan's relaxed lips. She was having a shower.

The image of her naked body, glistening with streaming water, bubbles of soapsuds clinging to her amazing curves filled his head. He groaned, opening his eyes in an attempt to remove the image. Regan *did* need a moment alone. Thinking of her wet and naked made him want to leap up the stairs, fling open the shower-screen doors and make love to her all over again.

His cock twitched between his thighs at the thought.

Mary, Mother of God, when did everything in his world become about Regan Thomas?

When you first saw her in Epoc's lab? When she first kissed you, back in her home?

He sat up, ignoring the blazing agony his side was becoming. Shit. Falling in love was not part of his plan. Get her out of Sydney. Take her far away from Epoc. Keep her there. Keep her safe. *That* was his plan.

She's never going to be safe with you, Dec. You know that. Not while Epoc is alive.

Cold realization closed over him and he clenched his jaw. As long as Nathan Epoc was alive, he had to stay away from Regan.

Another cold wave washed over him. Not only at the danger he'd brought into her life, but at the complete and absolute knowledge he could *never* stay away from her. Never.

He straightened from the chaise, walking across the ballroom in long, determined strides. The only way to never stay away from Regan was to wipe Nathan Epoc's existence from the face of the planet. And the only way to wipe Nathan Epoc's existence from the face of the planet was to take Regan farther away than he'd planned.

What he needed now was a fast car.

A *really* fast car.

Chapter Eight

Sydney's peak hour traffic turned the roads to sludge. Metal sludge. People sweated behind their wheels, hammered at their horns, hurled abuse out their windows and generally went nowhere.

Peter's grip on his own steering wheel tightened. The urge to activate the hidden red and blues on his unmarked car and part the gridlock like Moses parting the Red Sea made his fingers itch. One flick of a switch and he'd be moving. No closer to finding Reggie, but moving. If he were moving he'd be focusing on the road. Not the confusing, alluring and far too distracting female beside him.

"This is going to be a very poor partnership if you never speak to me again, Detective."

"I'll speak to you, Yolanda. Once I figure you out."

A throaty chuckle filled the cabin of his car. "Not until then? Then I guess we will never speak. A pity, really."

Irritation made him scowl. "Are you playing me for a fool, Vischka?"

"What do you mean?"

He glared at the traffic, muscles tense. "Nothing."

"Do you mean the attraction between us?"

His pulse kicked up a notch. "Drop it, *Detective.*" Anger rolled through him. At her unexpected statement and his physical reaction to it.

"If I tell you I was immediately attracted to you?"

"I said drop it."

"Why? Because you feel the same way?"

He shook his head. "What are you after, Yolanda?"

"After?"

"Call me suspicious, but I still have a problem with you becoming my partner the day my sister goes missing."

"And I had something to do with that?" She chuckled, low and throaty as always, the sound making his jaw clench and his balls throb. "You have seen too many movies, Detective."

He didn't respond.

"You need to trust me." Yolanda's warm hand smoothed over his thigh and her voice grew husky. "How can we work as partners if you do not trust me? *Verdammt,* Peter. You can feel the chemistry between us. I see it in your eyes, I feel it in your muscles. Imagine what it would be like if you only trusted me?"

He dropped a glance at her hand on his tense thigh before lifting his gaze to give her a level look. "Who are you, Yolanda?"

She blinked at him. "I am your new partner."

"No. I mean *who* are you? And the shit about transferring from Sydney West because your Area Command wanted to screw you doesn't cut it. I find it far too convenient my old partner breaks his shoulder on the very day my sister is abducted. And, apart from making my dick stand at attention with just a look, all you've done since we've met is ask questions about her."

A horn suddenly blasted. And again. Followed by a venomous shout from behind, *"Pull your fuckin' finger out, mate!"*

"The traffic is moving, Detective." Yolanda pointed at the growing space on the road before them, a languid smirk playing with her lips.

Peter turned his attention to his rearview mirror, scowling at the bird-flipping teenager in the lowered hatch behind him. The urge to open his door, walk back to the youth, flash his badge and teach the unsocial lout a painful lesson in patience was strong. But he couldn't. His cock—that traitorous, fervent organ—was growing stiffer with each passing second. He wasn't teaching anyone anything with a bulge in his pants.

Self-disgust curdled in his mouth and he pressed his foot to the accelerator, stomach lurching as his car roared forward. "I'm taking you back to Command."

"Why? Where are you going?"

The irritation in her voice made him want to smile. It was about time he got to her the way she was getting to him. "I have work to do."

"Without your partner?"

He pushed the car into a narrow gap. "Yes."

"You think I am involved with your sister's abduction, yes?" Yolanda's soft question filled the terse silence in the car. "You think I somehow had your partner injured so I could take his place? That I am using you to get to her?"

Peter turned his head, giving her a steady, silent look.

"And I am seducing you for the same reasons?"

He clenched his fists around the steering wheel. Refusing to answer.

For a split second, Yolanda's eyes seemed to shine with something dark and painful, before it disappeared behind a coolly poised glare. She lifted her chin. "You can not believe I find you attractive, even though I know partners should never feel that way about each other?"

"No. I can't."

She removed her hand from his thigh. "Very well. What if I tell you my life has been one bad choice after another? One shattered dream to the next? What if I tell you, the first time I met you, I thought maybe, just maybe, you were a man governed by his heart, not his fists, seeing the caring way you scratched the lizard perched on your shoulder? What if I tell you every time I see the worry in your eyes when you talk about your sister, I fill with hope? Hope fate has finally dealt me a hand I might win with? Can you believe that?" She tilted her chin. "Or am I playing you for a fool?"

Peter felt his heart hammer in his chest. Christ. What the fuck did he think now?

Yolanda scowled at his silence and turned to look out the window. "You have been a cop too long, Detective."

Unease twisted in his gut. Something didn't ring true. Didn't feel right. He'd listened to his instincts his whole life. Why was he not doing so now? What was it about Yolanda Vischka that threw him so far for a loop? "So, it's all a coincidence?" he asked, unable to keep the skepticism from his voice.

She turned back to him, eyes direct. "Yes."

"Prove it. Call your old Command."

"Now?"

Peter nodded.

Wordlessly, Yolanda removed her cell phone from her jacket pocket, dialed in a number and handed it to Peter. "Penrith Local Area Command," an indifferent voice said on the other end, the familiar sounds of a busy police station humming in the background.

"This is Detective Peter Thomas from Sydney City Homicide. Can I speak to your Chief Inspector, please?"

There was a slight clunk, followed by: "This is Inspector Wallis, Detective Thomas. How can I help you?"

"I just wanted to ask you a question about one of your detectives, Inspector. Yolanda Vischka. She was transferred—"

"To your command area," Wallis cut in. "And I'm bloody pissed off about it. Told her months ago I wasn't going to let her go. Too bloody good at her job to lose her. Pisses me off. I shoulda tore up the transfer papers when she put them on my desk. She started yet?"

Peter's chest grew tight. "Yes, Inspector. Today." He cast Yolanda a sideward glance. "When was her transfer approved, may I ask?"

"Three months ago. I refused to let her go until she'd closed off her cases." There was a heavy pause. "The place isn't anywhere near as enjoyable now she's gone."

Peter disconnected. He passed the phone back to Yolanda, unable to miss the smug expression on her face.

"Well?"

Her smooth and somehow throaty voice caressed his ears. Made his prick twitch with contemptuous attention.

"You want to say something to me, yes?"

"Your old Inspector says Hi."

"That is not what I mean, Detective."

He stared at the taillights of the car in front of his, sweat trickling down his temple. "You've got me so fucking mixed-up, Yolanda. I don't know which way is up. When I should be thinking about Reggie I'm wondering what it would be like to..."

He faltered, knuckles turning white on the wheel.

137

"To what? Kiss me?"

Self-contempt gnawed at him. "Drop it, Yolanda."

The hand returned to his leg. Caressed his knee. His thigh. "I can show you. If you let me."

Peter clenched the wheel, his balls beginning to swell with base interest at the lazy strokes Yolanda's fingers played over his leg. Resisting the urge to squirm, he studied her from the corner of his eye, knowing all too well she felt the tension in his body. Jesus. Everything in his gut told him she was wrong, that the whole situation was wrong, but with one touch of her fingers he was ready to fuck her senseless. *What does she really want? Get her to answer that at least. Maybe then you can get your focus back on the hunt for Reggie.*

"Tell me straight, Yolanda," he said, keeping his stare firmly on the road. "Are you fucking with me?"

Her responding chuckle—somehow both dirty and innocent—made his groin throb with hunger. "No. But I would like to."

He cast her a quick look, pulse pounding. "Do you seduce all your partners like this?"

"No."

"Why don't I believe a word you're saying, Vischka?"

The hand on his thigh inched high, making his blood run hot and his mouth dry. "Because you are broken."

Peter swallowed, the building tension in his lower body stealing his concentration. *Remove her hand, Thomas! For Christsake, remove her hand.* "Broken?" he repeated instead.

"Broken," Yolanda whispered.

He pulled in a ragged breath through flaring nostrils. "How do you know that?"

"It is in your eyes. And the way you react and recoil from

138

my touch. Like a man who finally tastes life after deprived of it for far too long. A man who hungers what he tastes yet fears it all the same, yes?"

Ravenous blood pumped through his veins at the thought of touching her. Touching her in ways partners never should. "Damn it, Yolanda. I don't need this now!"

"I'm not trying to deceive you, Peter."

He snorted, the sound sharp and scornful.

"Shall I tell you who I am?" she asked, angry, defiant and sad all at once. "I am single, my parents died when I was I seven, I have been in Australia for almost ten years, even when I was living in the orphanage in Germany I wanted to be a cop and I have a weakness for broken men." She slid her hand higher up his thigh, her knuckles brushing the swell of his crotch before slipping back down to his knee. "I will fix you, Peter. Let me in, *trust* me and I will fix it all." Her lips parted in a soft breath and she twisted in her seat, studying him with smoldering intensity. "Let me help you," she murmured, leaning slightly toward him, her warm breath kissing the side of his neck, his jaw, sending libidinous pleasure through his body. He stared out through the windscreen, the surrounding traffic and Sydney itself gone, the world narrowed down to the growing tension in his groin and the thought of Yolanda in his arms...

"Let me help you, Peter. Let me help you find Regan."

His sister's name was a shard of ice stabbing straight into his gut. He glared at Yolanda, the blaring horns and sweltering heat of reality crashing over him in crushing, contemptuous force. "Why are you so interested in my sister?" he demanded through gritted teeth.

Yolanda stared at him, face unreadable. Her lips parted...

And his cell phone rang.

Infuriated impatience tore through him. He snatched the

device from his jacket pocket, refusing to take his eyes from Yolanda's. "Detective Thomas," he snapped.

"Detective," a familiar voice said on the other end. "This is Sydney City Dispatch. Your sister's left a message for you."

Peter's heart slammed into his chest and for a moment everything felt frozen. "Yes?"

"It's in a private residence in McMahon's Point," Dispatch said. "Detective Huddart from North Sydney Command is waiting for you there."

Regan tried not to feel the luxury surrounding her. The stolen Jag purred north along the freeway, eating up the miles like an animal on the trail of prey both sweet and fast. The leather seat hugged her hips and back, the cool air-conditioned air kissed her bare limbs and cheeks and the mellow sounds of Miles Davis emanated from the speakers with such deep clarity her skin rippled with shivers. If she closed her eyes, it would be too easy to imagine she was heading to a secluded resort up the coast for a relaxing weekend away with her sultry, new lover.

But she couldn't close her eyes. Not when Declan looked so pale. She frowned at him. "You need help."

He grinned, looking far too at ease behind the wheel of the stolen sports car, despite the pallor to his skin and the sheen of sweat on his forehead. "What kind of help?"

"You're not well. You need to see a doctor."

Declan chuckled. "And what kind of doctor would you be having me see, love? An animal doctor?"

Regan glared at him, a faint blush heating her cheeks. "So, it's perfectly okay for you to risk your life to keep me safe, but when I make an educated statement you make fun of me?" She turned back to the window, watching low, rolling hills pass beside her in a green blur. "I don't like you, Declan O'Connell."

Declan chuckled again. "Yes you do."

Regan ignored him. Well, tried to. Her body was way too attuned to his presence, her heart too entangled with his. The blush in her cheeks growing hotter, she turned from the window and cocked an eyebrow at him. "So, your plan is to keep driving north until we get to where? Queensland? Will you see a doctor then?"

"Love, a doctor would run screaming from the room if he took a look at me. You know that. You've done it yourself a few times already."

"Declan, you *look* terrible."

It was a lie. He looked gorgeous. As dangerously sensual as ever. The clothes he'd "borrowed" this time suited him, the expensive, black designer jeans, black leather boots and a black polo shirt seemingly made for him. If it weren't for the sweaty forehead and pale skin she'd have thought him as healthy as ever.

Declan laughed. "You really know how to make a man feel good about himself, do you know that?"

She narrowed her eyes. The laugh was loud and totally at ease. But it also seemed controlled. Like he was holding it for some reason. "You're being stupid," she stated. "I spend every day working with animals in pain. I know you're trying to hide it from me."

Another laugh burst from Declan's lips, this one louder. "So, you've finally admitted what I am. Guess it was a vet you were talking about taking me to, after all."

Regan gaped at him. She wanted to slap him. Or hold him. "Watch it," she snapped, "or I'll be asking him to neuter you."

Declan laughed again, the rich sound a perfect foil to the bluesy trumpet tones wafting from the car's sound system. "I've never met anyone like you, Regan Thomas." He gave her a cheeky grin. "Are all Australian women as prickly as you?"

"Only ones abducted by Irish werewolves with a hero complex." She cocked an eyebrow at him. "You know, you're not doing much to dispel the old Irish stereotype here."

"And what stereotype would that be? That all Irishmen are amazing lovers?"

Regan felt her cheeks fill with heat. She rolled her eyes—both at Declan's statement and the way her pussy fluttered and pulse quickened at the thought of his sexual prowess. "No," she shot back, forcing her rapacious response away. She was *not* in love with him, damn it! She wasn't. "The stereotype that deals with an Irishman's intelligence." She folded her arms and tilted her chin. "Not getting medical care is just plain stupid."

"Aah, *that* stereotype. Just be calling me Paddy then, love."

Regan threw up her hands, exasperated to screaming point. She turned to her window and watched the eucalypts blur by. What did she do now? Knock him out the same way he had her?

She shot him a surreptitious look.

She'd laid out more than one male in her life—Peter had copped more than one punch to the jaw as they were growing up—but something told her Declan's jaw wouldn't succumb to mere human physics. Besides, she knew how he drove. There wasn't a chance in hell he was doing less than ninety miles an hour at the moment. She wanted him to get medical care—*not* put them both in an ER. She needed a different tactic.

Letting her lips curl into a seductive smile, she leant toward him, flitting her palm up his thigh. "I can think of another reason to pull over."

Declan burst out laughing, eyes sparkling with mirth. "Oh, lovey. As tempting as the offer is...I'm not *that* stupid."

Regan pulled her hand away. Well, tried to. Declan's fingers closed around hers before she broke contact, threading through them to hold her hand exactly where it had been on his thigh. She scowled at him. And at the sudden urge to inch her hand higher up the muscled hardness of his leg to the bulge of his crotch. "Yes you *are* that stupid." She gave a pathetic, little tug against his hold. "If you won't let me help you, that's exactly how stupid you are."

"Ha! You're a fine one to be lecturing me on receiving help. I've been kicked and thumped by you more times than I can recall since I started trying to help you."

Regan stared at him. Laughter laced his words and his fingers melded so perfectly with hers for a moment she wanted to lean over and kiss him deeply. "OK, Paddy," she said instead. "What is your plan? I think you owe me that much. At least give me a say in what we're going to do next."

Regan thought she saw a bleakness tighten his features seconds before he smiled at her. "I've always wanted to see the Great Barrier Reef."

"You're not serious?"

Declan's grey gaze fell on her. His expression *was* serious, but Regan suspected it had nothing to do with the fourth natural wonder of the world. "Here's the thing, Regan," he said calmly. "We can't run forever. Every second you're with me, you're in danger. Every second Epoc's alive, you're in danger. The only way I can keep you safe is to remove Epoc from the equation." His fingers closed more snugly around hers and his eyes shimmered silver. "I can't do that if you're with me."

Regan's mouth went dry. "So, you're planning to do what?"

He shook his head and turned back to the road. "I'm

assuming you left a note for your brother back in the mansion?"

Regan started at the unexpected question. "Why...?"

"Because he's your brother," Declan answered without looking at her. "Because you love him, trust him."

Regan licked her lips, unsure what to say.

"I knew you would. But it complicates things."

"In what way?"

"I told you earlier, Regan. Epoc owns the cops."

A sharp snort of disbelief shot from Regan's nose. "You think Peter's one of Epoc's lackeys? You truly are stupid."

Dark grey eyes flicked to her. "Not Peter."

Regan blinked at Declan's calm statement. The sound of an unfamiliar, arrogantly poised female on the other end of a phone connection echoed in her head and her heart thumped into her throat. Oh, God. Was Pete in danger now too? "What do you mean? Is my brother—"

Declan shook his head. "I don't know, Regan. But I'm not the trusting type. I have to take you somewhere no one will find you. Not until I'm finished with Epoc."

"And what? Lock me up? Chain me to a wall?"

Stiff silence answered her incredulous question.

"You're not serious?" Regan asked. Again.

"I lost Maggie to Epoc. I'm not losing you too."

"Lose me? Am I property now?"

Declan's eyes flashed with impatient irritation. "You know what I mean."

Regan tugged her hand from his grasp and folded her arms across her chest. "Excuse the cliché, Paddy, but I do know how to take care of myself."

Jaw clenched, Declan planted his foot harder to the

accelerator and the Jag roared forward with an aggressive growl. "Against a human," he said, stare fixed on the road, "I don't doubt it."

Anger—like a simmering volcano—bubbled up in Regan's chest. "I've sent you reeling twice."

"More than twice, Regan. Every time we touch you send me reeling."

The low statement caught Regan's breath. Heat flooded into her cheeks. Between the junction of her thighs. "Declan..." she began, unsure what to say.

"Which is why I have to take you some place safe," he continued without looking at her, his knuckles growing whiter on the wheel. "So you can keep sending me reeling for the rest of forever."

She gazed at his hard profile, at the hawkish nose, the messy tumble of ink-black hair brushing the brooding forehead, at the lips capable of making her weak at the knees and the jaw chiseled from granite. She wanted to kiss that jaw, wanted to caress its unforgiving hardness with her fingers and tongue, wanted to taste his sweat on her lips as she took away every moment of pain in his heart.

He'd opened her eyes to a world she'd never dreamed existed and now she wanted to do the same for him—show him there was a world without pain, without anger and blood and death. Fresh heat pooled between her legs and she pulled in a swift breath. Oh no. She *was* in love with him. In just one day. Irretrievably in love. She closed her eyes for a moment, shocked by the realization. *Mad, Woman. You're mad.* Maybe, but that fact didn't change a thing. Nor would she have it so. She'd deal with it all later, once she and Declan were safe. Opening her eyes, she placed her hand on his thigh once more. "Let me help you, Declan. Please."

Silence stretched between them as the Jag ate up the road. She stared at him, waiting. Praying.

Finally, after what seemed like a lifetime, he turned those stormy grey eyes of his on her, his face unreadable. "No, Regan. I can't—I won't risk it."

Cold heaviness fell over her. She withdrew her hand, glaring at him. "You *are* stupid, Declan O'Connell. Stupid and stubborn."

He chuckled—low, bleak and wry. "Then I guess the stereotype is..." A brutal spasm suddenly rocked his body and, like someone had reached into his stomach and yanked out his soul, he collapsed forward.

"Declan!" Regan screamed, grabbing at the wheel. The car lurched wildly to the right, flinging both her and Declan to the side. A solid thwack filled the car, bone on glass, as Declan's head smacked against the side window. Cutting heat ripped across Regan's neck, her seatbelt slicing at her flesh. She scrambled forward, desperately trying to gain control of the still-speeding Jag even as her seatbelt tried to flatten her back into the seat. "Declan?" she shouted again, fighting with the wheel. Blood oozed down his shattered side window in bright red streams, following the cracks like iridescent ink. *Oh, God. Declan.*

An ear-splitting horn blasted over the screaming tires and Regan snapped her head around in time to see a semi-trailer roar past them, so close she saw the dead, splattered insects on its metallic, cherry-red paintjob. The sucking force of its wake yanked the wheel from her hands in a violent spin, burning her palms and almost popping her right shoulder joint. The Jag lurched to the left and they were off the road, barreling through grass and eucalypt saplings, the rapid sound of dirt and stones spitting up into the car's undercarriage like bullets peppering a tank.

Regan cried out, reaching blindly for the spinning wheel, her seatbelt sawing at her neck. Metal creaked and squealed and, just as she closed her fingers around the wheel, the car came to an abrupt, jarring halt, smacking her forward into the dash.

White agony exploded in her head. Disorientated and confused, she pushed herself upright. Releasing her belt buckle, she slipped free, the narrow band of synthetic material lashing her neck one last time as it snapped back into its housing. Sucking in a ragged breath, she peered at Declan's slumped form through a hazy fog of pain.

"When you come to, you are in so much trouble," she mumbled, disconnecting his belt buckle. Gingerly, she twisted in her seat and opened her door, stumbling out of the car. Legs wobbly, head spinning, she gazed at the scrub and mutilated vegetation behind the Jag, following the path of destruction up to the bitumen. Her stomach clenched. How were they alive?

She turned slowly and staggered behind the Jag, leaning against it as she made her way to the driver's side. Pain throbbed in her head but she ignored it. She had to get Declan out of the...

"Oh, shit."

Frozen, she stared at the Jag's crumpled hood, wrapped around an immature tree like it was trying to devour it. Her heart leapt into her throat. After the tree, there was nothing. Just a drop-off. If it weren't for the eucalypt both she and Declan would be dead.

"Oh, Paddy," she growled, turning away from the chilling sight. "You are in so much trouble."

She opened Declan's door, gravity grabbing at his limp form and pulling him from his seat before she was ready. She caught him seconds before his shoulder hit the ground and, hooking her arms around his back, dragged him from the car.

Crouching beside his still form, she checked his pulse. Weak, but there. Looking about, Regan chewed on her bottom lip, ignoring the growing ache in her neck, shoulder and head. Rationality told her to flag down a passing motorist and get them both to a hospital, pronto. She probably had a concussion and who knew what was going on with Declan.

Yet at the very moment the thought of getting help surfaced, the sound of an unfamiliar female voice sounded in her head. The same arrogant, condescending yet almost desperate voice she'd heard on the end of Peter's work-line. *Tell me where you are and I will come get you.*

Was Declan right? Did Epoc have plants everywhere? She closed her eyes for a second. *Be safe, Pete. Be safe and watch your back.*

Opening her eyes, she listened to the cars tearing along the freeway, oblivious to her and Declan down the embankment. She could go up there now and have help in sixty seconds or so, but what if the person she flagged down was one of Epoc's grunts sent after them?

She scrubbed at her face, ignoring the pain the action caused. "C'mon, Thomas. *Think.*"

Looking up, she surveyed the area around her. They were approximately fifty-five minutes north of Sydney, which put them almost at the Central Coast. Hobby farming territory.

She knew the mentality of hobby farmers well. Rich city men, over-stocking their supplies just because they could, keeping every veterinary drug legally allowed whether needed or not in an attempt to out-do their neighbor. They were over-zealous, over-the-top and never there. Exactly what she needed.

Curling her fingers around Declan's wrist, she hitched his

arm around her shoulders, gritting her teeth. Bloody hell. He weighed a ton. White blossoms of pain flared in her head and she groaned, heading away from the broken Jag, the drop-off and the road. Damn, she was going to make him pay for this. For a very long time.

Fresh pain exploded in her head and she suppressed a moan, hitching Declan's limp form higher up her shoulders as the world swam in and out of focus.

If they *had* a very long time, that was.

Something deep in her gut told her falling in love with a werewolf shortened one's lifespan. Considerably.

Chapter Nine

Peter walked into the mansion, every fiber on edge. He pulled in a deep breath, detecting lavender, furniture polish and the faint ghost of expensive cologne. He crossed a foyer larger than his living room, scanning the opulence around him, looking for anything out of place, anything that may give a clue to what he wanted to know. Nothing however, told him Reggie had been there.

"Detective Thomas?"

A tiny woman appeared through a massive, white marble archway to his left, her petite, grey-suited frame positively dwarfed by the excess around her. She crossed the floor between the arch and Peter in long, confident strides, the sound of her sensible heels a drum tattoo in the silent house. She drew closer, and Peter made out a smattering of freckles across a pixie-like nose under light brown eyes completely free of make-up. Beside him, Yolanda gave a most inaudible snort. "Dressed by Wal-Mart," he heard his partner snarl under her breath, German accent thicker than normal.

Peter glared at her and she curled her lip at him.

"Detective Thomas?"

He turned back to the tiny woman and for the first time noticed the Glock in its holster beside her left breast.

You're slipping. Vischka's more under your skin that you realise.

"Yeah, I'm Thomas." He held out his hand. "You're Huddart?"

Detective Huddart nodded, shaking his hand. "Please, call me Jackie."

Behind him, he heard Yolanda growl. Low and soft.

Jackie Huddart raised her eyebrows, studying his partner with obvious indifference before seemingly dismissing her altogether. "Did you know your sister was missing, Detective?"

Peter's chest grew tight. Yes he did. And what had he'd been doing? Fantasizing about a femme fatale like a bad Hollywood gumshoe.

Huddart nodded her head again, obviously not needing an answer. "She's left you a message upstairs." Without pausing to see if he followed, she turned and climbed the large staircase dominating the foyer, tiny frame moving up each step with fluid, compact grace.

A hand fell on Peter's shoulder, followed by Yolanda's warm breath on his ear. Unreadable blue eyes held his. "Well?"

The contact got his feet moving. In what seemed like three giant steps he stood beside Huddart in a luxurious bathroom twice the size of his own bedroom, towering over her and staring at a message written in some sort of black marker on the wall-to-wall mirror over the sunken bathtub. He swallowed, throat tight and mouth dry.

Det. 45217

Heading Nth

Not hurt

Rex?

Peter read the message again.

"Do you know who Rex is?"

Peter traced the hastily written words on the mirror, recognizing Reggie's relaxed penmanship. "My sister's pet lizard," he answered Huddart. "If anyone called my Area Command and mentioned Rex, Command would know immediately Reggie was somehow involved."

"Ahh, that explains how Sydney City Dispatch knew the message was from your sister then." Huddart nodded. "The question mark threw us. We thought it may have been code for something."

He gave her a quick glance. "Do you know when it was written?"

The petite detective shook her head. "The neighbors across the road contacted us fifty minutes ago. They saw the owner's XKR Jaguar exit the garage, driven by a male, between the ages of 35 and 40, black hair, Caucasian. They were a little bit suspicious because the owner is bald, in his sixties and apparently in New York."

The click of six-inch heels on tile announced Yolanda's arrival. As did the musky scent of her perfume invading Peter's breath. He turned to her, body wanting to respond to her enigmatic presence. He controlled it. But with far greater effort than it should have required.

A cool, blue unreadable gaze flicked over him before she focused her attention on the mirror. "Kohl?" she asked, although it sounded more like a statement.

Huddart nodded. "Looks that way."

Peter read the message again. *Not hurt.*

What did *Not hurt* mean? Reggie was okay? A willing part of the whole thing? Was he missing something? And what did the mention of her lizard mean? Was she trying to tell him something, or just thinking about everyone else—including the bloody reptile—before herself again? "Do we have a track on the Jag yet?"

"Not yet. Area Command is still trying to contact the owner. He's proving a little tricky to track down. The car has a GPS based security system but we need the access PIN." A shadow of sorrow crossed Huddart's otherwise detached expression. "It shouldn't be long." She paused. "Do you know who has your sister?"

Peter's chest clamped tight. The Irishman? McCoy? He shook his head. "No."

He turned to see Yolanda's reaction to his answer.

And found the doorway behind him empty.

"Do you know why someone would abduct her?"

Huddart's question snapped his attention away from his partner's unexpected absence. "She's trodden on some powerful people's toes." He shoved his hands into his pockets, stare fixed on Reggie's message.

Not hurt.

Heading Nth.

"Such as?"

Peter huffed out a sigh. "Anyone who conducts animal testing knows who my sister is. She's had more than one cosmetic company CEO in—"

Huddart's cell phone burst into life and, pulling it from her jacket, she held up a pointed finger to Peter: "One moment."

Chest heavy, nerves strung, he left the petite detective to her call and exited the bathroom, heading back toward the stairs. Reggie *had* trodden on some powerful people's toes. When it came to animals, she didn't hold her tongue. She'd had more than one so-called professional animal breeder stripped of their license, had more than one animal shelter employee sacked for cruelty and that was in her *day* job. What she did in the wee hours of the mornings, in the dark, cold rooms of the city's science labs and cosmetic factories had caused many a powerful businessman or politician to scream for her arrest. Or blood. They had no proof it was her releasing their test subjects, but they had their suspicions, fed in part by Reggie's extremely verbose opposition to their actions. The list of people whom she'd annoyed was long and illustrious, but abduct her? Storming along the corridor, he dragged his fingers through his hair.

McCoy.

O'Connell.

The two names echoed in his head. Did one of them have her? Did both? He clenched his fists. The Forensic boys had phoned through the urine results as he drove to the mansion, reporting the samples as indeterminate, possibly animal. Which meant sweet fuck-all in helping him find Reggie. Locating the Jag was paramount. As soon as the McMahon Highway Patrol located the Jag he'd—

"I do not care." Yolanda's low growl from the bottom of the staircase cut the thought dead and he frowned at her tense back. "Just do your fucking job," she continued into the shiny black cell phone rammed to her ear, "Or I will rip your fucking balls off."

"Who was that?"

His partner started, snapping the cell shut and shoving it into her hip pocket. She spun about, staring up at him. "My landscape gardener." Without giving him any time to respond, she crossed the foyer in long strides, disappearing through the archway.

Gritting his teeth, Peter descended the stairs and followed her into an expansive, sparsely furnished room, the urge to strangle her almost as powerful as the urge to pull her into his arms and kiss her senseless.

"He fucked her here."

Yolanda's blunt statement froze his blood and he stared at her. "Who?"

"The man who has your sister." She pointed to the cushion-covered chaise she stood beside. "He fucked her here."

Peter studied the piece of furniture, noting numerous, tiny slashes in the tumbled cushions, frenzied gashes in the material that looked made by a small, wildly-wielded blade. Cold fury roared through him and an image of Reggie struggling to be free exploded into his head. "How do you know?"

"Can't you smell it?"

He pulled a deep breath, but all he detected on the air was Yolanda.

"Their sex stinks the place. His sweat..." She leant forward, plucking something almost invisible from one of the torn cushions. Holding it up, she studied him over her pinched fingers, eyebrows raised. "Your sister's?"

He focused on what she held, a single strand of long, chocolate-brown hair. At some stage, Reggie's head had been pressed to the chaise.

Why?

Rape?

His gut twisted at the word. His heartbeat tripled.

Yolanda watched him, the closed expression she sometimes wore back on her face. "We will find her, Peter." She placed her free hand on his shoulder, stepped forward so her thighs brushed his. A soft, almost sad smile curved her lips. "Trust me."

Peter looked at her. Felt the warmth of her hand radiate

through the icy rage consuming him.

Indeterminate.

Trust me.

Not hurt.

Do your job.

Fuck. What the hell was going on?

"Detective Thomas?"

Jackie Huddart's voice sounded above him and he blinked, turning from Yolanda's hypnotic blue gaze. "Yes?"

Huddart looked down at him from the top stair, conspicuously ignoring Yolanda's less than professional contact. "Command has located the stolen Jag, Detective. A unit's on its way."

Something scratchy pricked at Declan's neck. He opened his eyes—slowly—staring up into the dim shadows of a barn roof. Dusty cobwebs laced the beams, crisscrossed the framework in such plenitude the scattered gardening equipment hanging from the rafters almost seemed choked by the silken threads. He frowned. Where was he?

He moved slightly, waiting for an onslaught of agony in his side. Nothing. Just the scratchy prickling on the back of his neck and a strange, not entirely unpleasant numbness in his limbs. He rolled his head to the side. Hay. Lots of hay.

Why didn't you smell it, Dec?

His frown deepened. He should have smelt it.

You should also be in pain, but you're not.

The last thing he recalled was looking into Regan's

beautiful, stubborn face as they were driving north. Then...

He sat up, cold dread smashing into him like a wrecking ball. Regan. Christ, if she was hurt...

"How are you feeling?"

The wind burst from Declan's lungs in a relieved whoosh. He twisted on the hay and looked up into Regan's smiling green eyes. "Jesus, love. Thank God, you're okay."

She smiled, leaning back against the stack of hay bales behind her, crossing her slim ankles, her legs looking longer than ever from his low position. "No thanks to your driving. You know you pretty much totaled a two-hundred thousand dollar car?"

"Bugger. I liked that car." He moved slightly, waiting for burning pain to stab into his gut. It never came. In fact, he felt good. Better than good. His senses were a little numbed, but apart from the soft fuzziness...Suspicion stirred in his chest. "What did you do to me?"

A cheeky grin played over her lips, making his heart skip a beat. "The farmer here has quite a supply of Rimadyl in his cupboard."

"Which is?"

"A mild painkiller. Vets use it often on injured animals."

Declan cocked an eyebrow at her, choosing to ignore the mention of vets. "And he just gave it to you?"

She shook her head, green eyes twinkling. "You're not the only one capable of breaking and entering, Paddy. Remember?" She pushed herself from the haystack, dropping into a graceful crouch before him, her running shorts riding higher on firm butt cheeks he seriously wanted to squeeze. Tender fingers touched his temple, worry replacing the mirth in her eyes. "You know, I wanted to kill you earlier," she murmured, looking at something above his right eye. A dull throb was the only clue as to what she studied, but there was no pain. Just that fuzzy numbness. "As I was dragging your ass from the car and across the field getting here. Do you know how many cow-pats I stepped in?"

Her fingers trailed down his jaw, her thumbs tracing the swell of his bottom lip, making his body stir and his groin twitch.

"But now you're conscious, now you're looking at me with those storm-cloud eyes...Killing you seems such a waste. There are other things I want to do to you." She leant forward, coming closer—as if to place her lips on the very spot her thumbs caressed. But then she stopped, a very small frown creasing her forehead. "But I can't," she whispered. "Not yet."

She shifted away from him and everything in the way she moved told Declan she was about to rise to her feet. About to walk away from him.

No, he thought. Not without explaining that "not yet". Not without that kiss.

He reached for her hands, his own a blur of preternatural speed...until they jolted to a sudden halt. *What the—*

He looked down. And discovered thick, metal manacles locked around his wrists, two heavy steel chains attached to each.

Lifting his stare to Regan, he gave his arms a sharp jerk. The chains snapped taut, kicking straws of hay up into the air. Each length disappeared beneath the pile of hay he sat on, and something about the unforgiving way they stayed tight told him they were fixed to something solid.

"The Rimadyl is only a stop-gap, Declan," Regan said, inching away from him, cheeks red, eyes apologetic—but determined. "You need antibiotics. Quite possibly surgery. I'm going to find the closest doctor."

Declan shook his head, anger simmering in his blood. "No, you're not." Fists clenched, he jerked his arms upward, readying for the jolt as each chain shattered. They didn't. Not even close. He leveled a stare at Regan, surprise and, unexpectedly, admiration threading through his anger.

"They're high tensile steel," she said. "Australian farmers have to deal with some pretty feral pigs. Even this close to Sydney. By the look of this farmer's set-up, hunting pigs is more than just a hobby." A small, wry smile stretched her lips. "Which is lucky for me."

He tilted his head to the side, giving her a dark scowl and the chains another—futile—tug. "Pigs? You comparing me to Babe, love?"

Regan laughed, the sound rich and warm and so wonderful he almost forgave her for chaining him. "Babe is a cute, lovable character, Declan O'Connell. There's nothing cute about you."

"What about lovable, Regan?" he asked, mouth suddenly drier than dust. He paused, chest heavy. "Am I lovable?"

She stared back at him, a tiny pulse leaping to life below her ear. "Unfortunately," she said on a whisper, leaning toward him once more. "You are."

Her lips brushed his. Soft. Gentle. Her tongue flicked out and touched his, the tentative caress making his blood roar. He grabbed her ass, the chains clinking as he yanked her hips to his. She gasped, the sound captured by his mouth, and she plunged her tongue deeper past his lips, rubbing her crotch against his rapidly growing erection in small up-and-down strokes. Her hands slid up the back of his skull, tangled in his hair. She fisted them, little jolts of pleasure spurring across his scalp as she tugged on the strands she held.

He groaned into her mouth, sank his nails into her ass-

159

cheeks. The soft cotton of her shorts did nothing to hide the divine firmness of her butt and he groaned again, wanting to tear the material from her body so he could feel her flesh. He shoved his cock harder to the warm junction of her thighs, knowing—even if he couldn't smell it—she was wet there. Her sex called to his. He ravished her lips, drew her tongue into his mouth and sucked, a part of his passion-fogged brain wishing it were her nipples. Oh, to scoop both of her full, heavy breasts up, to push them together for his mouth to claim both dusky nipples at once. To have each perfect point between his lips, to have them sliding under his tongue at the same time...

His pulse thumped. Hard. Primitive. He felt his wolf flex. Dragging his lips from hers, he scored a line of savage kisses over her bowed neck, flicking at the frantic pulse below her ear before sinking his teeth into the sublime curve above her collarbone. She cried out, tugging on his hair again, ramming her cunt harder to his throbbing cock. "You scare me so much, Declan," she rasped. Her heart hammered, pounding against his chest in a rapid tattoo. "The way I react to you, the way you react to me."

He lifted his head, gazed down into her eyes, their smoldering, desire-clouded depths almost destroying his control there and then. "I don't mean to scare you. I don't want to." He raked his hands up the curve of her hips, under her top, over her ribs. Her flesh burnt his palms and his balls throbbed, spiking currents of pure pleasure into his groin. "God help me, Regan, you've got into my head and nothing matters but keeping you safe. Keeping you in my arms." He dropped his head and nuzzled on her neck, needing to taste her. "Keeping you on the verge of sexual rapture until time ends and we become creatures of pleasure."

She moaned and rolled her hips, grinding the heat of her sex over his straining cock. Hands curling tighter in his hair, she arched her back, directing his head to her breasts.

Suck them.

The order sounded in his head, a demand he neither wanted to ignore, nor could. He took the rock-hard nub of her left nipple in his mouth through the material of her shirt.

"Jesus, that feels so fucking good."

The raw words sent surge after surge of hot blood into his cock. His head swam but he didn't stop, torturing her nipple beneath its sodden cotton covering.

"Move it." She pushed her breast forcefully against his mouth and he knew exactly what she wanted, as if she'd placed the very desire directly into his mind.

Chains rattling, he lifted his hands to the neckline of her tank top and, with barely a pause, tore the already tattered garment open. Her breasts spilled free, creamy curves of swollen flesh. He stared at them for a frozen second before, breath shallow, nostrils flaring, he shoved them both together and captured the nipple of each with his mouth.

Regan bucked, her fists tugging brutally on his hair. "Oh, my fucking God!"

He closed his teeth down on each imprisoned tip of flesh, wondrous hunger consuming him at Regan's wild cries of pleasure. She wanted this as much as he. There was no doubt. No confusion. Everything else boiled in uncertainty—whether he would he survive the upcoming battle with Epoc, whether Epoc would finally have the test subject he always craved—but the way Regan felt about him, the way he felt about her, was as undeniable as the moon and the sun and the planets.

She raked her nails through his hair, over his shoulders. Her cunt rubbed at his cock. "Oh, Declan, that feels...that feels..."

Her words dissolved into gasps and whimpers. He suckled harder on her nipples, his hands mauling the soft heaviness of her breasts together, the chains slapping at his arms in stinging bites with every move he made.

His cock throbbed, pushing against the denim of his stolen jeans and the hot curve of Regan's mons with urgent insistence. He lifted his head from her breasts, blew on the two red peaks glistening with his saliva. She arched, the tips pinching even tighter before his eyes as the cool stream of his breath fell on their tortured surface. "How do you know what I want...?"

Her breathless question made him pause. How did he? She was human, not werewolf. Yet he seemed to sense her every thought, her every desire. Like their souls were inextricably entwined. As though she were his lifemate...

A shiver rippled through her body and she moaned, the low sound raising his gaze to her face. "Lifemate." The word fell from her lips as her eyelids fluttered closed.

Lifemate.

Blood roaring, head swimming, he stared at her. The need to claim her, to bury his manhood into the folds of her sex had never been so powerful. So commanding. He slid his hands from her breasts, the chink-chink of steel links slicing at the humid air. He watched the passion play over her face as he moved his palms down her ribs, watched her lips part as he removed his hands from her body...*please don't stop touching me, Declan*...watched those same lips curve into a sultry smile as he took her hands from his shoulders and place them on the burning bulge of his erection...*oh, yes, yes*...the chains clinking a rhythmic reminder of their presence as he did so.

"Release me, Regan," he murmured, dropping his head to brush a feather-light kiss on her lips. "Release me."

Her fingers cupped his swollen cock, his throbbing balls,

through the painfully tight denim. She opened her eyes, gazed up at him, her hand moving over his shaft in slow strokes.

"Release me, Regan," he repeated. His whole body was numb. Numb and gloriously aware. She was his lifemate. And he was going to claim her.

She stared at him, the heat from her body folding around him, her hands pressed to his sex and said, "I can't."

Declan's throat clamped shut.

Regan shook her head, and before he could stop her, she was on her feet, moving away from him in backward steps, reknotting the torn front of her top, her eyes never leaving his. "Not yet. Not until I know you're better." She reached the barn door and pressed her palms to its rough wooden surface without turning around. Her eyes beseeched him to understand. His body roared for her to come back.

"Regan."

"I'll be back soon, Declan. I promise."

She pushed at the door, a sliver of brilliant sunlight pouring through the thin crack she made.

And the stench hit him. Hard. Powerful. Malevolent.

Wolf.

Loup garou.

He leapt to his feet and the chains snapped tight, jerking him back to his knees with brutal force. *"Regan!"* he screamed. *"Behind you!"*

She turned. Just as the door swung wide and McCoy filled the glaringly bright opening, towering over her like the harbinger of Death, cold, red-gold eyes triumphant.

"Told you I was gonna fuck her," he smirked before, with frightening speed, he reached out, grabbed Regan by the arms and yanked her to his massive body.

Chapter Ten

She couldn't move. The man gripped her arms so cruelly tight, she couldn't move. Nails sank into her flesh like claws, right below her armpits. She felt them puncture her skin and muscle. She stared up into his face, into eyes of molten lava. Dread crashed through her like a wall of crushing ice.

"Leave her alone, you fucking bastard!" She heard Declan scream behind her.

McCoy laughed, his hideous burning gaze razing her flesh. "I'm going to have so much fun with this bitch, O'Connell." He pulled her harder into his body and she felt—oh, God help her—a long, thick and solid erection grind against her belly. "For every minute of trouble you've caused me, I'm going to stick my dick in her cunt and make her scream and curse your name."

Fear exploded in Regan's chest. She bucked against McCoy's brutal grip, lashing out with her feet. "Let me go, you fuck!"

He laughed again, and without effort, hauled her off her feet, snatching her in a crushing bear hug tight enough to send splintering pain through her ribs. His stare bored into hers and he bared his teeth in a terrifying smile. "Not for a while, lass. Not until I'm finished with you."

"Leave her alone, McCoy, or so help me—"

McCoy's laugh boomed through the barn, his hulky chest vibrating against Regan's body like an earthquake. "No one's going to help you, O'Connell. No one at all."

A movement in the corner of Regan's eye caught her attention. She swung her head around and her heart stopped at the sight of two men stepping out beside McCoy, each radiating menace and hate. *"Declan!"*

She thrashed in McCoy's hold, and he chuckled at her efforts. "Thanks for chaining him up for me, lass."

Regan spat in his face. "You fucking bastard! Let me go!"

"I like her spirit, O'Connell," McCoy commented, dropping her to the floor and snatching her flailing wrists in one large fist. He fixed her with a smoldering stare, wiping her spittle from his cheek with a casual swipe. He looked at the two men beside him. "Deal with the Irish mongrel. Remember, Epoc needs him alive." He turned his gaze back to Regan, fist crushing her wrist bones together. "I'm going to get acquainted with this little lassie here."

Regan's stomach rolled at the promise in his eyes. She yanked against his hold, her blood chilling her veins, her pulse pounding in her ears. Burning friction tore at the skin on her wrists and she cried out, McCoy closing his fist tighter as he began to walk, dragging her away from the barn.

Toward a familiar van parked under an ancient eucalypt.

Regan stared at the gaping back doors, at the darkness within. Every fiber in her being knew what was going to happen next. *Oh, God! Help me!*

Behind her, a wolf howled. Long. Wild.

McCoy leered at her over his shoulder, and her flesh crawled at the depraved hunger she saw glowing in his eyes. "I've always wanted to fuck an Australian." He grinned at her struggles, nodding in appreciation. "I really need to thank

O'Connell for giving me the opportunity."

"Go fuck yourself."

"When I have such a delectable piece of ass right here?" With a savage jerk on her wrists, he threw her through the van's back doors.

Her shoulder smacked against the steel floor. White pain detonated up her neck into her head, blurring her vision. She twisted onto her back and immediately leapt forward, desperate to escape, but McCoy shoved her back in, his palms punching against her chest like twin mallets.

She landed on her ass with a thud, staring at the man before her through the dark tangled strands of her hair. "I'm not going to make this easy," she growled.

McCoy's teeth flashed. "I'd be disappointed if you did."

He lunged forward, eyes ablaze.

She lashed out with her feet, striking his chest and gut with her heels. It made no difference. His weight whacked into her, ramming her backward, the ramrod shaft of his cock grinding into her crotch as he grabbed her wrists again, driving them to the van's floor. He shoved his hips forward, a wet grunt of pleasure heating her face as she bucked underneath him.

"You're a strong little bitch, aren't you," he panted, thrusting against her even as he fought to hold her down. "Just my type."

Cruel fingers sank into her flesh, ground her wrists together, and she bit back a squeal of pain, determined not to show him anything but hate.

"Go on, lassie," he drawled, hot breath assaulting her face, his right hand raking down her arm to cup her chin in an iron grip. "Scream for me."

"Fuck off."

"Not when I'm having so much fun." With a petrifying speed, he tore at her top, ripping the material apart. "Oh, yes." He gave her a smug smirk. "Very nice." And then his mouth latched onto her left nipple.

"NO!" Regan screamed, thrashing underneath him.

But it was no use. He was too big. Too heavy.

Too determined.

He shoved his bulk harder, harder between the junction of her thighs. Only the cotton of her shorts and the denim of his jeans kept him from invading her...

With a grunt and a shove, he yanked down the elasticized waistband of her shorts.

Oh, Declan! No!

McCoy lifted his head, leering at her. "Ready?"

He jerked up his hips and reached for the fly of his jeans, the bulge between his thighs straining at the stretch denim with hideous insistence, pushing at the unreleased opening.

Regan watched him fumble with his zipper, dread storming through her. *Now. While he's distracted. It's your chance.*

With a strength born of petrified desperation, she kicked out, knocking him off her. Enough to thrust her knees up and push him backward.

He stumbled from the van, rage and hunger flaring in his eyes. "Oh, that's my little lassie," he growled, immediately regaining his balance. "Keep it up and I might let you live."

He lunged again.

Regan screamed, scrambling backward. He landed on her, hands immediately hooking around her wrists. He yanked her arms wide and she fell to her back, the wind gushing from her in a harsh burst, her chest suddenly filled with lead. He pulled her wrists together and pinned them in one hand above her head, fingers sinking into her right breast as his mouth closed around her left nipple. He bit—hard—and agony flooded through her. She writhed underneath him, doing every thing possible to escape him.

His hand raked at her breast, mauled it, squeezed it. His tongue and teeth savaged her nipple. He sucked it into his mouth with such force Regan felt black spears of pain tear through her breast. She sank her teeth into her bottom lip and fought back again, pounding her heels against his thighs, his ass.

Yet all it seemed to do was ignite him further. With each blow she struck, he thrust harder at her crotch, his hips driving her legs further and further apart. His hand left her breast, nails slicing furrows down her rib cage to her stomach, ramming his hand between their pressed bodies until his fingers pushed past her shorts and found her sex.

"NO!" Regan thrashed violently, petrified. Furious. McCoy grunted against her breast, his fingers wriggling deeper past the folds of her cunt.

He lifted his head, grinned down at her, eyes like twin suns of depravity in his sweating face. "You're so tight, lassie. So fucking tight."

He plunged his finger in further, pushing at the inner wall of her sex. Regan cried out, squeezing her eyes shut, squeezing her muscles close. Trying to keep him from penetrating deeper.

His mouth latched onto her nipple again, sucking and biting and gnawing. She twisted her wrists, jerking against his clamped fingers. Sweat slicked her skin and her wrists moved. A fraction.

Yes!

Rage poured through her. Rage and determined hope. She thrashed beneath him, closing her mind to the brutal assault of his trapped erection between her thighs and concentrating on her wrists. Slipping them free of his grip. Pouring every ounce of strength, hate and fury into the muscles of her arms she jerked them apart...and her wrists ripped from McCoy's clenched fist with an audible pop.

She smashed her palms to his ears. Hard. Wanting—hoping—to shatter the bastard's eardrums.

A howl of agony tore the hot air in the van and McCoy's body arced backward, his head thrown back, his face scrunched in pain. Regan lifted her feet and punched them into his gut, launching him through the open doors behind him.

Go!

She scrambled into a frantic crouch, stare locked on McCoy's falling frame. His mammoth bulk cut through the summer heat, a wild arc of growling rage before, mid-plummet, he twisted into a fluid spin and landed on his feet and hands. Glaring at her from all fours with burning golden eyes. Wolf's eyes.

Regan's throat clamped shut. *Oh, shit.*

He bared his teeth in a silent snarl, teeth no longer human. "You are a little minx, aren't you?" he growled, unfurling into a menacing stand, the guttural words spitting from a mouth now more a blunt wolf muzzle.

"Come at me again and I'll rip your balls off."

"Rip them off, no. Suck them..." McCoy dropped her a lurid wink, his face more distorted and animalistic by the second. "Absolutely."

He lunged, a great black blur, ramming into Regan's chest and driving her against the metal floor. Claws ripped at her shirt, her shorts. His mouth sank into her neck, his teeth into her flesh. Her wild blows seemed to matter little to him. He rammed his cock at her crotch, again and again. Black pain exploded between her thighs, the soft lips of her sex pummeled by a ramrod shaft. He reared up, the split-second moment of freedom allowing Regan to see what he'd become—part wolf, part man—before grabbing the front of her shorts and shoving them down. He snatched at her wrists, almost popping her shoulder joints as he yanked her arms above her head and dropped back on top of her, his weight immovable. Inescapable. He pinned her legs with one of his and imprisoned her wrists in one cruel fist, plunging the fingers of his free hand past the bruised folds of her centre.

"No!" Regan screamed. "Get the fuck off me."

With grunting chuckles, he tore his hand from between her legs and yanked open the fly of his jeans. "Now this is gonna hurt, lassie," he panted, wolf's eyes boring into hers. "Quite a lot, in fact." He flattened his hand to her shoulder, nailing her completely to the floor, lining up his swollen erection with her now brutalized sex. He dropped his head, the contorted length of his muzzle-nose pressing to her ear. "Feel free to scream as loud as you like."

Regan clenched her fists. "You first." She lashed her head to side and, fury consuming her, sank her teeth into his stubble-covered jaw. Fur and flesh and sweat filled her mouth. He yanked back, leaving part of his skin behind. A maniacal light flared in his eyes and he wiped at the bloody wound she'd made, grinning. "Such a wild bonnie lass," he murmured. "I *really* need to say thank you to O'Connell."

"Not thank you, ass-wipe," a deep male voice sounded behind him. "You need to say goodbye."

And with that, Declan rose up behind McCoy, grabbed his head with clawed, bloody hands and snapped it to the side like it was a bottle top.

A sharp crack shattered the air. McCoy's body went limp

and Declan yanked it backward, flinging it from the van in a savage throw.

He turned to Regan, silver wolf eyes steady. He held out his right hand, wrist still encased in a now dented steel shackle, the wicked claws at the end of each finger retracting until they were but blunt human nails. "Did he...?"

Regan shook her head, colder than ice. She felt sick. Sick and angry and numb. "No. You stopped him." She stared at him. Wondering if he really was there. Blood splattered his body and numerous gashes littered his face, neck and chest. The black shirt he'd procured from the mansion back in Sydney was now a tattered rag, hanging from his shoulders in strips, barely intact. The wound in his side seeped fresh blood, his chest heaved with each ragged breath he drew and his hair was a stringy, tangled mess.

Ignoring his hand, she climbed from the back of the van. Her stare slid to McCoy's inert form, lying prone in the long, dry grass. Sick contempt flooded through her. She swallowed, turning back to Declan who watched her with such intent her skin prickled. "Is he dead?"

He looked at her with human eyes once again, their grey depths swimming with concern and anger. And something else. Something shadowy. "We have to go."

She hugged herself, the hideous memory of McCoy's touch on her flesh like acid eating her skin. Her muscles ached, like her body had been through a senseless war. But the ambiguous shadow in Declan's eyes...It made her scared. "Is he dead, Declan?"

Without a word, he skimmed his hand down her back and she flinched. "Don't," she murmured, hugging herself tighter, returning her stare to McCoy once again. The ice encasing her limbs cracked and suddenly, boiling, savage rage roared through her. She spun around. Fixed Declan with a hard stare. *"Is. He. Dead?"*

Declan shook his head. "Regan, you're not ready to—"

She snapped. Fear, fury, helplessness and shame erupted in her soul. Devoured her. "Don't tell me I'm not ready!" she screamed. "Don't tell me I won't understand!" She hammered his body with her fists, glaring at him through hot, stinging tears, hating herself, hating him. "Don't." She struck his jaw. His chest. His shoulders. "Fucking tell me..." He stood still. Took it all. Every blow. Every screamed word. Watching her. She thumped at him. "I'm not ready!" She stared at him, blinded by tears and agonized grief. *"He almost raped me!"* She smashed her fists against his chest, choking on the air. Tears ran down her face, burning trails of inexplicable shame. "He almost raped me," she sobbed, and suddenly she was burying her face into the chest that only seconds ago she'd been punishing.

"I know, Regan." Declan slid his arms around her body and held her, his breath soft and warm on the top of her head, his presence as solid as the ground on which they stood. "And I will never forgive myself for not being there."

For a still moment, he did nothing but hold her, his heart beating against hers, his lips pressed gently to her forehead. Before, with infinite care, he scooped her up and carried her to the driver's side door, the feverish heat of his body a furnace against hers. More comforting than anything she could imagine. He lowered her into the seat, buckled her in and placed a soft kiss on her forehead, brushing the strands of her hair from her face.

Regan curled her fingers around his wrists, stilling his hand. "I'm sorry I chained you."

He chuckled, the sound low and soothing. "Apologize later."

Empty numbness still holding her like a shroud, she watched him walk around the front of the van, following his every step. Heavy guilt unfurled in her stomach, cold and fierce. Jesus, he was hurt. Hurt so bad he could barely walk.

He climbed into the cab, a stretched tightness around his eyes, his skin slicked with sweat.

"Declan, you're hurt. I need to—"

"I haven't got time to be hurt, love. We have to go."

"But your side? Your head?"

"Don't argue with me, Regan." Declan buckled himself into the passenger seat. "Just start the car."

"Let me at least look at your wounds first."

Grey eyes turned to her, worry like a cold flame in their depths. "There's no time. He'll be after us."

"Who? Epoc?"

Declan didn't answer.

Fear tickled at Regan's chest and her throat squeezed tight. "McCoy?" The name tasted like bile on her tongue. "But I saw you break his neck. I *heard* it!"

A shudder wracked Declan's body, but he kept his gaze on her. "Most of the myths are crap, love," he said, his normally deep voice rough and somehow scratchy, "but Hollywood got two right. Silver bullets work really well if you want to kill a werewolf, as does decapitation. Anything else just pisses us off."

Regan swallowed. "Then McCoy is..."

She swung her head around. Stared out the window at the body of the massive man, lying face down in the long, dry grass. Watched it twitch. Watched wide shoulders bunch, elbows bend. Watched as McCoy began to move, to lift his torso from the ground. An inch. Two.

Ice ripped through her and she spun back to Declan,

mouth dry, chest tight. "What...what? The other men? Wolves...werewolves? Did you kill...Are they...?"

The worrying tautness around his eyes stretched and a fine sheen of sweat broke out on his forehead. "Turn the key and get us out of here, love." He coughed and Regan gasped as a spurt of blood left his mouth. He wiped it away, hands shaking. "I've little left in me and if we're both to survive the next few minutes we need to go. Now."

Regan turned the key.

She flung the van along the freeway, the stench of McCoy in the cabin threading through her every breath, an insidious reminder of a nightmare she hoped to forget.

You'll never forget that. Never.

She shot Declan a quick look. He slumped in the seat beside her, sweat pouring down his face, his body wracked by violent shudders. If he hadn't arrived when he did...A cold weight pressed on her heart and she turned back to the road, pushing her foot harder to the accelerator.

"North's the other way, love," Declan mumbled, voice weak and shallow. "Where are we going?"

"I'm taking you to see a friend of mine."

Heavy silence followed until Declan asked, "Who's Rick?"

Regan ground her teeth, gripping the wheel in a death vice. He was in her head again. "How do you *do* that?"

"Who's Rick?"

She swerved around a 4x4 moving at a snail's pace. "A vet in Sydney."

Declan growled. "It's not safe. I need to deal with Epoc before you can go back home."

She studied him, eyes narrowed. "Declan, we're almost a hundred kilometers out of Sydney and I've just been attacked. Do you really think we're safe anywhere?"

He opened his mouth to argue, but she shook her head. "After we get you better, than we can talk about how we're going to take out Nathan Epoc."

She heard Declan shift in his seat and a whisper of a word floated through her head. "Yes, *we*." She grinned bleakly at the road. "I'm a farm girl, remember. I know every way possible to kill a feral animal causing trouble."

The car was a wreck. Peter stared at it, taking in the crumpled metal and shattered glass. The powerful state-of-the-art engine now nothing but a mangled tangle of steel and hose, pissing oil and fluid and smoke. He ran his inspection over the splintered mess of bark, branches and leaves before returning it to the Jag, his nerves and chest so tight he could barely breathe. Shit, his sister had *been* in that. If it weren't for the one lone eucalypt, she'd probably still be in it. At the bottom of the ravine, her lifeless body as broken and shattered as the car itself, her blood soaking into the cream leather upholstery, staining it forever with her life. His gut twisted.

"She was not driving."

Yolanda's shoulder brushed his and he started, flicking his gaze from the stolen Jag to his partner. "That meant to make me feel better?"

She shrugged, a distant look in her eyes.

Peter released a long, silent sigh and approached the open driver's side door, studying the confined area within. Blood splattered the cracked side window, dry and dark. Whoever's head had smacked into the window would have a bloody big headache right about now. A grim smile stretched his lips, cold and mirthless. Good.

He studied the thick patterns of red on the broken glass. By his estimate, at least eighty-odd minutes had passed since the Jag left the freeway and hit the tree, maybe more. Long enough for whoever had been driving to now be nowhere about. Squinting into the blazing sun sitting low in the western sky, he scanned the area around the crash site, taking in the rolling hills, stretching fences, un-fleeced sheep and the occasional barn dotting the shadow-covered landscape. Hobby farming territory. The perfect place to lay low while recovering from a car accident. If Reggie's abductor hadn't decided to highjack another car, that was.

If he was still alive.

If he wasn't, wouldn't Reggie still be here? Or maybe trying to hitch back to Sydney?

Not if more than one person was involved in her disappearance.

Peter scowled at the dark thought and two names floated into his mind: O'Connell. McCoy. Two men. Who had her now?

"There is nothing here." Yolanda spoke at his elbow, agitation making her normal husky voice somehow sharp. "We are wasting time."

Irritation shot through him like a hot charge. "You told me on what piece of furniture the bastard possibly raped my sister but you can't tell me what direction they headed from here? Who's wasting whose time, Vischka?"

She shrugged again, blue gaze skimming over the horizon.

Peter scowled. "Remember that trust thing we've had so many conversations about?" He waved his hand at the driver's seat. "This is a perfect opportunity to improve on the situation."

"What do you want me to do? Sniff them out?" She curled her lip, chin tilted forward. "I am not a dog."

Anger rolled through Peter and he clenched his fist. The closer they'd drawn to the Jag's location, the lower in the sky the sun fell, the snippier Yolanda became. She'd even stopped those teasing little flutters of her fingers on his thighs that sent his pulse racing and his cock twitching. He'd told himself repeatedly over the forty-five minutes it'd taken to get here the lack of unprofessional, distracting—no, disturbing—contact made him happy, but deep in a dark, tainted place in his soul, he knew he was lying. He wasn't happy about it at all.

Jesus, you're pathetic.

He stared into the empty driver's seat, looking for anything in the shadows that might tell him something about Reggie's abductor, trying like hell to shut the traitorous realization he *wanted* Yolanda to seduce him—*wanted* her, period—from his mind.

"Where are you, Reggie?" he murmured, crouching down and studying the seat and steering wheel. The memory of her destroyed sofa and the tuft of grey animal fur he'd found on it crossed his mind and he frowned. Rising to his feet, he leaned into the wreck, peering at the gloomy area behind the front seats. Looking for...what? More animal fur? Signs an animal had been in the car? A leash?

His gut sank. *Shit.* "Nothing."

"Did you expect to find her there?" Yolanda asked, sarcasm rolling through her accent. "Maybe trussed up, waiting for you to save her, yes?"

He snapped upright, letting her see the cold contempt on his face. "Go."

She recoiled at the blunt force of the word. "Go where?"

177

"Away. From me."

Glossed lips pursed and she shifted her weight, jutting her hip forward—a spark of her old femme flaring like blue fire in her eyes. "Make me."

Anger exploded in Peter again. "Don't you get it, Yolanda?" He ground out. "This is my *sister* I'm trying to find. Trying to save." He shook his head, letting her see his rage and frustration and, yes, even his fear. "For fuck sake, I don't know who has her or what he's doing to her! All I've got to go on is an ambiguous scrawl on a mirror which may or may not be a lie and two names so common I'd be questioning half of the state!" He dragged his fingers through his hair, wanting to drive his fist through something—*any*thing—in an attempt to destroy the complete and utter sense of helplessness eating at him.

Yolanda gazed back at him, motionless.

"You want me to trust you?" he spat out, knowing breaking point was close but incapable of caring. "You want a relationship with me? Then stop making smart-ass comments and *help me find her.*"

She stared at him. Stared *into* him. "You love her, don't you," she finally said, her voice free of artifice for the first time since they'd met.

"Of course, I love her," he snapped. "She's my sister."

She tilted her head to the side, unreadable eyes hidden in shadows. "Blood? Is that the only reason? A sense of obligation because she is your kin?"

Peter clenched his jaw, throat tight, gut tighter. The late afternoon sun bore down on him, sucking the sweat from his body before it could bead on his skin. Yet he still felt cold. Cold, helpless and angry. "No," he said, holding Yolanda's stare. "I love her because she's got a heart the size of an elephant, a sense of humor sharper than a knife and a sense of loyalty that would make a Labrador envious. I love her because she'd give her life to defend those incapable of defending themselves and would do so willingly. I love her because she never thinks of herself first and has a stronger moral center than every High Court judge, social worker and religious leader I know." He paused, dropping his stare from Yolanda's eyes to the mangled Jag once more, picturing Reggie there in the passenger's seat, terrified, hurtling toward possible death along a road miles from her home. "And if—no, *when*, I find the bastard responsible for this, I will make him wish *I'd* never been born." He turned back to Yolanda, jaw clenched. "Because trust me when I say, partner, you don't mess with someone I love and expect to walk away from it."

Yolanda looked at him, silent, still, her eyes enigmatic pools of shimmering blue. A sad expression flickered over her features and she let out a soft breath. "I wish I'd met you about three hundred years ago," she said, the words a barely audible whisper.

Peter blinked, tension gripping him in vise. "What?"

Shocked surprise flittered across her perfect face and she gave her head a sharp, violent shake. "Never mind," she said, contempt so thick in her voice he almost saw it flaying her flesh.

"What do you mean, 'never mind'?"

"Nothing. It is of no consequence."

Peter narrowed his eyes. "Who hurt you, Yolanda?"

She froze, shoulders growing stiff. "I don't know what you mean."

"Who made you this way? You're like an abandoned puppy, desperate for affection yet scared of the hand that feeds you. Scared it's going to lash out and strike." He paused, his pulse pounding, his throat tight. "Who did this to you? Because I'd really like to meet him."

She cocked a contemptuous eyebrow. "And do what?"

"What do you think?"

For a moment, nothing, and then she looked away. "He would kill you before you had the chance."

An angry beat smashed through Peter's chest and he curled his hands into hard fists. "Let him try."

She opened her mouth, her eyes swimming with uncertainty, shining with barely contained tears, and her cell phone rang. Snatching it from her pocket, she dropped her head forward, the white-blonde curtain of her hair cascading around her face, hiding it from him as she studied the cell's small display. Her shoulders tensed and, without a word, she turned away from him, storming from the crash site, spine stiff, shoulders square, phone still ringing in her hand.

Peter watched her go, blood roaring in his ears, heart pounding in his chest. Everything about her body said, "leave me alone". Such a contrast to the woman he'd first met, perched on his desk at work, sultry sensuality oozing from her in waves. "What the fuck is going on?"

He turned back to the Jag, wishing to God and Jesus and the Devil himself it would tell him its secrets. Tell him where Reggie was, who she was with, if she was hurt or not, and while it was at it, tell him who the fuck Yolanda Vischka was, what she had done to him and how he was ever going to survive her.

He gazed blankly at the stolen car, heart thumping, body tense, and for a frozen, split second, the very last wish seemed to engulf him.

He dragged his hands through his hair. "Fair dinkum, I'm screwed."

Epoc stood in his private office, watching the eastern sky over the harbor turn to a pink and violet canvas as the sun began to sink below the horizon behind him. He studied a line of seagulls gliding north through the darkening dusk sky, heading, no doubt, to Manly and the hordes of tourists who populated the seaside suburb every night; tourists with too much beer in their bellies to read the signs plastered everywhere on the harbor promenade that read, *"Do not feed the seagulls".*

"It's time," he said aloud, admiring the effortless way the birds rode the sea breezes, as though gravity was a thing afflicting only man. "Bring him in."

"But..." A disembodied voice wafted from the telecommunication speakers embedded in the surface of his desk, soft but—unexpectedly—resistant. Defiant.

"Remember who you were before I took you in," he interrupted. "A homeless, unwanted female, lost, without family and struggling to survive. Easy pickings for those who may have wanted to do you harm or use you for their own nefarious purposes. Remember how grateful you were when I allowed you to become a member of my clan, when I gave you a sense of belonging. A sense of *place*." A small smile of power played over his lips. "You do remember, don't you?"

Silence stretched from the speakers for a long moment. Epoc's smile widened. His prick twitched with dark victory.

"I remember," came the answer. Low. Somehow dejected.

"Of course you do," he said smoothly. Smugly. "The sun has set, Yolanda. It's time to bring the brother in. Now."

Chapter Eleven

Regan directed McCoy's van through the darkening streets, flicking her attention continuously from the road to Declan beside her and back to the road. He'd fallen into a fitful sleep on the outskirts of Sydney, sweat wetting his skin, trembles shaking his body, and while she knew he needed rest, his silence scared the shit out of her. She wanted to wake him, but didn't. At least he wasn't arguing with her to turn around and head north.

Guiding the van through the traffic, she chewed on her bottom lip. The whole journey back into the city, she'd expected McCoy to somehow jump onto the moving vehicle, climb into the cab and finish what he'd begun. When she wasn't staring hard at the road, or shooting Declan worrying glances, she watched the rearview and side mirrors, positive she'd see an enormous wolf sprinting after her in the stretching dusk shadows, red-gold eyes burning with depraved promise and evil hunger.

But here they were, seconds from Rick's practice, and not a wolf in sight. Well, with the exception of the one beside her, although Declan still existed in his human form. For the moment.

She sucked in a slow breath, scanning the street for a parking spot outside the vet clinic, hoping Rick was already inside waiting for her. Manly was not the suburb to drag a semi-unconscious, half-naked bleeding man along the footpath, especially at this time of the evening when people descended on the suburb to eat, drink and party the night away. Too many tourists, too many curious eyes, too many waggling tongues. If Epoc *did* have plants everywhere, they'd learn very quickly where she was. Where Declan was. She needed to get him behind closed doors as quickly as possible.

Spotting an empty space not more than a few yards from Rick's practice, she swung the van in, bumping the front wheel to the curb with a clumsy jolt. Declan moaned softly, already-closed eyes closing tighter as pain etched his features anew. "Sorry, Paddy," she murmured, jumping from the driver's seat. She hurried around to the curb, studying the area around her with quick glances before opening the passenger door. She didn't know what she expected, but every fiber of her being told her to be on edge. Alert.

"Need help?"

She spun around, eyes wide, muscles coiled. "Rick," she gasped, slumping against the van's side, glaring at the tall man with light brown hair frowning at her on the sidewalk. "You scared the shit out of me."

Rick's eyebrows shot up, fudge-brown eyes immediately concerned. "You really *are* in trouble, aren't you?"

Regan scrubbed at her face with her hands. "You could say that," she answered into her palms. Pushing herself from the van, she stared long and hard at Rick. How the hell did she explain the last seventeen hours to him? She suppressed a sigh, reaching for the passenger's side door handle. "No questions, okay?"

Before he could answer, she opened the door.

Declan slumped in the seat, sweat-slicked face white, slight shudders wracking his body, blood—both old and new—staining his pale, clammy flesh.

"What the fuck?" Rick gasped beside Regan.

Declan rolled his head to the side, glassy-eyed gaze slipping from Regan to the man beside her. *"Ná bain di, tuili."*

"It's okay, Declan," she said softly, leaning across his body to unclip the seatbelt holding him upright. Blazing heat radiated from him in waves. Sick, insidious heat she knew all too well accompanied sick, insidious pain. Regan's stomach clenched and she quickened her pace, not wanting to send any jolting movements into his fevered limbs but knowing she raced the clock. "I'm here."

Delirious, grey eyes slid to her. "Run. Get away. I'm sorry. I never meant..." His eyelids fluttered closed and a grimace scrunched up his face. *"Scaoil í."*

"Jesus, Regan." Rick jumped forward, helping her remove Declan from the van. He wrapped one strong arm around his back, hefting him from the seat to the sidewalk. "What the fuck is..."

Declan stiffened, a suddenly lucid stare locking onto Rick. *"Bain di agus réabfaidh mé do scornach."*

"I've no fucking idea what you're saying, mate," Rick muttered, hitching Declan further up his side with the gentle skill of a person used to moving large creatures in agony. "But I hope it's thank you."

A sharp groan burst from Declan's dry lips, his eyes squeezed shut and he slumped forward again. Another wave a violent shudders took possession of his body, the short length of chain attached to the shackle on his wrist rattling with each.

Rick looked at Regan, his level stare speaking volumes—*I want answers*—before he turned and walked slowly toward the open door of his clinic, carrying most of Declan's weight with him.

Regan slammed the van's door shut and followed, worry eating at her like a cancer. What if she was too late? Declan's condition had deteriorated so quickly over the last thirty minutes. What if—

"Stop it, Woman!" she hissed to herself. Now was not the time.

Stopping at the clinic's door, she hurriedly studied the street. It was almost empty, Rick's practice situated as it was, two blocks from the main strip. Several people wandered around, mostly heading for the restaurant drag, but no one had bothered with them. Not even to cast a curious sideward glance. She breathed a sigh of relief and the sudden black lights swirling across her vision made her realize she'd been holding her breath.

The sting of disinfectant, ammonia and animal urine assaulted her nose as she stepped into the clinic's waiting room. The smell normally calmed her. It was a smell she associated with her uni days, made her think of recovery and care for those in need, but tonight it made her nerves string taut. In the back rooms, dogs locked in cages overnight awaiting surgery the following day barked and whined, the sound sad and somehow lonely. A lone cockatoo called for an owner not there, obviously disturbed from its sleep by the unexpected interruption. *"Mavis,"* it called repeatedly. *"The lights are on! Mavis, the lights are on!"*

The low nightlight on the front counter cast the area in looming shadows, the sinking sun adding its own through the louvered blinds on the windows and door. Anyone could be hiding, waiting in those shadows. Anyone...A chill rippled up her spine and she scowled.

Oh, for Pete's sake. McCoy is not here. Wake up, Woman.

She crossed the foyer, heading toward Rick's main operating room. Brilliant white light streamed through the thin cracks around the door, telling her the vet had wasted no time. He never did.

Declan lay stretched on his back on the stainless steel table when she entered the room, turbulent, grey eyes closed. A tube poked from between his lips, held in place by two strips of sticking plaster. The tattered remains of his black shirt were gone, now nothing but a crumple of blood-soaked material on the floor at Rick's feet. She ran a stunned gaze over his lean form, throat clamping shut at the hideous lesions and gashes crisscrossing his rib cage and chest. Jesus, it looked as though he'd been attacked by a pack of wild animals.

Which is exactly the case, isn't it? Two werewolves on one. Declan chained, the others free. Thanks to you.

Guilt consumed her and she bit back a moan.

"It'll take about five minutes for him to go under completely." Rick adjusted the controls on a large canister positioned at Declan's head, feeding a steady stream of anesthetic into his lungs. "That's five minutes of answers I want before I begin."

Regan stopped on the other side of the table, wanting to thread her fingers through Declan's, to make sure he was still warm. Still alive. "I can't, Rick."

Two very angry, very worried brown eyes snapped to her face. "I saw you on the six o'clock news, Reg. The report stated you were abducted by a dangerous criminal!"

Regan hissed in a breath. Bloody hell, what would her parents be thinking? They'd be going out of their minds.

"Is this the criminal?" Rick continued, anger making his words deep and hard. "This bloke I'm just about to cut open? Has he hurt you? Are you okay?"

Regan gave him a small smile. "I'm fine. Really. You know me, Rick. You think I can't take care of myself?"

Rick shook his head, refusing to let her gaze go. "I know you can, Reg, but you've a lump on your head the size of a tennis ball, scratches on your arms and neck that look like they're from an animal of some sort and your eyes look like you've been to hell and back. And whoever this bloke is, he looks about twenty minutes away from death, babbles on in a language I don't understand and seems to have a bullet wound in his side." He rounded the table, smoothing his palms up her arms and staring hard into her eyes. "I'm sorry, babe," he said, voice soft with worry. "But I don't believe you. I want answers. I want to know what the hell is going on."

"Something you'd never hope to understand, pup."

Declan's low growl spun both their heads around, and Regan gasped, watching the man sit up and swing his legs around, plant his bare feet on the floor and stand up, his eyes cold with deadly rage, the plastic tube only moments ago in his throat now crushed in his clenched fist.

"Declan!" Regan began.

"Hey!" Rick shouted, stumbling backward a step. "You can't do that!"

"Watch me," Declan snarled, glaring at the stunned vet. Muscles coiled, he took one step. Another. Another.

And then his eyes rolled back in his head and he crumpled to the cold, tile floor. Still.

Rick raised his eyebrows. "Guess I was right," he murmured.

Lifting her gaze from the sight of Declan laying motionless on the bed and covered only by a thin cotton sheet, Regan studied her surroundings. Rick used the spare room in his apartment as an office-cum-storage room. Stacks of thick veterinarian journals covered the small desk under the only window in the room—as well as the floor and side tables—surrounded by folders of paperwork, cardboard boxes, a neat pile of unironed laundry and a weight bench complete with cobwebs.

She shook her head, a wry smile playing over her lips. Rick to a tee. Solid, dependable and a touch messy. Organized to the outside world, organized disorder within.

Returning her attention to Declan, she chewed on her bottom lip. The Irishman on the other hand, was the embodiment of chaos, in little under a day turning her life upside down and inside out, turning it into a roller coaster of emotions and events she'd never forget or recover from. So different to Rick it made her head ache. She gently brushed a few strands of black hair from Declan's forehead, noting his temperature seemed back to normal.

Normal? What is normal for a werewolf?

Regan pulled a face. She didn't have a bloody clue. Not yet. But she would. Eventually.

She let her gaze move down his bare torso, forcing herself to focus, not on the lean perfection of his body, but on the freshly dressed wounds scattered over his frame and the stitched incision on his side. It had taken Rick about fifteen minutes to find the bullet embedded in Declan. Another twenty-five to remove it and clean up the lacerated mess it had left. The x-ray he'd taken of Declan's mid-section before the operation had bleached his face of color and his normally laughing, brown eyes had turned almost cold. For a moment Regan thought he wasn't going to help her, especially when she refused to explain what Rick most obviously saw—a skeletal and muscular structure not entirely human—but after a long look both regretful and irritated, he'd begun slicing into Declan's flesh with steady hands. Doing what he did best—tending to an animal needing his care.

Regan released a sigh. Was it enough?

Rick wouldn't tell her. But he'd agreed to take Declan back to his apartment after the surgery, depositing him on the clean, spare bed with gentle care. He'd said nothing to her before he left, just gave her another long sad look as he'd closed the door behind him, leaving her and the still-sedated Declan alone.

Regan sighed again, threading her fingers through Declan's limp ones.

What next?

Ring Pete? Her parents?

If she did, was she putting them in danger too? Was her brother already in danger? What would she do if Declan didn't survive? How would her heart handle it?

She closed her eyes. Too many questions and not enough answers.

A dry snort escaped her and she shook her head slightly. At least she now knew how Rick—

Declan's fingers clamped down on hers and she snapped open her eyes. *"Where's my sister, you flea-ridden fucker?"* he snarled, staring up at her with wild and glassy eyes.

"Declan." She tried to remove her hand from his crushing grip, keeping her voice calm and her actions smooth. Her heart thumped. Bloody hell, he looked savage. And lost. "It's Regan. You're going to be okay."

"Where's Maggie?" he roared, body arcing as he tried to

lunge upward. *"What have you done with—"*

He slumped backward abruptly, lids fluttering closed, body limp once again.

Regan sucked in a sharp breath, staring, waiting, her fingers free of Declan's grip, her throat tight. Dear God. What should she do now?

Peter slammed his cell to his ear, his heart leaping into frantic flight. "Thomas."

He studied Yolanda from the corner of his eye. She sat silent in the passenger seat, staring out the window at the passing traffic, gnawing on her bottom lip as if the troubles of the whole world weighed down on her. Silence had stretched between them since they'd left the crash. She hadn't uttered a sound. Hadn't even looked at him.

"Peter?"

A familiar, male voice sounded down the phone. A *worried,* familiar, male voice.

Peter frowned, steering his car one-handed as he pressed his cell harder to his ear. "Rick? Is that you?"

"She's here, mate," the man on the other end almost whispered, thick worry rolling through each word. Peter's blood ran cold. "At my apartment. Get your arse here. Now."

"Is she okay?" Peter demanded, and out of the corner of his eye he saw Yolanda shift in her seat, twisting to face him.

"Just get here as soon as you can," Reggie's long-time friend muttered, low and harried. "And bring your gun."

The disconnect tone drilled into Peter's ear, loud and cold.

He lowered the phone and turned to Yolanda, pulse pounding, chest heavy. "I know where Reggie is."

Yolanda stared at him, every muscle in her body tense, her fingers curling tighter around her own cell phone, eyes sharp. Eager. "Tell me."

His mouth felt dry. Like it was stuffed with cotton wool. Opening his eyes slowly, he peered into the darkness around him. He was in a room and on a bed. Better than the last time he'd regained consciousness, at least. No prickly straw scratching at his neck this time.

He shifted his wrists slightly, waiting for the sound of chains. None came and he smiled.

"Rick offered to cage you." Regan's husky voice caressed his ear and he turned his head, finding her standing beside by the bed. "But I said no."

"Gee, thanks." He rose up into a sitting position and studied her, frustrated at the shadows of the room hiding the expression on her face. Was she angry? Worried? He couldn't sense anything. He pulled a quick breath and her soft, delicate scent filled his being like ambrosia. His heartbeat tripled and he swallowed. Had he thought his mouth dry before? "Are you okay, love?"

She placed a gentle hand on his jaw and leant forward, her green eyes hidden in the darkness. "Haven't I already told you not to call me love?" she whispered, before brushing her lips over his.

Electricity surged through him. Cut through his body like a charge. He reached up and tangled his hands in her hair, holding her to the kiss. Praise Mary, he was never going to let her go. He flicked at her lips with his tongue and she opened to him willingly, her mouth a sweet, warm well that gave him life.

A life so much more now she was in it.

He broke the kiss, pulling away from her a little to stare into her eyes. "God forgive me, Regan. I never meant for you...for McCoy..." He stumbled over the name, chest clenching, jaw bunched.

Regan gave him a small, warm smile. "I know." She kissed him again, her lips velvet-soft. Forgiving. "Just don't let it happen again, okay?"

"Never." He smoothed his hands from her hair to cup her face, holding her gaze with his. "Which is why you have to stay here when I leave."

She cocked an eyebrow, her smile turning sardonic. "You going somewhere?"

"Yes. Nathan Epoc's private residence."

She rolled her eyes, stepping backward. "Not this again."

Pulling the sheet free of his limbs, Declan swung his legs around and placed his feet on the floor, ignoring the slight stab in his side. He'd find out what the vet did to him later. After he got this sorted out once and for all. "Yes, this again. Do you really think I'm going to let you come with me after what happened?"

She folded her arms across her chest, glaring at him. "And do you really think I'm going to let you out of my sight after working so hard to keep you alive?"

He stood up, wrapping his fingers around her arms, holding her still. Her heat seeped into his hands, up his arms into his body and he dragged in a deep breath. "Don't you get it?" he growled. "I couldn't survive if something happened to you, something I could have prevented. Losing you would mean losing myself. Losing who I am, who I've become *because* of you. It would mean the death of my human soul and if that happened I'd become the monster Hollywood so loves to portray—an ancient creature more savage and wild and deadly than any on this earth. I can't risk that. I can't risk *you*. Not after losing Maggie. I can't."

Regan regarded him silently for a still moment, her eyes unreadable in the dark room, before the corners of her lips curled gently. "What was I doing when we first met? I mean, as wolf and human?"

Declan frowned. "Trying to save the animals in Epoc's lab. Why?"

"You were one of those animals, Paddy. I wanted to save you—help you—then and I want to help you now."

His frown deepened. "It's not the same, love. Breaking into science labs is a bit different to storming a psychotic werewolf's personal territory. And if I remember rightly, your rescue mission went belly-up."

Her smile stretched wider. Grew almost predatory. "There are five things I know about you, Declan O'Connell. You're Irish. You're a werewolf. Your sister was murdered, you hate Nathan Epoc and you're ruled by your emotions."

He opened his mouth to argue, but she shook her head, cutting him short. "Let me finish. There are three things you should know about me. I'm stubborn, I hate being cornered and in just under a day I've fallen irretrievably, madly and completely in love with you. And if you think I'm going to let you face Epoc and his mongrel alone, that *I'm* going to risk losing *you*, you really are monumentally stupid!"

Declan gazed at her, mouth open, heart hammering. Did she say what he thought she said? Did she just say...

"Yes. I did. Now shut up and kiss me. I've been sitting here watching you recover for almost half an hour. I think it's time the attention was reversed after everything you've put me through."

A growl rumbled in Declan's chest and he yanked her to his body, crushing her mouth with his. Her tongue plunged past his lips immediately, mating with his in untamed strokes and flicks. He met it with equal passion, sucking it into his mouth as he grabbed her ass, pulling her hips harder to his. His cock—rigid and throbbing with desire so blistering hot he could barely breathe—ground against the smooth curve of her mons and she moaned, the raw sound tickling his lips and igniting his lust.

He tumbled backward onto the bed, taking her with him. Her weight pressed upon him, light and hot, an intoxicating force he was now incapable of living without. He raked his hands up her back, snaring the hem of her tank top as he did so, pulling it from her body. Her breasts flattened to his chest, soft and full and exquisite, her pinched, rock-hard nipples rubbing against his. "Christ, I want you so fucking much," he growled against her lips, thrusting his hips upward, pushing his cock closer to her cunt. His lungs felt bereft of air, his blood on fire. He dragged his hands around her rib cage, cupped the glorious swell of her breasts in each, rolling her nipples between his fingers.

She moaned, bending her knees up beside his body, spreading her legs wider, moving her sex up and down the length of his cock in slow strokes. "The feeling's entirely mutual," she answered, voice low and shallow.

She touched his chest, hands sliding over his skin, fingernails tracing little circles around his rock-hard nipples. A sigh slipped past her lips, the sound intensely erotic in the silence of the room, the feel of her breath on his skin more so.

She dropped her head, flicked at his left nipple with the tip of her tongue. He sucked in a sharp breath and grabbed her hips, holding her still as he moved his hips backward and forward, fucking her sex without penetration, his balls and cock swollen with molten desire.

"I should be petrified," she whispered, rising slightly to gaze down at him. "After..." Her eyes gleamed in the darkness and she dropped her head, her hair cascading forward, hiding her face. She smoothed her hands over his chest, her right stopping over his heart, pressing to its pounding beat. "But I know you'll never hurt me." She lifted her head again. "No matter what you are."

Declan stared up at her, his blood thick. "Regan," he breathed, wanting her to hear the tension in his voice. To hear his pain at her memory, as well as his desire for her touch. "I will never do anything but love you."

She moved, rising up to her knees. For a moment he wondered what she was doing, and a stab of fear shot into his chest. Was she going away? The sound of material rasping against skin made his pulse quicken. His throat grew tight with relieved anticipation and he watched her remove her shorts, sliding them over her hips and down her thighs, shucking them free of her legs.

His stare fell to her exposed pussy and his breath caught. *Oh, Sweet Mother of Jesus.*

She straddled him again, gazing down into his face for a long moment, the darkness of the room shrouding her in shadows. "Let me love you first," she murmured as she repositioned herself, her limbs brushing against his hot flesh. She turned around, slick skin against slick skin, presenting him the divine line of her spine.

He reached up, encountering the smooth, firm curve of her

ass, the delicate angle of her hips before moving around to the flat plane of her stomach. His heartbeat tripled. She was facing away from him on all fours, her body suspended above his. "Regan," he said again, hearing the tremble in his voice.

She dipped her head, something silky feathering over his bare hip and across his thigh. He sucked in a ragged breath, realizing it was her hair. Fingers played along his legs, traveling down and up their length in slowly delicious lines drawing closer and closer to his rigid shaft with each journey, tangling ever so briefly in the tight thatch of his pubic hair before beginning their trip anew. And all this while, as her hands set fire to his blood, her hair tickled his burning flesh and her breath fanned his throbbing cock.

"Jesus, Regan. What are you doing to me?"

She didn't answer. Not with words, at least. Her breath grew hotter on his cock, her fingers cupped his balls and her tongue flicked over the tiny slit at the end of his shaft.

Pure pleasure crashed through him. Intense and consuming. He arched beneath her, driving his head into the mattress, digging his fingers into the softness of her belly. "Oh, yes!"

Her tongue left his cock, replaced by a cool stream of air he knew blew gently past her lips. It sent ribbons of rapture through his body. Made his pulse quicken, his blood roar. Christ, he was drowning. Before he even touched her.

Touch her. Taste her.

He smoothed his hands over her hips, her ass, her skin like satin under his palms and dipped his fingers into her wet slit.

She gasped, sharp and shallow. The noise excited him and he delved deeper, wriggling one finger, another and another into the gripping slickness of her pussy. She arched her back, pushing her cunt onto his hand, her own fingers wrapping

196

around his cock in a hold both harsh and exquisite, stroking and pumping up and down its length until his balls felt ready to burst.

He sucked in a steadying breath and the musky scent of Regan's pleasure filled his nose. It was too much. He pulled his fingers from her cunt and replaced them with his tongue, flicking and teasing at the hot folds of her sex. Seeking the small nub of her clit.

She bucked against his mouth, fingers squeezing his cock. "Yes!"

He lapped at her, the taste of her cream on his tongue a sensation he could not comprehend. There was power in it. Power and existence and intoxicating rapture. He drove his tongue deeper into her sex, wanting to feel the centre of her heat. Wanting to bring her to the pinnacle of desire with him. Where she should be.

Just when he thought he couldn't wait any longer, that the pulsing strokes of her hand on his cock were going to push him over the edge, she took him into her mouth. Her tongue slid over its eager head, her lips wrapped around his solid length completely and she sucked.

He drove his head back into the mattress again, clenching at her hips as he bucked against her mouth. "Jesus Christ!"

She sucked at his cock, drew her mouth up and down, flicked at the sensitive web of skin just below its head with such savage need he cried out, sinking his nails into her flesh. Her tongue wrapped around his turgid length before she plunged lower again, lips pressing to the swollen sac of his balls, fingers squeezing his ass cheeks.

Oh fuck, oh fuck, oh fuck.

The words tumbled through his head, a fevered echo growing louder and louder with each sucking force Regan's mouth bestowed on his cock. He was going to come. He couldn't stop it. No more than he could stop loving the woman driving him rapidly to release. He couldn't stop it, but he could take her with him. Wanted to take her with him. Wanted her to feel what he was feeling. Wanted her to tumble over the precipice with him.

He raked his hands up the curve of Regan waist and over her rib cage, seeking out the heavy swell of her breasts, teasing her tight nipples with his fingers as he returned his lips and tongue to their lavish attention of her sex. Flicking at her clit, drawing it into his mouth and biting on its tiny formation.

She pushed her cunt harder to his face and moaned around his cock. The soft vibrations on his shaft sent ripples of concentrated bliss into his balls, ass and spine. Liquid heat erupted. He rammed his hips upward, thrusting deeper into Regan's mouth, feeling like his life-force pumped through him, *from* him. Rendering him utterly weak and totally invincible at once as it left him in explosive, surging spurts.

She took it all, swallowing his seed, feeding the scorching pleasure consuming him body and soul, her hands cupping and massaging his balls every time he bucked, her mouth milking him until he dropped back to the mattress, drained and slicked with sweat.

His breath burst past his lips in short, ragged pants and he closed his eyes, struggling to bring his heart under control. His wolf lingered below the surface, its heightened senses thrumming, its desire so powerful his cock continued to throb.

"Finish me, Declan," Regan murmured against his groin. Her lips, moments ago having rendered him spent, began to explore his hips, the inner-flesh of his thigh, her tongue leaving a wicked, hot trail over his skin. "I'm so goddamn close..."

He felt himself stiffen, felt his still-turgid shaft spasm with eager want as Regan's wet, masterful tongue investigated his testicles. His breath caught in his raw throat and his hands flattening against her ass, her waist.

"Regan," he choked, stunned at how quickly she had returned him to the edge. Werewolf or no. "Regan, I want to be inside you. I need..."

She raised her head, the night air cool where her wet mouth had been. She moved, straddling his hips, her breasts brushing his face as she slid down his body, nudging the straining head of his cock with the moist lips of her pussy. "...to make me reel," she finished, gazing into his face.

He nodded, nostrils flaring. "Yes."

She planted her hands on either side of his torso, shifted her weight ever so slightly and impaled herself on his cock. He heard her sigh his name as he filled her, a moan in her voice. She gripped him with muscles that felt like hot fingers, and tangled her hands in his hair.

He sat up, holding her still with his arms, his own fingers burying into the cool strands of hair at her nape, arching her neck so his lips and teeth devoured the satiny-smooth skin.

"Declan," she moaned his name again, wrapping her legs around his hips, her heels pressing against his ass cheeks, forcing him closer to her, deeper into her. "Don't stop."

"Never," he replied. How could he? He wouldn't know he was alive if he didn't feel her, smell her. Hold her.

Thrusting deeper, he captured her lips with his, fierce and hungry. A sound escaped her—a whimper, a hitching of her breath telling him without words she was there, ready to fall and explode and implode. "Yes, Declan. Yes!" she moaned. "Oh, God, *YES!*" Her fingers dragged across his shoulders and into his hair once more, holding his head still as her hips began to buck. Wild. Erratic. Powerful. He felt the pulses rocking through her. Clenching and releasing, clenching and releasing. Charging him with life.

It consumed him, surged through him. Erupted from him in a violent, liquid force, scalding him from head to toe and making him howl.

He collapsed backward, Regan coming with him, lying along his chest, her heart hammering against his, her ragged breath fanning his sweat-slicked skin.

Closing his eyes, he listened to her heartbeat slowly return to normal, letting his fingertips trace small, aimless patterns over her back. He felt utterly at peace. An emotional state he'd never experienced before.

"Don't stop," she whispered against his chest, wriggling her shoulders under his caressing fingers.

"Never," he replied.

"Good," she murmured back, and he felt her smile.

They lay, limbs entwined, hearts beating in harmony, for many minutes, and as each one passed Declan felt more and more calm. He gazed up at the black ceiling, listening to the sounds of nightlife beyond the room's walls: people laughing, enjoying their existence. He smiled, letting his hands skim down the delectable curve of Regan's waist to her hip. For the first time in his life, he understood what they felt. His existence had purpose now beyond death, beyond vengeance. Because of Regan.

He let his eyelids flutter closed, opening his senses to her. Letting her fill him on every level.

"Declan?"

Her voice, soft and somehow hesitant, made him open his eyes and he tilted his head, looking down into her face. "Yes?"

"Are werewolves like other members of the canine genus?"

He frowned.

"Do you rut with any bitch that catches your attention, or do you..." She trailed off and he heard the uncertainty in her voice.

He gave her a slow grin. "For a such an expert at animal behavior, you're lousy at the human kind." He ran his hand back up her body, drawing her closer to him, letting her look directly into his gaze. "No," he answered. "When it comes to mating, werewolves are just like people. Some fuck around, some find their lifemate and never let them go."

She studied him intently, as though looking for—wanting—an answer she didn't yet have. "Which type are you?" she whispered.

He let his grin turn into a smile, reaching up with his free hand to tuck an errant strand of her hair behind her ear. "The latter."

She gazed into his face for a moment, body still, expression revealing nothing, before rising up onto an elbow. She lowered her head, her lips brushing his in the softest of kisses. "Me too."

A chuckle rumbling up his throat, he wrapped his arms firmly around her body and flipped her to her back, catching her squeal of delighted shock with his mouth. He loomed over her, snaring each wrist, pinning her to the mattress with his hips, thighs and hands. He grinned at her, nestling his rapidly growing cock against the soft heat of her pussy. "You doubted me?" he growled, the sound coming out more like a laugh.

Eyes twinkling with a devilish glint, she shook her head, rolling her hips under his. "A girl can't be too careful. Especially one hopeless on human—"

An explosive bang shattered the air and the door flung open, flooding the room with bright, glaring light.

"Get off her, you bastard!"

Declan flung his head to the side, just in time to see a hulking great man storming through the door. A man with light green eyes and dark brown hair. A man with fury in his stare and a Glock nine millimeter in his hand.

"*Peter!*" Regan yelled, squirming in Declan's hold. "*Peter, it's—*"

"*Get off her now!*" The man bellowed. Aiming the gun straight at Declan's head.

Chapter Twelve

"Peter!" Regan shouted, struggling in Declan's crushing hold. "Don't! It's—"

But Peter's stare was locked on Declan, and, dread cutting through her, she saw his trigger finger squeeze.

"No!" a blonde woman in skin-tight denim jeans cried, suddenly charging through the door and leaping at Regan's brother from behind. She shoved at his shoulder, sending him tumbling forward—the very second he fired his weapon.

A deafening crack filled the air, and a split instant later something small and hot hit Regan in the shoulder. Slamming her backward to the mattress.

"JESUS CHRIST! REGAN! NO!" Peter's voice, horrified, punched at her ears.

Hot pain ripped through her chest. Up her neck.

"NO!" Declan screamed, staring down at her.

Slow. Everything felt slow. Like some celestial power had decided to mess with time. She frowned up at him, confused. What was going on? Why was Peter screaming "no"? Why was Declan? Who was the blonde? "Declan?" she said, but her voice felt weak. Insubstantial. "Why does my shoulder hurt?"

"Jesus," he whispered, eyes wide. Wild. "Jesus, love. He shot you." Fury fell over his face—cold and murderous—and those traumatized grey eyes changed. To the savage, silver eyes of the wolf. He swung his head to the side...

...and time caught up.

"You fucking bastard!" he roared.

He leapt off her, and just as his words sank into Regan's confusion, just as the pain in her shoulder erupted into unbearable agony, she saw him transform. One second a man, the next a wild, mammoth wolf.

Lunging straight for her brother.

The massive animal struck Peter in the chest, sending him reeling backward.

"Declan, no!" she yelled, struggling to sit up. White pain exploded in her shoulder. Black stars exploded in her head. She cried out, dropping back to the mattress, bolts of agony tearing through her as she watched Declan—now more than a wolf, now something from a nightmare—snap at Peter's neck with wickedly pointed teeth.

Eyes bulging, Peter whipped his head away staggering under the weight of the attacking creature. His broad back smacked into the wall, his thick, muscled arms flailing wildly at Declan, barely deflecting his snapping muzzle and lashing claws. Her brother was huge—a childhood spent wrestling wayward bulls and cows, and an adulthood spent wrestling the scum of the city wouldn't let him be any other way—but Declan, or the creature Declan had become was bigger. And more deadly.

"Declan!" Regan pushed herself upright. Agony ripped through her. Bright red blood pumped from her shoulder, warm and wet. The sharp sting of copper bit at her sinuses, but she didn't care. She had to stop her lover killing her brother. *"Declan! Stop it!"*

The creature swung its head toward her, insane silver eyes

shimmering for a second with confused lucidity.

And Peter struck out. His booted foot landed in Declan's gut with a whoosh and the werewolf stumbled backward, a growl of surprised anger bursting from its lathering muzzle. Its hackles rose, its clawed fingers curled into tight fists and it leapt forward again. Meeting Peter's own attacking lunge in mid-air.

Regan's blood turned to ice. Oh, God. She had to stop this. She had to—

Two strong hands curled around her wrists. "You are Peter's sister, yes?"

She snapped her head around, gazing at the worried blonde crouched beside her. "Who..." she began, tugging at the woman's hold on her wrists. "How did you find..."

The blonde's attention flicked to Regan's shoulder before returning to her face. "Your boyfriend, the vet." Her fingernails dug deeper into Regan's wrists, an ambiguous gleam in her blue eyes. "Lucky for Peter, he called." She sprang into an alert stance, jerking painfully on Regan's arms as she did so. She shot Declan and Peter a hurried glance. "You have to come with me."

Regan shook her head. "I'm not going anywhere." She yanked her arms downward, but the blonde's grip only grew tighter. "Let me go." She glared at the woman. "What did you mean, lucky for Peter? Who are you?"

"Run, Reggie!" Peter's scream rose over Declan's deafening growls, over the smashing of furniture. *"Get away!"*

Regan tugged on the woman's wrists, flinging her stare to her brother.

Declan had him pinned to the wall, teeth-filled muzzle snapping at his face, claws tearing at his shoulders. *"Declan! He's my brother! Leave him alone!"*

205

"Reggie!" Peter roared back, drenched in sweat and blood, wild green stare fixed on the creature attacking him. *"Get away! Get away NOW!"*

"Yes." The blonde pulled at Regan's wrists. "Come with me. Your brother wants you to."

Fury and fear pounded through her veins. "Let me go!" she snarled, twisting at her punishing grip. "Let me—" Suddenly cold realization hit her. She stared at the woman, every fiber of her being turning to ice. "You didn't freak out when Declan transformed," she whispered.

Blood-red lips curled in a slow smile. "No," she growled, eyes dilating. Changing. From blue to golden-amber. An animal's eyes. A *wolf's* eyes. "I didn't." With unnatural strength, she yanked Regan to her feet. "And whether you like it or not, you're coming with me."

"Declan!" Regan screamed, heels scuffing the floor, seeking traction. *"Peter!"*

"Go, Reggie!" Peter yelled back. Just as the creature—Declan—sank his claws into Peter's shoulders and flung him across the room.

The woman hauled on her wrists, pulled her off her feet. "Yes. Let's go."

"Fuck off," Regan snarled, and smashed her forehead into the blonde's.

Bright, white pain erupted in her head. Blinding stars burst before her eyes. She staggered backward, eyes closed, feeling like she'd run headfirst into a brick wall.

The grip on her wrists squeezed tighter. "This is how you do it, human," the blonde drawled, yanking Regan forward and slamming her forehead into the bridge of Regan's nose.

Agony detonated in her head. Consuming, absolute agony.

The world turned to a thick, dark, silent fog and she slumped forward. Straight into the blonde's snatching arms. A long, savage and blood-curdling howl filled her ears.

Declan...

Followed by a single shot from a gun.

Peter...No...

And then nothing.

Only blackness.

Peter smashed into the wall. Blood streamed from a gash in his forehead, stinging his eyes. He stumbled to his feet, swiping at his face, desperate to clear his vision. The animal—the *creature*—circled him on long hind legs, wild silver stare boring into him like a drill, teeth dripping saliva. Its massive chest rose and fell, each breath it pulled forcing fresh blood from the wound high on its chest. But it didn't seem to notice. Peter sucked in his own ragged breaths. Christ! He'd shot the fucking thing point-blank in its heart and nothing.

His blood ran cold. Was this the man who'd abducted Reggie? This monster? He gripped his gun tighter. "What the fuck are you?"

The creature bared its fangs and lunged.

Peter dropped into a crouch just as the animal slammed into his bunched shoulder, sending him to the floor. He twisted, striking out at its soft underbelly with his heel, desperate to get back on his feet. The animal flipped in the air, landed on all fours and came at him again.

He scrambled backward, staring at the creature through

blood and sweat. It launched itself through the air, hideously clawed fingers sinking into his shoulders as it drove him to the ground. Claws like steel punctured his flesh, stabbed into his muscle. He bucked, thrashing under the thing's massive weight, tearing pain ripping through him. Fuck! He had to get it off.

Wicked teeth snapped at his face and he flinched, hot saliva splattering his cheek. His blood pumped from the holes in his shoulder, the wound on his forehead. He gazed up at the creature through a translucent crimson curtain. He'd fought with some mean bastards before—both in training and on the job, but nothing like this. Currents of agony tore through his arms but he continued to fight. He had to get the thing off him.

He writhed underneath it, striking out with his foot, his knee. Each made connection, but the animal didn't budge. Jesus, was it real? He shoved at its chest, his palms mashing against muscle that felt like hot steel covered in fur. If he could get his gun to its head...If he could just blow the fucker's brain out.

He moved his arm a fraction. And stopped the second pointed teeth almost tore a chunk of his face out. Fuck. It was no use. It was only by sheer muscle and frantic determination he kept the animal from tearing out his throat. How the hell was he to move enough to shoot the thing in the head?

Energy poured from him in draining, depleting waves. Joining his blood in its exodus of his body. He tossed his head to the side, desperate to see if his partner had dragged his sister from the room. A flash of blonde running through the door made his heart burst with relief. *"Run, Yolanda! Get her away!"*

The creature froze above him, its silver stare locked on his, burning with hate. Peter tensed. *Christ, I'm dead.* The wild eyes grew wider, and suddenly a slight shudder rippled through its form.

The hideous, elongated limbs shivered, the fur covered muscles rippled again, and then it was a man staring down at him. Not a monster but a man, dripping in sweat and blood, fingers digging painfully into Peter's arms, knees ramming into his thigh and hip. The *very* man who'd been lying on the bed with Reggie, pinning her to the mattress. "Yolanda?" he snarled, the sound animalistic.

Peter gazed up at him, incapable of speech. Incapable of anything, in fact.

"Yolanda?" The man growled again, more human this time.

Peter started. Did he just hear a soft Irish accent cutting through the growl? The same Irish accent haunting him for the last nineteen hours?

Strong fingers dug into Peter's shoulders. "Damn it, man. Did you say Yolanda?"

"O'Connell?" The name fell from Peter's lips. *The accent. The name.* "You're O'Connell, aren't you!"

The man leapt to his feet, fluid and fast. He flung his gaze around the room, dragging trembling, bloody hands through tangled black hair. "Shit. They're not here!"

Peter climbed to his own feet, staring at the naked man. He raised his gun. Pointed it at the man's bare chest. "Tell me who the fuck you are now!"

"Look around you, Peter," the man snapped, ignoring his order. "Your sister. She's gone."

Peter closed his finger firmer on his trigger. "Good. At least she's safe from you."

Those grey eyes turned cold. "But not from your partner."

"What do you mean, my partner?"

"The blonde. Slight German accent? How long she been

your partner for?"

Peter's chest tightened. "Why?"

"She's a plant. I'm guessing she's been playing you from the start." O'Connell stepped forward, completely mindless of the fact he had a blood-oozing bullet wound in his chest and a loaded Glock aimed straight at it. "Yolanda Vischka works for the very man I've been trying to save your sister from!"

Peter's mouth turned dry. He shoved the Glock's barrel harder to the man's chest, punching the raw flesh of the wound with its metal tip. "What the fuck are you talking about?"

O'Connell's lip curled and his grey stare flicked over Peter's body. "I can smell her on you. She's marked you as her own. She's touched you just about everywhere."

Peter's eyes widened and he bit back a curse, blistering guilt surging into his gut. Christ. How did the man know? Another surge of guilt crashed over him and he choked back a groan. What had he been doing all day? Trying to find his sister, or letting a woman he barely knew control his actions? His heart squeezed, as if a force stronger than the creature he'd fought was trying to rip it from his chest. "What the *fuck* are you?"

Hand a blur, O'Connell snatched Peter's gun from his grip before he could react. "The same kind of monster after Regan. A werewolf." His stare turned dark. Dangerous. "And if I don't go after her now, Nathan Epoc will kill her before you can draw her face into your mind."

Peter stood, frozen. For exactly one second.

He spun on his heel and sprinted across the room, heading for the door.

A dark blur whipped over his head, a gush of displaced air sucked at the hair on his crown and suddenly O'Connell stood between Peter and the door, snatching his arm in a brutal, inescapable grip. "No. You haven't a hope. Only I can take Epoc out."

Peter glared at him, tugging against his hold. "Get the fuck out of my way."

O'Connell's eyes flashed silver. "Don't be an idiot. I almost killed you."

"Get. The fuck. Out of my way."

Those eyes shimmered silver again before, hands raised to his shoulders in a display of surrender, his right still gripping Peter's gun, O'Connell stepped aside.

Peter tore through Rick's house, his chest growing tighter with each pounding step. Fuck! Reggie? Yolanda? Every second of the day ripped through his head in multi-colored, sickening detail. Yolanda's arrival, her seduction, her supposed vulnerability, his stupid, stupid capitulation to the power she held over his body, his hungry longing for every inch of her, despite his suspicions.

He'd thought there was something wrong about her from the beginning, but his growing desire for her had taken control. Lust and his desperate desire for her to be something she clearly wasn't. Bloody hell! Could he be that stupid? That lonely?

Fuck, Reggie. I'm sorry...

He burst through the front door, staring wildly up and down the night-shrouded footpath. Empty. He spun about, sprinting to his car, hope and fear crashing over him, through him.

It sat, exactly where he'd parked it. Locked. Empty. No Regan. No Yolanda. Nothing.

Snapping about, he stared up the street again, pulse thumping in his neck, blood roaring in his ears. Where was his sister? Where was Yolanda? An icy fist squeezed his heart, his throat. *"Reggie?"*

"She's gone. Your partner's taken her to Epoc."

Peter spun around and glared at the man standing behind him. Cold fury and burning guilt consumed him. "Where is she?"

Hooded, angry grey eyes bored into him. "I told you. Vischka's taken her to Nathan Epoc."

"Give me my gun," Peter demanded. "I'm going after them."

"You don't have a ch—"

"She's my sister, mate," he snarled through gritted teeth, cutting O'Connell short. "I'm going after her."

"You'll be killed before you get past the gate." O'Connell shook his head again, his pale torso almost ghost-like in the engulfing shadows of the night. "What is it with you Thomases? Didn't you hear me say werewolf? Didn't you just spend the last fifteen minutes fighting to stay alive as one tried to kill you?"

Peter stared hard at the man, keeping his voice low, controlled. "That one being you." He stepped forward, clenching his fists to stop jabbing a finger into O'Connell's chest. "Now listen to me, mate. She's my sister. My *sister*. I'm not going to trust her life to someone, *something*, who just tried to kill me." His knuckles cracked and he shook his own head. "You obviously don't have one or you'd understand."

Dark rage rolled over O'Connell's features, before—with a blink—his grey eyes grew lost, swimming with a grief so intense Peter found them almost too painful to look at. "I do," he whispered, shoulders slumping slightly. "I did." He took a step back. "And I understand completely. Let's go."

Gut churning, Peter narrowed his eyes. "What? Am I to trust you now? A man standing naked in the street with a bullet wound in the heart, who only seconds earlier tried to tear my throat out?"

The man gave him a wry grin, his pale, muscled body already taut and sprung for action. "I plan on becoming your brother-in-law someday soon," he answered, holding Peter's gun out to him, butt first—an offering of peace. Of partnership. "If we both live through the night. Does that help make up your mind?"

Muffled voices wafted through her head. Indistinct. Distant. Like the speakers spoke through cotton wool from the other side of the world.

Awareness returned slowly. A slow incoming tide bringing with it a world of pain. Dull pain in her jaw. Hot, angry, terrible pain in her shoulder.

Regan moaned, her head lolling to the side. A low roar vibrated through her aching body and she shifted, her hip grinding against something cold and hard.

Vivid images ripped through her mind and she snapped open her eyes, staring in horror at the bare white, metal wall before her. The sound of an engine changing gears filled her head and fear sank into her gut. Shit. She was in a van.

Shit! Declan! Peter!

The vehicle hit a pothole in the road and she bounced, head and shoulder and hip smacking the metal floor in a sharp series of agonizing thumps.

Fuck, that hurts.

Warm liquid seeped from her shoulder and down across her chest. Blood. Her blood.

213

Anger rolled through her and she tried to move.

Slicing pain cut into her wrists and ankles and she bit back a curse. Cable-ties. The blonde bitch had cable-tied her. What the hell was she to do now? How was she to get back to Declan? To Peter? Where the fuck was the blonde taking her?

Epoc.

The name floated into her head and she sucked in a swift breath.

Oh, no.

"So you are awake, yes?"

The woman's voice came from Regan's left and she twisted on the van's floor, pain shooting into her shoulder. The blonde looked at her from the passenger seat, her face composed, the fingers of her right hand loosely gripping a Glock nine-millimeter. Her eyes however, looked uneasy. "I thought I may have hit you too hard."

Regan glared at her, struggling against the thin strips of plastic cutting into her wrists and ankles. "Untie me, bitch and I'll show you what a hard hit feels like!"

"Told you she had spirit."

A low chuckle followed the accented words and Regan's blood froze, her heart leaping into her constricting throat.

The van's driver swung his head around, leering at her from behind the wheel, his red-gold eyes glowing with a hunger Regan recognized all too well.

God, no. No no no no.

"I'm so glad to see you again, lass," McCoy drawled, lips stretching into a cold grin, long, sharp teeth glistening in the dim dashboard light. "We've got some unfinished business to attend to, don't we?"

Chapter Thirteen

The table pressed against her back, butt and shoulder like a block of ice, its chilly surface biting at her hot flesh. Ignoring the dull ache in her shoulder from Peter's gunshot, sweat trickling into her eyes, Regan tugged at the thick metal shackles locking her wrists beside her. They didn't budge an inch. She wasn't going anywhere.

She pulled in a deep breath, staring at the high ceiling.

McCoy had dragged her from the van after what felt like hours driving through the streets of Sydney, his hands mauling her breasts as he did so. He'd thrown her over his shoulder, chuckling at her struggles. His long fingers had found her ass, squeezing at each cheek with punishing pressure until tears stung her eyes.

She ground her teeth, trapped immobile on the table. She'd be damned is she'd cry out though. She wouldn't give the bastard a single sound. No matter what he'd done to her.

Studying the ceiling, she gnawed on her bottom lip, unease churning in her stomach. Apart from carrying her from the van and fastening her to this table inside a mansion that made the one she and Declan hid in at McMahon's Point look like a shack, McCoy had done nothing to her. Not even given her a leering grin. The moment he stepped foot inside the quiet, mausoleum-like building, he'd become different. If he'd been a dog, Regan would've said he was almost cowering. As if a more dominant animal lurked nearby.

A chill rippled over her flesh and her nipples pinched into tight points of fear under the light sheet covering her. A more dominant animal...Epoc.

Neck straining, shoulder throbbing, she lifted her head from the metal surface and looked around the room as best she could. Harsh overhead fluorescent light bleached all color from the space, making it hard to see anything. Apart from the table she lay strapped to and two smaller, stainless steel ones on either side, it seemed empty. And very inhospitable.

Sudden movement in the corner of her eye caught her attention and she rolled her head to the side. Anger crashed through her. Cold and absolute. The blonde.

The woman walked toward her, a small metal tray in her manicured hands, the same apprehensive expression in her cool blue eyes. She stopped by Regan's table, giving her a troubled look. "Your shoulder hurts, yes?"

"My shoulder?" Regan creased her forehead in mock confusion. "No. Not at all. Why?"

The blonde cocked one perfectly arched eyebrow, pursing her lips. "Just as stubborn as your brother, it seems." She deposited the tray on a bench beside the table before turning back to Regan, a cloudy-filled syringe in her hand. She lifted it, examining its contents in the glaring fluorescent light. "This will not hurt," she murmured, flicking at the glass tube with one blood-red nail. "In fact it will give you a small..." She paused, as if searching for the word she wanted, "...buzz."

Before Regan could react—and really, strapped to the table like she was, what could she do?—the woman plunged the needle into the crook of her arm. A sharp sting, like the prick of a pissed-off wasp, punctured her flesh and she bit back a hiss.

"What was that?' she demanded through gritted teeth. The inside of her elbow tingled.

"An experimental concoction designed to heighten your physical awareness of stimuli." The blonde returned the now-empty syringe to the tray. "Epoc wants to see how a human responds to it."

Regan narrowed her eyes. "So, Declan was right. Epoc does own the police."

The woman tilted her head to the side a bit. "Not all the police."

"But obviously my brother's Command Area. What happened to his *real* partner? Is he dead?"

White-blonde eyebrows rose. "I don't kill indiscriminately, Regan. I'm not a monster."

Regan snorted. "Sure about that?"

"I see you share your brother's trust issues, yes?"

Hot anger tore through Regan's veins, and her skin tingled. Pulling at her restraints, she glared up at the woman. "He didn't trust you? What a surprise."

Cool fingers pressed to her shoulder, sending tiny licks of rippling ice down Regan's arm. "You need to stay calm," the woman murmured. "Remember, you've just been injected with an experimental sensory accelerant."

A warm throb pulsed in Regan's elbow and she fidgeted, growing increasingly aware of the soft caress of the sheet covering her naked body, of the cool touch of metal on her wrists and ankles. She pulled in a short breath and the gentle feathering of air on her tongue felt like a soft kiss.

The woman watched her, eyebrows dipping into a small frown. She picked up a folded cloth from the tray and touched it to Regan's shoulder, patting at the bullet wound in almost hesitant strokes.

A slight sensation whispered down Regan's arm, like a single sliver of ice and her breath caught. She stared up at the blonde and for a moment her vision blurred, before coming back, sharp and clear. "What did you do to me?" she demanded, lips dry.

No reply.

"What did you do?"

Again, silence.

Regan shifted on the table, her skin prickling. She felt odd. Like she was standing too close to an immense electrical charge. A biting metallic taste coated her tongue, sharp and bitter. Her nipples pinched into harder, puckered tips, pushing at the sheet draped over her. Squirming twists of heat unfurled low in the pit of her stomach and she dragged in a hitching breath, pulse pounding in her throat. "Please..." She gave the woman beside her a beseeching stare, hating herself for it. "Please, what did you inject into me?"

The cloth continued to pat at her shoulder, cool and damp, and ripples of delicious chills ran across Regan's skin. Blue eyes studied her, and once more, even as her body reacted, Regan couldn't miss the apprehension in their clear, direct depths. The woman was troubled about something. "The wound will heal," she said softly. "Despite the amount of blood, the bullet was shallow. I removed it in the van." She lifted the cloth from Regan's shoulder and touched the flesh there with gentle fingers.

Ribbons of delicate pleasure spiraled out from the contact. Made Regan's breasts swell with a base response.

"It seems to have an aphrodisiac affect, doesn't it, Yolanda."

Icy alarm rolled through Regan as a gravelly male voice filled the room. She turned her head, staring at the short man

218

with the gleaming scalp and amber eyes crossing the floor toward her. "You're a dreadful host, Epoc," she stated with a sarcastic reproaching tone, trying to ignore the sinful sensations licking up her limbs from the cold, hard manacles. "I've been here for ages and no one's offered me a drink."

His shining golden gaze bored into her, making her flesh crawl. "Regan Thomas, animal-rights activist and all-round annoying female. You've made this day quite entertaining." A wide smile stretched his mouth and his stare grew malevolent. "Hasn't she, McCoy."

Regan's heart froze. *Oh, no.*

She twisted her head, trying to see the man Epoc spoke to. Overwhelming dread and hate crashed into her. She did *not* want to be trapped on her back. She couldn't be trapped on her back. Not with that bastard walking toward her. Her blood roared through her veins and she tugged at the restraints on her wrists. Exquisite ribbons of slicing pain shot up her arms, made her nipples pinch harder again. The sheet slithered across her body, and Regan's flesh—fuelled by whatever Yolanda had pumped into her—responded, rippling into tiny bumps of delicious pleasure. Shame and rage consumed her. "Come near me, McCoy and I'll rip your balls off, you bastard!" she snarled, twisting her head from side to side, trying to find him. If he touched her now, with the shit in her veins perverting her system...

Epoc smirked. "I don't think she's that happy to see you, McCoy." He pressed his hand to Regan's shoulder, forcing her shoulder blade to the metal table and her pussy constricted at the chill of the surface on her hot flesh. "Do not worry yourself, Ms. Thomas. McCoy will not touch you unless I say he can." He drew small circles on her skin with the tip of a finger, sending shards of sinful sensations down into her breasts. Amber eyes locked on hers. "Believe me, he has been reprimanded for his

219

inappropriate behavior at the farm."

"And I should believe you because?"

"Because I am the Alpha of this clan. And as such, my word is law. Yolanda can vouch for that. She was meant to bring your brother in at sunset for...Ah, 'questioning' but failed to do so." He lifted his head and studied the blonde standing beside the table. "She was punished for failing to follow my orders."

Regan watched Yolanda's high cheeks fill with pink heat before the woman dropped her stare from Epoc to the floor.

"But never mind," he continued, returning his attention to Regan. "It is of no consequence. Fortunately for her she delivered you instead. A much more valuable subject." His hand lifted slightly from her shoulder and smoothed along the line of her collarbone, her body thrumming with a charged electrical current at the contact. "Such lovely bone structure," he murmured, his stare following the path of his tracing fingers. "So delicate. Fragile." He flicked his gaze back to her face. "Surely the *Onchú* piece of filth told you how order is kept in our kind? The Alpha has the right to anything in the clan." He dropped his head lower to hers, his lips almost touching her cheekbone as he stared into her eyes. "Whatever I want is mine."

Pussy clenching, stomach churning, Regan spat at him.

A shocked gasp cut the air and from the corner of her eye, Regan saw Yolanda take a step back, looking more uncomfortable than before. Epoc however, only chuckled, slowly lifting his hand to wipe the spittle from his face. "Now, now, Ms. Thomas," he smirked, straightening at the hip. "I thought you were an intelligent, articulate woman?" He stared at her for a moment, before—abruptly—cold anger twisted his expression and he grabbed a fistful of the sheet covering her body and yanked it away.

"You stink of O'Connell, Ms. Thomas," he snarled, drying his hand on the bunched strip of material. "His mark lingers on your flesh like a stain." Dropping the sheet, he razed her naked limbs with a golden-yellow stare, teeth glinting in the light as he sneered his appreciation. "I must admit though, now I see you stripped, I understand the Irish *conriocht's* attraction. For a human you are quite—" He placed a pointed finger on Regan's chest and ran it slowly down to her navel in a lazy line, "—delectable."

Regan jerked away from his touch, the table refusing to let her move far. Shivers of traitorous response trickled through her body, radiating from the still-felt contact of Epoc finger, and she choked back a sob of disgust. "The Lord help you, Epoc," she growled. "If you're ever stupid enough to let me off this table..."

Epoc laughed, removing his hand and looking to his right. "Remember how O'Connell reacted when he smelt you on his precious sister, McCoy? How he lost control?"

"Yes, Epoc."

McCoy's voice reverberated above Regan's head and she forced it back as far as she could. Nothing. Her mouth went dry. Wherever he was, he was still too far away for her to see.

Epoc returned his hand to Regan's stomach, his fingertips brushing over the soft edge of her pubic hairline. "I wonder how he will react when he smells *me* on *this* bitch?"

Regan's stomach lurched. "Get your fucking hand off me!" She bucked her hips, panic biting into her anger, desperate to be free of the restraints and Epoc's vile touch.

Savage amber eyes fixed on her. "No." He rammed his hand down hard, flattening her ass to the table, plunging his fingers between her spread thighs. "Do you know what my mating with you will do to O'Connell, Ms. Thomas?" He pushed at the folds of Regan's sex with a brutal finger. "It will destroy him. After he's finished tearing your brother limb from limb he will come to save you, the noble bastard he is. When he comes for you— and he will come for you—he will smell my mark on your flesh." He buried his finger deeper, wriggling it in slow, cruel circles. Pain shot through Regan—pain and hideous, drug-induced pleasure—and she whimpered, writhing her hips in a futile attempt to be free.

Epoc's eyes flickered and he laughed lowly. "He will smell my seed as it dribbles from your cunt and he will lose control. He will become more than a wolf. He will become a creature of myth. A creature of incomparable strength. A creature more powerful than any in existence." He dropped his head to hers, grinding his knuckle against her mons, his eyes slitted. "And when that happens, when that last little link to his humanity is destroyed, I will immobilize him and cage him and drain every last drop of his *croi* from his body and make it my own." He pressed his lips to her ear, his breath hot and wet on her skin. "The last of the *Onchú* devoured. Rendered an empty shell. By me."

The mansion loomed before them, huge and imposing.

Rubbing at his wrist where the manacle from the hobby farm had been, Declan stared up at it, counting the number of windows blazing with light and the number shrouded in darkness. He studied the immediate area. Night claimed most of it, the low mottled glow of expensive garden lighting the only relief from its concealing blackness. The breeze cooling his skin only moments earlier now pushed against him, aggressive and insistent. A bad omen. Declan scowled. If he were a superstitious man, he'd be worried.

"Best entry point?" Peter whispered beside him, drawing his mind from the changing weather.

Declan frowned. "South. Under those low branches of the fig tree growing on the fence line."

Peter nodded, and even in the darkness Declan saw his face tense and his grip tighten on his gun.

"Remember." He gave Regan's brother a hard look. "Wait until you hear my howl before going in. You won't stand a chance if..."

"If I go in before you distract the guards," Peter finished, voice sharp. "I'm not stupid." He quickly checked the chamber of the ornate double-action revolver in his hand. "Fuck, I wish we had more of these," he muttered, the wind almost snatching the words away.

Declan didn't know if he meant the weapon or the ammunition nestled within. Either way, he agreed with him. Loaded in the archaic gun was a single hollow-tipped silver bullet, both items appropriated by Peter with a quick flash of his badge from a very unconventional antiquities dealer on the way. Declan didn't ask how Peter knew the dealer had such an unusual weapon. It didn't matter. But one look at the guy behind the counter told him it was the real deal. Ancient tattoos covered the man's sunken cheeks and skinny arms, tattoos designed to ward off evil spirits and demons. Declan had seen his type too often in Europe, although he'd never expected to come across it in Australia. Losers dreaming of being heroes. Submerging themselves in the paranormal and occult—enough to believe, not enough to know better. Hunting werewolves and demons and vampires. Pissing themselves when they finally came upon one.

Just as *this* man had done, although it had been Peter's police badge, not Declan's lycanthrope genes rupturing his bladder.

Face white, hands trembling, eyes scared and wistful, he'd handed the bullet and the gun over to Peter immediately, begging not to be arrested. One less hero in the world.

Declan felt his bile rise. *One* less hero? Maybe after this, the count would be three. What he and Regan's brother were attempting was the closest thing to a suicide run Declan had ever been on. Jesus alone knew if either of them would return.

He ground his jaw. For Regan's sake, he hoped at least one of them did.

A dull ache throbbed in his chest and he pressed his hand to the hot but healing wound there. Peter's earlier shot back at Rick's had, thankfully, missed his heart. Just. Even though *that* bullet wasn't silver, a direct puncture to the heart was not something quick to recover from. If Peter had fired his police-issued Glock a fraction to the right, he—Declan—would be in enough pain now to adversely affect his raid on Epoc's territory. More pain than he already was in, that was. When all this was over, he'd get Regan's vet to work his magic again. After he demanded an apology from the guy.

A small smile pulled at the corner of his mouth. *After* he'd made long, passionate and tender love to Regan. A few times, actually.

Sucking in a slow breath, he studied the blackness before him. Four lycanthropes still stood guard to the east, five to the west. He'd detected their scent as he and Peter did their first perimeter sweep. All nine were currently in human form. All nine armed. He'd smelt the silver of their bullets before he'd tasted their cringing nervousness. As always, Epoc had surrounded himself with those easily controlled and dominated.

It seemed being in a different country made no difference. Declan prayed to God it would bring about his downfall tonight.

He clenched his fists, letting his wolf come closer to the surface. Ready. Eager. He'd make a ruckus on the mansion's northern perimeter, drawing the guards and leaving Peter a—hopefully—free run to the building from the south.

After that, the cop was on his own. Declan would be dealing with his own entry.

For Peter, the plan was simple. Get in. Get Regan. Get out.

Declan's plan included an extra element. Kill Nathan Epoc.

He closed his eyes for a second, picturing the smug man. Hate roared through him and his wolf stirred again, its strength flooding his limbs. He opened his eyes. It was time.

"Remember," he said to Peter without looking at him. "In. Out. No heroics. Just get your sister and get her safe."

From the corner of his eye, he saw Peter shift slightly. "Remind me to buy you a beer after this."

Declan chuckled softly. "Deal. But it's gotta be a Guinness. I'm not drinking any of that Fosters."

Peter laughed, muscles bunching as he readied to spring forward. "Me either. Real Aussies don't drink Fosters." And then he was gone. Into the blackness, devoured by the night.

Declan's eyebrows shot up—*Jesus, he's a fast bugger*—before he too, took off, leaping over the sixteen-foot, spear-topped iron fence in a single bound. Heading north across Epoc's manicured lawn. Vengeance boiling in his veins.

A loud howl cut through the air, rising above the wind,

long, savage and angry, followed by the sharp report of a fired handgun. Another, and another. Epoc lifted his head, turning from the appealing sight of the female's bruised lips, a smug smile stretching his own wide. Running his tongue over them, he tasted her fear and spirit. Delicious.

He bared his teeth at the hovering Yolanda and McCoy in a gleeful grin. "He's here." He dropped his gaze back to the human bitch, chuckling at her hate-filled glare. Tracing a claw along the line of her full bottom lip, eager to taste it again, to feel warm blood beading on its soft surface with his teeth and tongue, he raised an eyebrow. "I told you he would come. As predictable as ever." He let his finger score a line over her chin, down her neck to the little dip at the base of her throat, pushing the tip of his claw at its sensitive, delicate surface. "Are you ready?"

Another howl rose over the wind. Closer. Louder. Angrier.

A twist of apprehension knotted in Epoc's stomach, unnerving and completely unexpected and before he could suppress it, a worried frown creased his forehead.

Regan Thomas looked up at him, a perceptive light suddenly flaring in her ice-green eyes. "*I'm* ready, Epoc," she said, voice steady and unafraid. Knowing. "How about you?"

He ran, paws barely touching the ground as he did so. Behind him he heard the other wolves. Chasing him. Gaining on him. Nine different scents. All fired with nervous excitement. They may be submissive mongrels to Epoc's Alpha, but the *Eudeyrn* werewolf guards took their job seriously. They were out to catch Declan and bring him down. He smelt it in their radiating stink. He heard it in their yips and snarls.

Opening his gait, he headed for the northern boundary, forcing more speed into his sprint. They'd transformed shortly after realizing they couldn't intimidate him with bullets. Declan knew Epoc wanted him alive, which meant his guards would be under strict orders *not* to shoot him. After the fourth bullet buried into a tree trunk, they'd discarded their weapons and shifted. It hadn't made it easier for him, however. Shaking nine adrenaline-charged werewolves was never going to be easy.

Fighting them would be harder.

He needed to enter Epoc's home on his terms, and to do so, he needed to shake the pursuing guards, not be taken down by them. Which meant he needed to clear the high fence, draw them away from the property and into Peter's hastily organized trap, an anonymous tip-off to the local Animal Control authorities about a pack of savage dogs roaming the area. The officers wouldn't find any dogs, of course, but hopefully the threatening distraction of men and guns would send Epoc's guards running far enough away to transform back into human form, allowing Declan to slip back into Epoc's territory without notice. If the plan didn't work...

His claws dug into the warm soil as he pushed another burst of speed from his legs. For Regan he'd fight the devil himself.

Isn't that what you're about to do, Dec?

He snarled silently, teeth and tongue wet with exertion. Yes. To his kind, Epoc *was* the Devil.

The growing wind rippled through his fur, ruffled its length along his spine. He weaved through the trees, knowing the guards almost snapped at his heels but loath to run any faster. Not until the north fence-line came into view, at least.

After that, even a cheetah would be humbled by his speed.

The gusting, hot wind shifted, blew into his face, flattened his ears to his head, and with it came the strong scent of the *Eudeyrn* Alpha. Anger roared through Declan. At the exact moment the northern boundary came into view.

Behind him a wolf howled, an ear-shattering alarm that their target was about to escape.

Declan creased his muzzle in a wolfish grin and he finally let his full speed surge through his legs. *Come and get me, you flea-bitten whelps.* With an image of Regan smiling and laughing in his mind, he vaulted the fence, hind legs clearing the razor-sharp steel points a heartbeat before Epoc's Beta guard tried to snap his jaw shut on them.

He pounded into the night. Heading toward the distinct and belligerent scent of the Animal Control officers, his blood roaring, Peter's bullet wound a burning throb in his chest. If the cop's trap failed...

Let's hope Animal Control in this country know how to do their job, Dec.

Nine different growls followed him over the fence. Filled his ears. Close. Very close.

Too close.

Ears flat, Declan pushed forward harder.

Jesus, please let the Australians know what they're doing.

Peter moved through the dim hallway, revolver raised, nerves tight. His gut churned, telling him everything was wrong. O'Connell had warned him they were walking into a trap, that Epoc would be waiting for them, but he'd expected something other than empty, quiet hallways. Where *was* everyone?

The sound of his footfalls on the marble floor echoed off the richly-painted walls, and it seemed to Peter the eyes of the massive portraits hanging on them followed his progress. Sharp, almost animal-like stares weighed down on him, each subject wearing a look of arrogant contempt, as if they knew who and *what* he was—mere human—and only waited now to witness his impending death. It was complete rubbish, of course. He'd seen enough B-grade movies to know about the "ubiquitous stare" phenomenon but *knowing* didn't make walking under the ancient paintings any less disconcerting. For fuck's sake, until an hour ago he hadn't believed in werewolves. Now he was raiding one's house to save his sister. Who knew if the eyes of the paintings really were just pigment and linseed oil?

He moved his stare from the portraits, studying a collection of swords hanging from the wall in an ornate display. Long, bronze and obviously heavy, each bore engraved images of wolves in their shiny blade, wolves who looked like men. A chill rippled up Peter's spine. Those swords seemed to radiate death, as if countless men had lost their souls to their wicked edges. Wielded with lethal grace by those not entirely human. Waiting to taste blood once more.

Peter ground his teeth and raised the revolver closer to his shoulder, disgust roaring through him. *Jesus, you're getting yourself worked up over—*

"Hello, Detective."

He spun, gun raised, heart thumping.

Yolanda Vischka stood behind him, her lush, sensual body encased in snug, black leather. An unreadable, blue gaze studied his face, a small wry smile pulling at her full, blood-red lips. "You are planning to shoot me, yes?"

Peter aimed the revolver at her left breast. "Yes."

Her smile turned sad and for a moment her eyes seemed to

shine with tears. And then she blinked and the same lofty expression she'd worn for most of the day returned. "'Tis a pity. After everything we have shared."

Peter's blood turned hot. He glared at her, anger and self-contempt stringing his nerves tight. "After the way you played me for an idiot, you mean? Perfect reason to shoot you, if you ask me."

She shrugged, but a flash of what looked like sorrow crossed her features. "If you must."

Keeping the heavy revolver leveled on her heart, he closed the distance between them. "Just who the hell are you, Yolanda?"

"I work for Nathan Epoc."

"No shit, Sherlock." He shook his head, disgust coating his mouth. "How could I have been so stupid?"

Indignation flared in her eyes and her shoulders snapped straight. "I think it had something to do with your cock."

Fury thumped at Peter's chest. He rammed the gun against the swell of Yolanda's breast, his pulse a rapid tattoo in his neck, his gut a churning mess. The urge to shoot her was powerful. His gut told him to do just that. To make her pay for her deception. To make her suffer the way Reggie may be suffering now. But his heart...His heart wanted him to throw the gun he'd taken from the antiquities dealer away, crush her to his chest and demand an explanation for her behavior. Demand an apology he would accept, before kissing her passionately until both their heads spun. He bit back a curse. Christ. He was more screwed up than he thought. "Where's my sister?" he ground out, hating himself as much as he hated the woman before him.

Yolanda met his level gaze. "Being used as bait." A shadow fell over her face—sad, regretful—and she took a slight step back. "As am I."

Peter narrowed his eyes. Gripped the revolver harder. "What do you mean, 'as am I?' Bait for who?"

"You," a deep growl sounded behind him. Seconds before a weight like a wrecking ball crashed into his back.

Chapter Fourteen

Declan padded on silent paws up the marble staircase leading to the entryway of Epoc's mansion, the sound of wolves howling, men shouting and gunshots firing a faint smudge in his head. His right hind leg ached from a bullet graze, a testament to the skill of the Australians. He'd been lucky to escape with just the one. The men from Animal Control had been on him before he knew it, guns tracking his mad, darting sprint. If it hadn't been for the snarling arrival of Epoc's guards—all still in wolf form—he'd probably be hiding under a tree somewhere in excruciating pain, waiting for his body to deal with multiple bullet wounds. No good to Regan, whatsoever.

Heart thumping, head low, he nudged open the heavy, steel door with his nose and slipped through, leaving the sounds of the guards and Animal Control behind him.

Immediately, the smell of Epoc assaulted him. Dominant. Arrogant. Violent. He bared his teeth in a soft snarl, hate licking through his blood. The man's scent had haunted his dreams for a lifetime. He drew another breath and his hackles rose. Threaded through the scent, like cheap dime-store incense, was an underlying tinge of McCoy. Cold contempt crashed over him. He looked forward to meeting the Scottish son of a bitch again. Next time, he wouldn't stop with just breaking his neck.

Tail motionless, he walked deeper into the cavernous foyer, tasting the air, trying to detect any hint of Regan.

Nothing. Wherever she was in the building, she hadn't been here.

A faint whir tickled Declan's senses and, ears pricked, he froze.

The sound was high. Mechanical.

He lifted his head, spotting a small security camera fixed high in the far right corner of the vaulted ceiling. Pointed straight at him.

Wherever Epoc is, he knows you're here now, Dec.

Declan stared at the camera for a still moment. Felt cold, golden eyes staring back at him through the lens.

And he's watching you right at this very second.

Crossing the foyer, he sniffed at an ancient Celtic armoire standing below a moody painting of the Austrian Alps. Once. Twice. Staring straight into the camera's lens, and with a thump of his tail, he cocked his leg on the beautiful piece of antiquity and urinated. A primitive act. A simple message that clearly said, *I am not afraid of you.*

Tail wagging again, he padded out of the foyer, his mark seeping into the old wood behind him, staining it forever, the soft whir of the camera following him as he left.

He let a low *gnarr* rumble in his throat. *The last of the Onchú is back, Epoc. And I'm going to wipe your existence from the face of the planet.*

A dark and surreal thought flashed through Peter's head—

not again—seconds before he crashed, shoulder first, to the floor.

Thick, strong hands knotted in his hair, yanked his head backward and whacked his forehead into the cold marble tiles underneath him. Bright pain consumed him, ripped down his spine into his chest.

"You've got to be the lassie's kin," the man mashing his face to the floor growled, pushing down harder on the back of Peter's head. "You share her same tempting scent." The fingers in his hair tugged, and a pair of glowing red-gold eyes stared into the side of his face. "Not that I'd fuck you, mind. Your sister however..."

Fury roared through Peter. He bucked backward, throwing the heavy man off him. Leaping to his feet, he spun about, glaring at the leering bastard. "Your dick goes anywhere near my sister and I'll rip it off and feed it to you. Followed immediately by your balls."

The man—a fucking giant—raised eyebrows the color of cayenne pepper, leer stretching wider. "O'Connell obviously didn't fill you in, lad. About who I am and how well I know your delightfully spirited sister."

Peter's fingers closed tighter around the revolver and he barely controlled the desire to shoot the werewolf there and then. "I know all about you, McCoy," he said instead.

Those red eyebrows shot up further and McCoy chuckled, the deep sound reverberating through the room. "So we can dispense with the pleasantries then."

And he lunged forward.

Peter sidestepped him. Just. Nails like talons shredded his left sleeve, the material ripping as loud as a gunshot. McCoy twisted, an angry snarl rumbling in his throat as he threw himself at Peter again. Peter ducked, punching his fist up into a barrel-like chest harder than steel. A low *oof* burst from McCoy and he swung his arm downward, his bunched fist smacking against Peter's temple with a solid crack.

Black stars exploded in Peter's vision. He dropped to his knees, almost losing his grip on the gun. McCoy snatched a handful of his hair and jerked him to his feet, hammering a punch straight into his gut.

"McCoy!" Yolanda's cry cut the air, high and wild. *"Stop it!"*

"What's the matter, Vischka?" McCoy chuckled, stare boring into Peter's as he yanked him bodily from the ground by the hair. "You got to liking the taste of this pathetic human?" He ran his tongue over the tips of his teeth. "Finally found someone who likes you for who you are—a soulless bitch?"

Hot agony tearing at his scalp, Peter glared up at McCoy. "Bet I taste better than you, McCoy," he growled, and clamped his hands down on each side of McCoy's fist, grinding the man's knuckles together.

A roar of surprised pain burst from McCoy and he flung Peter away, eyes molten pits of rage. "You fucking bastard!"

Peter stumbled to a halt against the wall, desperate to stay on his feet. The top of his head felt like it had been torn off. He gave McCoy a wide grin, shoving the revolver into the waistband of his jeans with a deliberate show of contempt. "O'Connell told me I wouldn't need a weapon to beat you. Looks like he was right."

McCoy's face warped with red rage. "Why you insolent fucking bastard!" He charged forward, body shifting mid-stride. Transforming into a colossal, terrifying wolf.

The surreal thought—*not again*—whipped through Peter's head once more before he dropped to the floor and rolled aside.

McCoy, or rather, the slathering, snarling creature he'd become, landed on its muscled hind legs, its clawed feet shattering the marble in the exact spot Peter had stood but a second earlier. It spun, red stare locking on him. With a roar so loud the chandelier rattled, it threw itself at him, claws sinking into his shoulders. Flipping him onto his back, the creature snapped at him.

Peter twisted his head to the side, hideous agony tearing through his cheek as McCoy's teeth ripped a chunk from his face. He smashed his arms upward, palm heels punching into the creature's neck. It recoiled, eyes bulging, a choked gurgle sounding in its throat.

Blood streaming down Peter's cheek, his head, body and face a screaming world of pain, he shoved his feet into McCoy's gut and kicked out. "Get off me!"

The creature staggered backward, shallow breaths rasping from its throat. Its body shuddered and, as Peter scrambled to his feet and pulled the revolver from his waistband, its muscles bulged and contorted, molten red eyes locked on him, teeth lengthening into horrific fangs.

Peter's heart froze. *Oh, fuck.*

"STOP!" Yolanda's scream cut the air.

She moved—a black and blonde blur—and threw herself at McCoy's arched back. The creature lashed out and Yolanda went flying through the air, smacking against the far wall with a crunch.

"Yolanda!" Peter shouted, watching his partner slump to the floor in a limp heap.

The creature turned back to him, a deep hideous sound rumbling in its chest.

Peter glared at it, fury boiling his blood. "You fucker! You're laughing!"

He raised the revolver. Aimed it at the werewolf's

heart...and it charged him. With a savage swing of its arm, it swiped his gun from his hand, dislocating his shoulder in a bone-cracking snap and sinking its claws into his neck before he could squeeze the trigger.

It rammed him to the wall. Again. Again. Showers of plaster and concrete dust rained down upon him, choking him as surely as McCoy's claws strangled him. Right arm dangling free by his side, sickeningly unattached, he flailed with his left at the hand closing down on his neck. Struck out at the creature's face, its bunched shoulders.

Another one of those hideous chortles sounded in its throat, and it squeezed its fingers harder.

Peter stared at it, the world growing faint. "Laugh at this," he muttered through a thickening grey fog, and rammed his shin straight up into its groin.

A howl rent the hallway. McCoy reeled backward, grabbing at its fur-covered genitalia.

Sucking in lungful after lungful of air, Peter searched for the revolver. *There. Near the swords.*

He lurched forward, vision blurred with pain, blood still deprived of oxygen. *Five steps, Thomas. Just five steps.*

An ear-shattering snarl filled the hallway and Peter's throat clamped shut. He spun around. In time to see McCoy launch himself into the air, teeth bared, claws extended...

"NO!" Yolanda yelled. And threw herself at Peter.

It happened in the space of a heartbeat.

Yolanda crashed into him, her long-fingered hands—the very hands only hours earlier she'd danced over his thigh—flattening against his chest, sending him sprawling to his ass. He skidded along the marble floor, back smacking against the wall, stare fixed on the horrific sight of his partner landing on her feet. Turning into McCoy's attack, blue eyes wide. Furious. Sad.

Unable to look away, incapable of doing anything but, he watched as McCoy's jaws closed around Yolanda's smooth, creamy neck and tore it open.

"Yolanda!" he screamed.

He lurched to his feet. Stared in horror as the massive creature thrashed its head from side to side, ripping Yolanda's throat apart, blood and saliva coating its muzzle, the walls, Yolanda, in glistening red splatters.

Blue eyes bulging, body wracked in spasms, Yolanda hung in McCoy's grip, growing more limp with each violent shake of his jaw. She reached out a hand to Peter, fingers spread.

Heart squeezing, breath rapid, Peter spun around. Fuck! The revolver was too far away. His frantic searched fell on…

Leaping forward, he snatched one long-bladed sword from the wall with his left hand. Turned back to McCoy. To the sight of the creature bathing itself in Yolanda's blood. "Hey, dickhead," he shouted.

McCoy lifted his blood-soaked head, twin orbs of glowing red insanity turning to him…

And Peter swung the sword, its weight heavy and powerful, slicing its long, deadly blade straight through McCoy's neck. Decapitating him.

McCoy's head fell one way. His body another.

Both returning to human form before they hit the floor. Both motionless. Dead.

For a split second, Yolanda hung suspended on the blood-soaked air, before, with a wet and seemingly boneless thud, she fell to the ground.

Peter dropped the sword and leapt to her side, his knees

slipping in McCoy's, Yolanda's and probably his own blood. "Yolanda," he cried, grabbing at her still hand with his left, threading his fingers through hers. "Yolanda?"

He stared at her, refusing to look at the gaping mess of her throat.

"Damn it, Detective," he ground out, squeezing her hand harder. "Don't fucking ignore me!"

"Found it impossible...ignore you."

The gurgled words were soft, almost impossible to hear, but Yolanda's all the same. Peter swallowed, staring at her. "Jesus, Yolanda. Your throat—He almost tore it out."

She shook her head. Ever-so slightly. "Will heal," she whispered. "It may...while, but...will heal."

"Jesus, Yolanda," he murmured again, dropping his forehead to her chest. "I don't know..."

"You are...not allergic...puppies, are you?"

Her husky question made him lift his head and he squeezed her hand. Relief and pain and worry crashed over him. Tears threatened to fill his eyes. "Jesus, I hope not."

"This...good." She smiled softly. "I told you you should trust me, Detective," she whispered, fingers weakly squeezing his hand back. "You...listen to me from now on, yes?"

He returned her smile, incapable of doing otherwise. "Yes."

Her eyelids fluttered closed, the grip on his fingers growing stronger by the second, and her smile stretched a little wider. "Finally, you see reason."

Declan sniffed at the steel table centered in the middle of

the almost empty room, his tail swishing in agitation. Regan had been there. Her delicate scent teased his senses. He moved his muzzle down to the manacles, her sweat strong on the cool metal arc. She'd been angry. Very angry. He tasted her rage not just on the air, but on the steel as well. His tongue lolled past his teeth in a bleak grin. Good. Hopefully, even Nathan Epoc would be wary of an angry Regan—whether strapped to a table or not.

He turned, studying the open door on the far side of the room. The *Eudeyrn* Alpha's arrogant stench permeated every molecule he pulled into his lungs, like an acrid mist that made it difficult to breathe. He snarled, detecting a concentrated band leading from the table to the door. Focusing his nose on its path, his tail thumped once, wolfish grin growing wide with satisfaction. Under the thick conceit of Epoc's scent lay a tinge of apprehension. Cold and niggling.

He crossed the small space to the door, the click-click of his nails on the chilly, marble floor the only sound in the room.

It hit him. Abruptly and inescapably.

As he passed the threshold into a long, dimly lit corridor.

Fear. Absolute fear.

Regan's fear.

Whatever lay at the end of the corridor, whatever Epoc was doing to her there, she was petrified.

He burst into a dead sprint, ears back, teeth bared. His right hind leg began to throb, rivaling the pulsing ache in his chest from Peter's bullet, but he ignored both. Worry ate at him. Took massive chunks from his control with each pounding beat of his heart. The corridor twisted, grew darker, and then he rounded a corner and a sprawling room opened up before him. The main wall was made entirely of glass revealing the moon-reflecting waters of Sydney Harbor beyond. Two enormous, low-hanging crystal chandeliers flooded the room with warm, golden light, illuminating the large four-poster bed standing on a centre dais. Beside which stood Nathan Epoc. Holding Regan, naked and trembling, close to his wiry body, a large syringe pressed into her neck just below her right ear.

Declan skidded to a halt, his paws slipping on the smooth floor. He stared at Epoc, locking his focus on the smugly smiling man. If he looked at Regan he would lose all control. The overpowering tang of her horror filling the room almost pushed him to the next stage of his transformation as it was. He had to keep it in check. For her sake and his own.

"We're so glad to see you, O'Connell." A smirk creased Epoc's smooth, unlined face. He moved slightly, pressing the syringe harder into Regan's neck. "I was just telling this delightful young woman here how boring it was without you."

Epoc gripped Maggie's elbow, his claws sinking into her flesh, his canines lengthening with each chuckle slipping past his lips. "She's been a wonderful test subject, Onchú," he said, eyes boring into Declan's, "but now with you here, finally in my control I don't need her anymore." He flicked a silent message to McCoy and the loup garou lashed out, ripping Maggie's throat out with his claws.

Time froze. Maggie's eyes met Declan's. And then her head lolled forward. There was a sickening, wet tearing sound and, with a dull thud, it dropped to the floor, her beautiful, blue eyes staring sightlessly up at Declan. "NO!" he screamed. He leapt forward, the primeval werewolf, the ancient monster, bursting free. Gone was the world. Gone was Declan O'Connell. All that existed now was heart-crushing pain. And the hungry, demanding, insatiable blood-lust for revenge...

Declan held himself still, ears flat, tail motionless. His blood boiled. His muscles tensed, the monstrous beast pushing at his control, fighting for release. Epoc returned his level stare, the hand on Regan's arm closing tighter on the smooth column of her biceps. From the corner of Declan's eye, he saw Regan flinch, but he didn't move. He needed to focus.

He concentrated his strength—his *croí*—on his form. A ripple went through his body. His limbs tingled. His muscles shifted, and he stood. On two feet.

"Ah, the *man* of the moment," Epoc sneered. He flicked his gaze over Declan's body. "You seem to be missing some clothes." His eyebrows shot up. "But gained some new wounds to go with the scars I've already marked you with."

Declan gave him a toothy grin. "Well, you know me, Epoc. I've never been one for material possessions."

Epoc puckered his lips, his golden eyes turning to Regan with deliberate malice. "No, you've always been one for possessions of the heart, haven't you."

Hot anger crashed through Declan but he remained motionless.

Epoc laughed, the sound soulless and smug at once. "Such a familiar situation we find ourselves in, isn't it, *Onchú*. Me, holding the woman of your heart, you standing there, as useless as ever." He pulled Regan closer to him, and for the first time since entering the room, Declan let himself really look at her.

She appeared almost catatonic, her eyes glazed, her body somehow limp, despite standing.

He sucked in a sharp breath and turned back to Epoc, jaw

clenched, fists balled. "You know I'm going to kill you, right? I mean, surely you're not that dumb?"

Epoc's smile grew wider, teeth glinting in the warm chandelier light. He moved his head, ran his nose slowly up the side of Regan's face until his mouth drew level with her cheekbone, his amber gaze still locked on Declan. "She smells almost as good as your sister, O'Connell. For a human. Just as feisty too, I must say." He flicked out his tongue and ran it in a small line up to Regan's temple. She flinched—the only sign she registered he was there at all.

Declan suppressed a growl. He couldn't move. Not until he knew she was safe. *Regan...?*

He strained to hear, to feel a response. Nothing.

"Did you know I passed Maggie around my clan?" Epoc commented, returning his full attention to Declan. He unfurled one finger from his hold on Regan's arm and drew a tiny pattern up and down her arm. "She was a tasty bitch. And a wanton one. She begged for every sexual depravity known to man and lycanthrope." He smiled again, canines now long and curved. "But you would know that, wouldn't you, being her brother and all."

Fury, like a scalding river of lava, flooded through Declan. The primal beast locked within his body roared for release. He clenched his fists harder, struggling to control it, the stinging puncture wounds of his own lengthening nails in his palms only feeding the creature's rage. He narrowed his eyes, studying the man before him. Epoc was baiting him. Taunting him to react.

Don't let him. Focus. You lose control, Regan will die.

"Pity you couldn't save her," Epoc murmured. "The same way you've failed entirely to save this female." He smiled, saliva-slicked incisors flashing. "Have you truly smelt her since slinking into this room, O'Connell, or have you been too focused on me?"

Declan's throat clamped shut. Still staring hard at Epoc, he pulled in a deep breath.

And smelt Epoc's saliva on Regan's flesh. His mark imbued in her sweat.

"She is a delicious one, I must say," Epoc went on, eyes blazing, thumb growing white on the hypodermic's plunger. "And a screamer. My ears are still hurting with how loud she screamed as I stuck my fingers, my tongue in her cunt. I've never had so much fun on my bed." He paused, expression melodramatically curious. "Have you fucked her on a bed, *Onchú*? Or was it just in the cars you stole and the homes you broke into?"

Declan ground his teeth, his heart thumping in his chest so hard he could barely breath.

"I must admit," Epoc continued. "I can see your attraction to her, despite her human DNA. She has a tight, wet cunt that's heaven to eat. Like mulled wine. I smelt you there, but, like you yourself, your mark was weak. It didn't take much to replace it with mine. A quick thrust here, a bite there."

"Keep talking, fucker. Every word's just another reason to tear you apart."

Epoc chuckled. "Hmm. Still the hero, I see. Good to see love hasn't made you soft. Although, I'm not sure the female here shares the same feeling. She wasn't happy with you at all while I entertained her on the bed. Cursed your name every time I touched her." He paused, eyes flaring with cold, smug triumph. "Much like your precious sister."

The snarl burst from Declan's throat before he could stop it. His muscles bunched. Flexed. Fury consumed him. The antediluvian creature in his blood bellowed and he let it. Welcomed it. It was time to succumb to its...

Declan.

The soft whisper tickled his mind.

Declan.

He flicked his stare to Regan, icy hope stirring in his chest, and found her staring back, green eyes shining with pain and anger and intractable fortitude.

Shut this fucking bastard up, please.

Declan returned his gaze to Epoc, a slow grin stretching his lips "Actually, Epoc, I think it's *her* name *you'll* be cursing." And he transformed.

The very second Regan snapped her leg up and stamped her heel down hard on Epoc's foot.

Regan stumbled away, staring dumbstruck at the sight before her. Declan, or rather, the great, grey wolf he'd become, slammed into Epoc, front paws thumping against the smaller man's chest with an audible crunch. Epoc fell backward, stunned disbelief on his face. He staggered once under Declan's weight before, with a shudder and an ear-shattering growl, transforming into a black wolf larger than a buffalo.

The two animals snapped and tore at each other, saliva and blood splattering their muzzles and thrashing bodies. Epoc's bulk dwarfed Declan's, but Declan was quicker. Each time Epoc lashed out at Declan's neck, Declan whipped it away, flinging the wolf off him and snapping at its exposed belly.

Frozen to the spot, Regan watched. The icy sting of Epoc's hypodermic radiated up into her head and she pressed her hand to her neck. He hadn't injected her—she didn't think—but her neck hurt like hell from the needle's brutal puncture. A small trickle of blood seeped from the tiny wound, probably caused by the needle's abrupt withdrawal when he'd jerked away from her. It was nothing however, compared to the bloody gashes and gouges the two werewolves inflicted on each other now.

Howls and snarls rent the air. Turned the room into an aural nightmare.

Declan pinned Epoc to the floor, front paws driving into his shoulders, muzzle clamped shut on his throat. He thrashed his head side-to-side, fresh blood spurting past his fangs and curled lips, staining his fur a dark crimson.

Regan's heart hammered. Declan was winning. Holy shit, he was—

Epoc growled, gold eyes wide, bulging. He bucked wildly, his massive bulk dislodging Declan in a sickening pitch that hurled him through the air. Flinging him, spine first, against the solid corner post on the bed.

"Declan!" Regan screamed, leaping forward.

"The suffering I will cause you!"

At the roared words, she spun about and her blood ran cold.

Epoc—*human* Epoc—stalked toward Declan's prone form, sweat and blood slicking his naked body, muscles coiled and ready to attack, the syringe he'd pressed to her neck back in his hand.

"Declan!" Regan screamed again.

With a grunt, the grey wolf lifted its head from the floor and twin silver eyes locked on her. A ripple ran through its body and, before she could blink, it transformed back into a man. Back into Declan.

The very second Epoc launched himself through the air and thumped down upon him.

"Finally," Epoc snarled, and plunged the needle straight into Declan's neck.

A howl, louder than the shattering of an iceberg, tore from Declan's throat.

Regan cried out, slapping her hands to her ears. Oh, God! What had Epoc done to him? Terrified, she watched him snap into a violent arc, head thrown back, arms flung wide, hurling Epoc from his body and across the room. He leapt to his feet and spun about, glaring at the man struggling to stand on the other side of the room. "No, Epoc," he growled, stalking toward him, fists clenched, eyes burning. "It is *I* that will make *you* suffer."

"How can you be moving?" Epoc cried, shrinking back into the wall, his face draining of all color.

Declan lips parted in a deadly grin. "Easy." And then a spasm rocked his body and he collapsed to the floor.

"Interesting." Epoc straightened, all sign of his horrified disbelief gone. Crossing the room, he stopped at Declan's side and gazed down at him. "A delayed response to *Plumbago zeylanica*." He lifted his foot and slammed it down on Declan's chest, grinding his heel into the weeping wound near Declan's heart. "I've never seen that before. It had an instant affect on you in Dublin. Interesting."

Regan leapt forward, anger and fear roaring through her veins.

An insane gold stare snapped to her. "Come any closer, cunt, and I'll rip O'Connell's arms and legs off right here and now. *Plumbago zeylanica*, or White Leadwort, if you prefer, is a paralyzer—of sorts—and there's nothing he could do to stop me doing so." He gave her a malevolent grin, canines crimson with saliva and blood. "Or save you, for that matter."

Regan faltered, staring hard at Declan. His gaze locked on

her, wide and anxious.

Don't.

Only one word. Whispered in her mind. But it kept her still.

Epoc smirked. "Smart girl. What a pity you're just a human. Intelligent, feisty and entirely fuckable. A rare find. It will be almost a waste to kill you." He dropped his gaze to Declan, ground his heel harder to his chest. "I have longed for this day for centuries, *Onchú*. You truly have no idea how much. The night your clan—*your* ancestor—took Aine's life, my beautiful, sweet, gentle Aine, your own life was forfeit. Before you were even born, you were dead. With the extraction of your *croí*, not only will I fulfill a promise I made to my lifemate's departed soul, I will become *more* than any of our kind ever dreamed, in all the millennia of our existence. Once that happens, the true lycanthrope war will begin. And *I* will be the sole victor."

"Sole fuckwit, you mean," Declan muttered, voice choked and barely audible.

Epoc's eyebrows shot up. "You can still talk?"

"Let's hope he can still move, too."

The familiar male voice made Regan spin around.

Standing in the doorway, an old and somehow strange looking gun gripped loosely in his left hand, bloody, bruised and obviously wracked in pain, was her brother.

Epoc snarled. *"You!"* He lunged across the room, knocking Peter backward. The exact second Peter flung the gun through the air.

"No!" Regan cried, watching Peter crash backward, Epoc on his chest.

"Epoc, you flea-bitten son of a bitch!" Declan shouted.

Regan turned. As did Epoc.

In time to see Declan, face bleached white with exertion, stand and aim the unusual gun at Epoc's head. "For my sister."

He squeezed the trigger.

"*NO!*" Epoc screamed. A split second before a tiny, red hole materialized on his forehead and his body disintegrated, instantly burning from the inside-out. Consumed in black flames in the space of a heartbeat.

For a moment no one moved. Regan stared, first at her brother, second at the greasy residue coating him in a fine dust, and finally at Declan. Who, with a deep exhale of breath, crumpled to his knees, eyes closed, head drooped.

She ran to him, dropped to her own knees and placed her hands on his arms. "Declan?" she whispered, concern twisting in her chest like a snake. "Declan, are you...?"

"Jesus, Mary, that took a lot of effort," he mumbled.

Regan's breath caught. "Declan?"

The black head lifted, slowly, and two storm-cloud grey eyes met hers. "I've been meaning to ask you, love," he said, voice weak and hoarse yet still reverberating with strength. "Does your love of animals extend to wolves?"

She stared at him. Felt her heart swell. Leaning forward, she placed her forehead to his, basking in the warmth radiating from his body. "That depends," she whispered, lips brushing his. She reached up, threaded her fingers through his hair and kissed him. Soft. Gentle. "How do you feel about lizards?"

Epilogue

Declan rolled onto his back and threaded his fingers behind his head, watching the play of early morning light on the white surface of the ceiling. He smiled to himself, the action languid and relaxed. A warm summer breeze wafted through the open window, bringing with it the soft, briny tang from Bondi Beach. Later in the day, he'd meet Peter down at the beach and go for a swim. It hadn't taken long, a matter of days really, but Declan had developed a deep love for the surf. There was nothing like diving into the crashing waves, submerging oneself completely in the invigorating water, letting its powerful force wash away decades of pain and memories and nightmares, before bursting up through its foamy surface— renewed, refreshed. Reborn.

He pulled a slow breath, exhaling it even slower. There were things he had to do before he escaped to the beach. People he needed to see. It would take some time, but he'd eventually get used to being the new *Eudeyrn* clan's Alpha. Eventually. Tradition was paramount to his kind and the ancient clan had accepted it as such. A superior alpha wolf had defeated Nathan Epoc and they were ready to move into a new era. It helped greatly Epoc's rule had been one of fear, degradation and brutal humiliation.

Declan's forehead creased into a slight frown. He hadn't planned on becoming the *Eudeyrn* Alpha when he'd sworn to destroy Epoc. All he'd been thinking of was making the bastard pay for Maggie's death. Retribution of the most basic, savage kind. Now...A dry grin pulled at his lips. Well, he'd always disliked the idea of being a lone wolf. Almost as much as he disliked the cliché.

"I hope that smile's for me?"

A voice husky with sleep caressed his check and he rolled his head to the side, casting a lazy gaze at the woman lying beside him. "Actually..."

Regan grinned at him, her fingers tiptoeing up his bare chest to flick at his nipples. "Oh, I get it. You become the Alpha of a pack and suddenly there's no room for me in your head." She sniffed melodramatically. "I should have known you were a workaholic." A pout quivered on her lower lip and she made to roll away from him. "I'm getting up to feed Rex. At least he loves me."

Declan moved, covering her body with his and pressing her back to the bed. "Rex can wait," he growled on a chuckle. He smoothed his hands down her arms and snared her wrists, sliding them above her head. She arched her back, pushing her breasts up and against his chest, rolling the smooth curve of her mons against his rapidly growing cock. He bit back a groan of delight, the gentle friction of her flesh on his making his head spin. "As for me being a workaholic..." He dropped his head, nibbling at the delicate line of her collarbone. "Work's not what I'm addicted to, Regan Thomas."

She moved underneath him, undulating her hips until her thighs spread enough to let his shaft nudge her soft pussy lips. "And just what are you addicted to, my animal?"

He traced the smooth column of her neck with a string of

tiny kisses, up to her jaw and over her chin until his lips came to rest on hers. "Now who's being stupid?"

Regan chuckled, the action sending gentle waves of vibrations through her body, down to the warm, damp junction of her thighs hugging his cock so snugly. "Well, seeing as you're awake and *not* making wild, passionate, untamed sex to me, I'd say *you*." She slid one long, bare leg up the back of his, her calf muscle doing things to his sanity no innocent body part should. "Still furthering that Irish stereotype, are we?"

Declan lifted his head and gazed down at her. Drinking in her beauty, her sensual spirit. He curled his lips in a languid smile, shifting his hips until the throbbing head of his cock parted the velvety lips of her sex. "For the sake of my nationality's reputation," he murmured, dragging his hands down her arms to cup the heavy swell of her breasts, "I best be making love to you, then. I wouldn't want the world to think we Irish aren't all that quick on the uptake." He rolled her pinched, puckered nipples between thumb and forefinger. She sucked in a hitching breath and shoved her breasts harder into his hands, her eyelids fluttering closed. "Now," he continued, teasing and twisting each rock-hard nipple. "That was wild, passionate, *untamed* sex, am I right?"

She opened her eyes, their green depths smoldering with desire and rapturous hunger. "Oh, God, yes," she sighed, raking her nails across his back to bury her fingers into his hair.

Declan let his smile grow wider. Devilish. *Wolfish.* "Untamed I can do, love. Anytime and every time you want." And, with a powerful, fluid thrust, he plunged his shaft deep into her sex.

About the Author

To learn more about Lexxie Couper please visit www.lexxiecouper.com/. Send an email to Lexxie Couper at lexxie@lexxiecouper.com or join her Yahoo! group to join in the fun with other readers as well as Lexxie http://groups.yahoo.com/group/LXC_Newsletter or http://groups.yahoo.com/group/Australis-Eros/

The best way to tempt a wolf?
Offer something irresistibly sweet.

To Tempt a Wolf
© *2008 Colette Denee*

Cadon Sterling thought retirement would be easy. Then not only does a new Rune show up in his town, but his successor isn't living up to expectations. Plus, his best friend is driving him crazy. On top of that, he just met a human who could tempt a saint to sin with the smallest whiff of fudge. Oh, yes, and there will be hell to pay should he fail to complete his task. Did he mention the fudge?

Brielle Austin lives a simple life. Make sweets, sell sweets. But simple doesn't quite cover it when she meets Cadon, leader of a local pack of wolf-shifters. She's afraid to offer her heart, but learns the hard way that some things just aren't a matter of choice. As her safe little world slips from under her feet, Brielle struggles to accept the true nature of her magic, and her soul.

Blessed by Odin and targeted by two rival races, Cadon and Brielle fight to stay alive—and together—long enough to see the Rune gets where it needs to be. Enemies lurk around every corner, but it is the demons inside that will either kill them, or set them free.

Available now in ebook and print from Samhain Publishing.

Overshadowed by the rising threat of the werewolf mafia, Ben and Tegan struggle to stand united.

Wolf Unbound
© 2008 Lauren Dane
A Cascadia Wolves story

Werewolf Enforcer Tegan Warden has been alone since the death of her mate four years ago. Until she meets Ben Stoner at a local club and she feels something she thought died inside her. Things move very quickly and she finds herself mated to a human man who's not altogether sure he wants a forever kind of love with a woman he's just met.

Ben realizes in short order Tegan is not only worth forever love, but a woman who'll stand at his side without tolerating anything other than a full partnership.

In the bedroom it's another story, as Ben has finally found a sexual submissive with a spark, and Tegan a man worthy of her submission. Together they work toward building a permanent relationship even as the specter of danger from the Pellini Group grows in the world of wolves.

All around them, the rising violence threatens the Packs and the only thing they know for certain is one another.

Warning: Naughty language that might get your mouth washed out with soap, domineering alpha males knocked down a few pegs by their women, smoking hot bedroom action including always consensual BDSM type action, werewolf mafia and the violence that loves them.

Available now in ebook and coming soon in print from Samhain Publishing.

GREAT
CHEAP
FUN

Discover eBooks!

THE FASTEST WAY TO GET THE HOTTEST NAMES

Get your favorite authors on your favorite reader, long before they're out in print! Ebooks from Samhain go wherever you go, and work with whatever you carry—Palm, PDF, Mobi, and more.

Samhain
publishing
Ltd

WWW.SAMHAINPUBLISHING.COM

CPSIA information can be obtained at www.ICGtesting.com
Printed in the USA
LVOW130030271212

313372LV00002B/80/P

9 781605 040196